Acclaim

"Romantic and heartfelt, Andromache delivers a powerful message in the midst of a clever dystopian landscape. Richmond's world is *The Selection* meets *Hunger Games* District 1 with unique twists and a completely fresh approach. I couldn't get enough of the romance, the challenges, and the seemingly insurmountable odds. This is a tale for dystopian die-hards and new fans alike!"
—E. A. HENDRYX, award-winning author of *Suspended in the Stars*

"Laundry overflowed, my stomach growled, plants wilted . . . all unessential tasks were dutifully ignored as I devoured pages like there was a pot of gold on the other side of this story. And there is so much treasure to be found within the pages of *Andromache*! This is not only an action-packed tale with fantastic world-building and characters that steal your heart, but it is a book that testifies to the immense value of human life and the dangers of pretending otherwise. As someone who's personally walked the path of infertility, I found Andi to be a unique and inspiring heroine. With dashes of *The Hunger Games*, *The Selection*, *The Handmaid's Tale*, and the Biblical story of Esther, *Andromache* is a book you don't want to miss!"

—J. J. FISCHER, award-winning author of *Calor*

"A gripping tale of love, loss, and the value of human life. A beautiful, poignant reminder of what is truly important, and that every life has purpose."
—APRIL J. SKELLY, author of *A Lethal Engagement*

"Intrigue, romance, and dangerous alliances await readers in the dystopian adventure, Andromache. Be prepared to get swept away in a story that will leave you breathlessly turning the page to find out what happens next, swooning over the sweet romance, and cheering on characters who will stay with you long after the book is over. L. E. Richmond delivers a spell-binding tale that touches the heart and reminds readers that no life is meaningless or disposable. This book is not to be missed!"
—CJ MILACCI, award-winning author of the Talionis series

"*Andromache* delivers a thrilling romantic adventure, full of unexpected twists and turns! Perfect for fans of *The Selection* and *Matched*, this whirlwind of a tale hurtles you through a fractured world, leaving you breathless as you reach the end."
—CANDACE KADE, author of the Hybrid series

ANDROMACHE

ANDROMACHE

Quill & Flame
PUBLISHING HOUSE

L.E. RICHMOND

Quill & Flame
PUBLISHING HOUSE

Andromache

This one is for the niece or nephew I will never know. The world sees your life as a barely-there flicker on an ultrasound screen, but to the God who made you, you are a valued and loved eternal soul whose time on earth was cut short by the curse we live under. Love you, baby - I'll see you when the "last enemy" is destroyed.

A Note

It has been said that we read books to find ourselves and understand the world around us. The world is a complex place with many different and complex people. There are monsters in the real world, and we find a safe place to slay those monsters inside the pages of books. Because of these monsters, sometimes books handle really hard topics.

This is one of those books.

This book deals with infertility, abortion, killing in the name of convenience and "betterment" of society, and abuse.

Opinions on these matters vary widely, and some of these topics are best avoided if a person has a particularly painful past with some of these issues. While all of these things are presented at a PG-13 level on the pages, these topics can still be acute.

If you pick up this book, we hope you find light in the midst of the darkness, and that you are moved to protect society's most vulnerable members.

If you or a loved one are struggling, call 988 and speak with someone who can help. The Crisis Hotline is open twenty-four hours a day, seven days a week.

You are not alone. Pain does not need to define who you are or who you become. There is hope, and there are people willing to help you.

May you find the strength to slay your monsters.

-April J. Skelly
CEO of Quill & Flame Publishing House

PROLOGUE

Andromache.

Ten letters that trace out the name of an ancient princess who watched her world crumble into dust under the onslaught of the enemy.

An impossible-to-spell name meaning "fighter of men."

But I don't fight with anyone.

Because where I come from, resistance gets you killed.

And those who are clever live out their days in the shadows, because a half-life is better than none at all.

Those who love me best call me Andi.

It means brave.

But I'm not that either.

Because I am afraid to leave this broken world that is all I've ever known.

And there are only three people on the entire planet I love enough to die for.

CHAPTER 1

"**I**t's tomorrow, you know."

Sasha's hands are sure as she washes the tiny, silent baby girl who was born less than half an hour ago. The water in the chipped porcelain basin turns pink, chunks of congealed blood and strands of white mucus floating to the surface around the infant's frail limbs.

"Give her to me," I say, holding out my hands with a glance toward the bed. The mother's ashen face blends with the dirty gray of the pillowcase, the rise and fall of her chest barely lifting the blankets.

Sasha raises her eyebrows as she reaches for a towel, loosely wrapping the baby before placing her in my arms. "That's not exactly an answer, love."

I place the baby on the corner of the bed, knowing that nothing I do will disturb the mother in her exhausted state.

I unfold the towel and place my hand against the delicate chest. A flicker of movement against my palm tells me the mite is alive. But barely.

My fingers find the baby's feet, alternately tickling and lightly slapping. I begin a full-body massage, rubbing hard enough to excite a pink flush in her skin. My stomach clenches with the irrational fear that always comes when I first handle a newborn, that I will snap the bird-like limbs. I sing under my breath, bending low so that tendrils of my straight black hair brush the baby's face as I squish her cheeks in one hand, wiggling to try to induce a rooting reflex.

Come on.

The two words—soft as a breath against my consciousness—make me recoil.

No caring, I remind myself.

Because death comes.

For one out of two of the babies Sasha and I deliver. For one out of three of the mothers. And for the babies who survive?

Life is misery for every one of them.

Watching disease and poverty take the lives of those they care about. Working at jobs so hopeless and backbreaking that they force themselves to believe the lies about the boats carrying those too old for work or childbirth to "Paradise." Exposing their baby sons to the elements because they can't afford to keep them. Grooming their daughters in the hope that one of them will be picked to travel east, to marry some man they've never met and produce children to rule the robot-dominated population of the East Coast.

A soft mewling sound, growing gradually louder and more hysterical, causes me to look down. The face of the child in my hands is screwed up with fury, and the sight delights me.

"She'll be all right," I say to Sasha, wrapping the towel back around the infant and turning her into a neat bundle.

I look down into the mite's wrinkled red face, her button mouth open as she bellows her wrath against the cold, hard world she has entered, and without thinking, I lift her, nuzzling my nose against her cheek and her soft dark hair. I know that I am being a fool—that the day I hear of this baby's death, another piece of my calcified soul will chip away—but for an instant, I stay frozen and drink in the new baby scent of her. Then I turn and march across to the bed to give the mother's shoulder a gentle shake.

"She's hungry."

Jez moans and tries to swat my hands away, but I continue to shake until she opens one bleary, red-rimmed eye. "She's hungry," I say again, tucking the baby into the crook of her elbow, which is encased in a dirty satin robe.

"She ain't the only one," Jez grumbles, but she pulls the front of her robe down as the baby begins to root against her skin. "Hey, Andi. You seen Heath lately?"

"Why?"

Jez purses her bright-red lips. "His father keeps asking about him. Says the farm could use more pickers."

"How do you even know Doug is Heath's father?"

The baby has finally managed to latch, and Jez leans back against her pillows with a sigh. "Not that it's any of your business, but I had dysentery that entire month. 'Cept for one week. Doug was my only client." She gives a snort of mirthless laughter. "Besides, Douglas Insley is the only man alive who could make Jezebel Modos produce a boy." Her eyes are filled with a strange expression of mingled pride and shame. "Thirteen girls. And one of them's gonna be my ticket out of this life. Ceci's fifteen. Only three more years 'til she can enter."

"Speaking of the Invitation," Sasha says, "Andi and I have to be up early tomorrow for the ceremony. We'd best be going."

"Oh, yeah," Jez says. "You're nineteen. I forgot. And this year is an Ascension Year. Lucky."

"I'm not going East," I respond calmly.

"You will if you're picked."

"I won't be picked."

"Oh, sweetheart." Jez's voice drips with condescension. "That's what I told myself the first night I stood on a street corner."

Sasha's hand closes around my elbow. "Goodnight, Jez," she says, steering me toward the door.

"If you see Heath," Jez calls after me, "tell him to come home to his mama."

I make no reply.

CHAPTER 2

Sasha silently loops her arm through mine as we stroll away from the crumbling apartment complex. I reach across and take the midwife bag from her shoulder, slinging it over my own back. Sasha's left hip has been bothering her lately.

After a few blocks of quiet, the edges of the buildings around us growing blurrier as dusk settles over the city that was once San Francisco, I say, "So...dinner?"

"Jez hasn't paid me for a delivery since baby number five, Andi."

"I guess there's always eggs, then." My stomach growls.

Sasha sighs. "What can I do, Andi? It's not her children's fault that Jez is what she is."

"I know." The words are sharper than I intend, so I soften my tone. "You're doing the right thing, Sasha. I just can't stand her."

Sasha gives my arm a light squeeze. "My personal feelings aside, we need Jez, Andi. *You* need Jez."

"Shh," I hiss, glancing around the bomb-splintered street we are currently traversing.

"There's no one here, Andi. Don't you think I already checked?"

"I thought you might be trying to get me disqualified so we wouldn't have to attend the Ceremony tomorrow."

Sasha throws back her head and laughs. I smile into the darkness. Lots of people don't understand my sense of humor. But Sasha gets my jokes. Every single time.

"You'd be more likely to do that than I, dear," she says after her laughter subsides. Then, "You never answered my question."

"What is there to say?" I ask, looking through a gap in the dilapidated, crumbling buildings. The Pacific Ocean glimmers in the light of the setting sun. "Besides, 'It's tomorrow, you know' isn't a question."

Sasha exhales. "Most of what I say to you holds an underlying question, my Andromache. Your mother was an open book to me. It felt as though our brains were connected by some sort of invisible wiring. You? I can never tell what is going on in that brilliant mind of yours." When I don't respond, she squeezes my arm again. "I didn't mean that as a reproach, Andi. I just want to know. So badly."

"Like I told Jez, I'm not going to get picked. So, what's currently in my mind is an advanced state of indifference."

"Come on, Andi. Mathematical mind like yours? You know there's a chance of you getting picked."

I stop in the street and turn to look down at her. I'm six feet tall—or 5'12", as I tell most people—and Sasha is just shy of five feet. In the darkness, I tower over her. "I don't know what kind of Higher Power controls this planet," I say. "But given the purpose of the Invitation and given what I am, getting picked would be a sick joke. A sick joke."

"And you think Earth's Higher Power doesn't have a sick sense of humor?"

"I don't know," I say, turning again to catch the shimmering strip of titian between the buildings. "But sometimes, when I look at the stars or hold a newborn baby or hear the ocean's roar in my ears, I think not."

"I know you're there."

My words cause a shadow to detach itself from the darkness outside the glow of the single lightbulb. There is a scuffling sound, and the stack of crates leaning against the garage's wall sways. "Get down from there," I say, eyes still trained on the equation-covered sheets of paper littering the folding table in front of me. "I haven't time to patch you up if you fall."

"When have I ever fallen?"

"There's a first time for everything."

"Even you getting picked at the Invitation tomorrow?"

I look up at the scrawny urchin, who is grinning at me from atop his precarious throne. "Hoping to get rid of me?"

The child shimmies to the edge of his box and drops with a thump to the garage floor. The box tower sways ominously, and I leap forward to steady it before glaring at the boy. "Your mother was asking about you."

"You didn't tell her where I'm hiding out, did you?"

I study him before turning back to the table. "Would I?"

Heath blows his breath out in a relieved sigh. "You're the best. I hope you don't get picked tomorrow."

I drum the end of my pencil lightly against my calculations. "Why, thank you."

"I don't understand why we even have the Invitation," Heath says, leaning against the table beside me. "I was two when the last one happened, so I didn't get to hear the spiel. And I'm a boy. I don't have parents constantly clucking over whether I might get picked or not."

The sight of his expression makes me put my pencil down and reach for a crate, dragging it across and sitting down on it. I pat the empty space beside me. "You know I'm not a great storyteller. But I can give you 'the spiel' if you'd like."

Heath cackles. "If you told stories on street corners like old Martin, I bet you'd have one rusty euroyen by the end of the day."

I push off the box, towering over him in mock fury. "You want me to kick you out of my lab, little boy?"

Unfazed, Heath saunters past me and makes a great show of dusting off his side of the box with a corner of his grubby shirt. "Even if you get chosen tomorrow, you'll never get picked as Consort. No man wants a woman who's taller than he is." He lowers himself onto the crate. "All right. You can give me 'the spiel' now."

Laughter bubbles out of me, destroying the menacing expression I'm attempting to level on Heath. "Fine, brat." I reseat myself and clear my throat. "Once upon a time..."

"Is this a fairy tale?" Heath interrupts scornfully.

I pause before saying, "Wait until the story's over. Then you tell me.

"Once upon a time, there was a country called the United States of America, one of the most powerful nations on Earth. But the country wasn't united at all. Increasingly, its citizens were moving, seeking others whose political and ideological values aligned with their own. In time, the country became polarized into an Eastern half and a Western half. And in 2234, there was a civil war. Neither side could justly claim any victory, but millions died and the central portion of the country was laid to waste. The survivors fled to the opposing coasts, forming the Federation in what was once the original thirteen colonies and the Commonwealth in what was once the states of California, Oregon, and Washington.

"Time passed. Nuclear war erupted between the Commonwealth and The People's Republic of China. All but the remnants of five coastal cities were destroyed—Los Angeles, San Francisco, Florence, Vancouver, and Seattle—and the Commonwealth became known as Cinq. Most means of food production were destroyed, and crime and disease began to skyrocket. Meanwhile, in the Federation, the years immediately following the civil war were marked by a growing economy and rapid technological advances. But a silent devastation was moving, unnoticed at first, through the already diminished society. Due to abortion and declining birth rates, the population was rapidly shrinking and growing steadily older and more male-dominated.

"Then a virus struck the Federation. A virus that spread like wildfire, killing the elderly and damaging the reproductive capabilities of the few remaining women. By the time a scientist named Dorian Xavier developed a vaccine for the virus, there were only five human families left on the East Coast, each with two young sons. In a move to combat the crisis, Dorian Xavier named himself Elector of the Federation with his friend, technological guru Tristan Grimsby, as his second-in-command. Together, they ensured that, through the aid of the robots in charge of all production and manufacturing, the supply chains remained open and technological advancements continued. But even as the country stabilized, the two men were in despair. Without the possibility of reproduction, their sons and the sons of the other three families who had survived the epidemic would be the last of the human population."

"But if they were such geniuses," Heath interrupts, "why didn't they just grow girls in labs?"

"The only remaining female DNA was that of the boys' mothers," I say, and Heath makes a disgusted face. "Besides, since abortion and other tampering with human reproduction had partially precipitated the crisis, Dorian passed legislation that only 'natural' means would be used to rejuvenate the population of the Federation. He sent messengers to the governors of each of Cinq's five cities."

"By plane?"

"Why on earth does it matter?"

"I'm just interested. I mean, if you're picked tomorrow, how are you going to travel three thousand miles? Plane? Train? Military vehicle? Boat?"

"There's no river that flows unobstructed from Cinq to the Federation."

"Not by boat, then."

I huff. "On the *miniscule* chance that I get picked tomorrow, I'll be flying back to the Federation. That's how the vast majority of communication between us and the Federation happens. It's the quickest method, and they have plenty of aircraft." Heath nods, looking impressed. "Xavier proposed a treaty between the Federation and Cinq. In exchange for medicine, vehicles, and communication technology, we would send five girls—one from each of the five major city-states—to marry the oldest sons of the five remaining families of the Federation. The girls selected must be virgins between the ages of eighteen and twenty-five and have had blood testing done to determine that they were fertile. In five years, when the younger brothers of the five families had come to marriageable age, another five girls would be sent."

"Hang on," Heath interrupts, narrowing his eyes at me. "Do they still do blood testing to determine fertility?"

I fiddle with a thread unraveling in the knee of my pants. "Every girl in Cinq has to start sending in blood samples when she turns fourteen."

"And you've been sending in blood since you were fourteen?"

"*Every* girl, Heath."

"Then..." Heath's voice is uncharacteristically hesitant. "Why haven't you been sent to Paradise, Andi?"

I bite my lip, contemplating how much to tell a seven-year-old. Then again, this particular seven-year-old is one of my three best friends. "Sasha has sent in samples of your mother's blood, labeled as mine, for the last five years. Jez had your oldest sister by the time she turned fourteen. She was never eligible to send in blood samples of her own."

Heath's expression becomes stonier with every word I utter. I touch his shoulder, half expecting him to flinch away from me, but he just stares straight ahead. After a moment, he says, "She owes you. And everybody knows she's fertile. It's a good thing you took her blood."

"Your mother's life hasn't been easy, Heath."

"Neither has mine! Thanks to her."

"I'm not saying she's not to blame for her actions," I say quickly. "But think, Heath. She became a mother months after becoming a teenager. Would you be ready to be a father in six or seven years?"

"I'm never going to be a father. No way am I going to be responsible for bringing a child into a world like this."

"A good family makes a lot of difference in how we experience the world," I respond, pushing away the thought that, unlike Heath, I will not get to choose whether to forego parenthood.

Heath's expression doesn't alter. "And after the treaty?"

"That year, five girls were randomly selected and sent to the East Coast. Upon their arrival, one of the girls, Elvira Costales, helped Dorian's oldest son, Dominic, to develop a solar panel more efficient at utilizing the sun's weakening rays. He chose her to be his wife, telling his father that since their country was built on technological prowess, intelligence was a vital trait in the next Consort of the Federation."

"Did Dominic become Elector as soon as he got married or did he have to wait until Dorian died?" Heath asks.

"The heir becomes Elector immediately upon his marriage. The previous Elector and his Consort become regents, acting in an advisory capacity to the new Elector and Consort."

"And the girls Dominic didn't pick got married to the other sons."

"Yes," I say, even though Heath phrased it as a statement rather than a question. "Within a year, all five of the girls from Cinq, including Elvira, were pregnant. By chance, all of their children were boys. Five years later, another group of girls arrived from Cinq to marry the younger brothers of the five founding families. Again, by chance, the first children born to all five of these couples were also boys. Guided by his father, Dominic again approached the leaders of Cinq. He proposed that a lasting treaty be established between the two nations—one in which, starting the year his son came of age, five girls would be sent to the Federation every five years. Through a series of challenges designed to test their physical strength, mental acuity, and leadership abilities—called Gauntlets—the heir to the Federation would select his wife, while the remaining young women would be auctioned off to the young men willing to pay the highest bride price."

"Auctioned off?" The horror in Heath's voice causes my lips to tip cynically.

"The Federation didn't call it that. The treaty stated that each family of a young woman selected to go east would be reimbursed for the rest of her married life. So, the arrangement is that for the girls not chosen to be Consort, four young men of marriageable age from the founding families submit sealed bids of how much they are willing to pay the girls' relatives each year, and the man who submits the highest bid gets first pick of the Elector's rejects."

"That sounds like an auction to me." Heath sounds nauseated. "A wife auction."

"It's not like the governors of Cinq were forced into it," I say. "What works out to one girl from the Western population per year in exchange for technology and medical supplies, plus support for an entire family, seems like a raging good deal. Which is why the 'amendments' that have subsequently been added to the treaty have been allowed."

"What amendments?"

"Sending infertile girls and women too old to bear children to Paradise was the biggest one," I say. "Dominic and Elvira Xavier said that—as evidenced by the dire situation on the East Coast—the ability to bear children is a woman's greatest asset, and without it, she is worthless."

Heath's shoulder bumps mine, but I continue to stare into my lap. "What really happens to the women who go to Paradise?" he asks quietly. "I saw a boat being loaded a few days ago, and I asked one of the dockworkers. He said that the women were all going to live out their days on the islands of Hawaii—truly Paradise on Earth. But I know that can't be true. Not when your face looks like that."

It takes effort to speak. "Hawaii? You want to know where they actually go? Davy Jones's locker."

"They—they sink? All of them?"

"There are Eastern aircraft waiting for them just out of sight of the mainland. Bombers."

"How do you know?"

"The year I turned fourteen, after the blood sample results came back, the girl who had sat next to me in school from kindergarten through eighth grade failed the test. Her FSH levels were too high." I swallow. "I wasn't even particularly close with her, but I went to the docks to say goodbye. Most of the women getting on the ships were happy, spouting about this amazing, all-expenses-paid relocation to Hawaii. But Noreen, my classmate, was distraught. 'Something terrible is going to happen,' she kept wailing. 'I just know it. I just know it.' So, when the boat set sail, I smashed the camera lens on one of the Watchdogs patrolling the beach and hopped on top. Watchdogs are shockingly easy to take control of, since most of the drone maintenance workers here aren't skilled enough to work on them from a distance."

I swallow again. "I followed the ship, staying low to the water. I was just starting to think about turning back when I heard the first explosion. When a massive wave of water crashed toward me, I turned the Watchdog and fled. I only glanced back once." My teeth clench involuntarily, and I remember them chattering frantically together as I watched the ship on which Noreen and so many others had set sail sinking slowly beneath the waves, as seven black planes circled above like monstrous vultures.

"Did you get caught coming back?"

"No. As soon as I could see the docks, I cut the power so the Watchdog and I dropped into the ocean. Then I swam to shore."

Silence stretches between us. The weight of Heath's head descends onto my shoulder. Words rise to my lips, questions about whether he's been able to sneak into any classes lately and whether his burn-pile searches have turned up any more books. Few boys in Cinq go to the government-run schools that provide basic classes in reading, writing, and arithmetic until the eighth grade. Most parents have their sons work as soon as they can do anything that will supplement the family income. Daughters, on the other hand, are encouraged to go to school as much as possible, since learning is highly valued in the Federation.

I coax Heath to go to school every chance I get, but he is afraid that his mother or father will come there looking for him, so his attendance is sporadic. Most of his education has come from the books he steals from burn piles. My books—old chemistry and biology textbooks that my father hid when the Enforcers came collecting textbooks to use as extra fuel—do not interest him. But books from the burn piles are his own personal bounty, and he will pore over them for hours on the floor of my lab, asking me for help with difficult words now and then.

I sit still and silent until his weight sinks even more heavily against me. Then I shift, looping one arm around his bony little back and the other under his knees, and carry him to the moth-eaten duvet in the corner of my lab.

When I settle him down, he shifts, fingers closing around my wrist as I drag a blanket over him. "I meant to ask what you're working on," he mumbles, gesturing toward the papers scattered across my table.

"I'll tell you tomorrow. After the Invitation."

"What if you're not here then?" Without waiting for an answer, he curls up on his side, pulling the blanket up to his chin as sleep claims him again.

He looks so small.

His usually tough, street-urchin face is childlike for once.

And I know that my "no caring" rule has been broken for a long time.

Reaching down, I smooth his tangled hair out of his eyes. "I'm not going to be another person that leaves you," I whisper, and then I throw a prayer skyward.

I pray that whatever God or First Cause or Higher Power rules this spinning blue planet really doesn't have a warped sense of humor.

CHAPTER 3

S*pluck. Splat. Squuuish.*

My bare feet strike the wet sand.

Sweat and spray-dampened strands of hair slap back and forth across my cheeks.

Foam hisses up the beach to lick at my bare toes as I dance toward the harder-packed sand higher up, rather than the granules slipping back into the surf.

"Girl!"

The rhythm of my feet falters for a moment. I glance around, expecting to see a bored Enforcer tucked behind one of the logs further up the beach, just woken up and wondering at what point in last night's drunken revels he ended up on the sand.

"They don't let you shower before the plane ride east, you know."

I come to a full halt and scan the beach for the owner of the voice I now recognize. A wisp of smoke catches my eye, and I jog toward the pile of rocks and driftwood dragged into a crude structure. I don't see her until I'm a stone's throw away, since her sand-speckled gray T-shirt and tan cargo pants blend into the rock and sand around her. She lifts a dark bottle to her lips, and I notice the sand coating the cracked edges of her mouth. The smoke is from a tiny driftwood fire—barely a spark hiding in the shadow of the rocks.

I stalk forward and kick sand over it. The woman glares belligerently up at me.

"That was for breakfast."

"What breakfast, Lida?"

"What breakfast?" Lida mimics in a singsong voice, raising her bottle for another swig. "Shouldn't you be getting ready for your tête-à-tête with the Elector's son?"

I reach over and yank the bottle out of her hands, sparks of anger, hotter than the just destroyed fire, flickering to life inside me. "You promised," I say, clenching the neck of the bottle so hard it creaks.

Lida looks past me to the swelling and receding waves of the Pacific. "You made me."

"Yes, I made you!" The alcohol swishing at the bottom of the almost empty bottle feels as though it has been poured on the sparks of my anger, turning them into a raging inferno. "Because I don't want to watch my friend drink her life away!"

"What life?" Lida's voice is dull and toneless—slate-gray sandstone to my boiling-red magma. "You know as well as I do that thirty days from now there'll be an Enforcer knocking on my door to register me for the next boat to 'Paradise'."

"What door?" I ask dryly, gesturing at the driftwood and rocks around us. Lida lets out a harsh cackle of laughter.

"Touché, girlie. But you know as well as I that my days are numbered."

"I'm living on borrowed time as much as you are, Lida. Do you see me spending my days lying like an alcohol-soaked sponge on the beach?"

"Ah, but there's the difference between us, Andromache. No one gives a rusty euroyen if I spend my last few days sitting and staring happily into the waves. You have people who need you. Who want you."

"Funnily enough, there seems to be someone standing over you right now who wants you."

"That someone is about to get on a plane. I can't care about someone who I'll never see again after today."

"I think you do care," I say. "I'll wager you a pint of"—I raise the bottle to my nose for a quick sniff—"rum that you do."

"Think you're clever, don't you?" mumbles Lida, slumping against the rock behind her and closing her eyes.

"No, I think I'm fed up." I turn and fling the bottle, watching it roll away with rum burbling out of the open top toward the foam swishing up to claim it. Reaching down, I clamp onto Lida's bony wrists and haul her to her feet. "You want breakfast? I know a place."

"I don't want eggs," Lida whines, staggering behind me as I drag her back toward the city.

"Tough. And in return for three *delicious* fried eggs, you can help me get ready for the Invitation."

"I'm not going to the Invitation."

"Wrong again. As my stylist, you most certainly are going."

I think I hear Lida mumble, "Send me to Paradise already", but I just give her my sweetest smile and quicken my pace.

They say that eight hundred and seventy-five thousand people once lived in San Francisco. I stare around the square beneath the city's monument, an enormous spinning wheel that people used for entertainment hundreds of years ago. My eyes skim the crowd, counting heads and multiplying bodies. Attendance at the Invitation is mandatory for all citizens of the city-state. I catch sight of Jez, surrounded by her daughters, with the baby I delivered yesterday strapped to her chest. I know I'm estimating, but there can't be more than three thousand people in the square. Point-three percent of the population that used to live here.

Heath spots his mother too and ducks behind me. Seconds later, a whisper drifts from his hiding place. "Hey, you smell different."

"All thanks to my stylist," I say. Lida rolls her eyes. I had been half joking when I first called her that, but I am shocked by the transformation Lida managed to effect with the limited contents of Sasha's and my cosmetic drawer. For the first time in weeks, I can tell what color the skin of my hand is—light, creamy brown with pale-pink nails, whose ragged edges Lida filed into smoothness. My hair hangs in straight black curtains around my face, the clean smell as unfamiliar to me as it is to Heath. Occasional tiny braids are laced with threads of silver Lida painted into my hair from an old half-dried bottle of nail polish Sasha bought me on my fifteenth birthday. I had thought all of my clothes were practical or stained, but Lida had rummaged in the back of my closet and come out holding a white dress with a long skirt and bell-like sleeves fringed with tassels. A broad red belt with a design made from shells was cinched around the dress's waist.

I remember the day I was given that dress. It was the middle of winter, the days as short and cold as they ever get here. Pink streaks of dawn painted the sky as I stood over a woman staring down into the blue-purple face of her stillborn daughter.

"Eleven," she had said dully. "Mother to eleven. But my home is still empty."

I stood there silently, unsure what to do or say.

"Take the dress," she said suddenly, gesturing to the broken closet door leaning clumsily against the wall. A fringed white sleeve was visible through the opening. Reaching to pull it out, I stared down at the beautiful soft fabric, the red of the belt drawing my eye. "I wore it at my wedding." The words were almost inaudible as she bent over her baby. A tear slid down her cheek, a gleaming thread of pain. "I meant to give it to my oldest daughter. But there will be no more children."

I looked around for Sasha before remembering that she had gone around the corner to the public phone to call the mortician. "Don't say that," I mumbled, my fingers bunching into the fabric of the dress's skirt. "You never know what might happen."

"My husband left last night." The words are jagged with pain. "I told him the baby had stopped moving. He said he was done. 'What use is a woman who can't bear children? What kind of woman's body rejects her own offspring? I'm not bearing your curse anymore.'"

"Curse?" The word is thick in my mouth.

What use is a woman who can't bear children?

What use?

"After the fourth miscarriage, he started to say that I was cursed. He believed in such things. I didn't. But now I'm not so sure." Her voice breaks on a dry sob.

"You're not cursed." My fingers close around her wrist, harder than I mean to. Her eyes, tear-filled and red-rimmed, flicker up to meet mine. "But he should be. How dare he leave you? How dare he say this...this pain, *this loss*, is your fault? You're better off without him."

"Andi." Sasha's voice pulls me back to the present. "That was the last call to ascend the stage."

Fear twinges in my gut, but I tamp down on it firmly.

I'm not going to get picked.

What are the odds, really?

I look down at Sasha. Something about her expression makes me suddenly see the resemblance to her sister, my mother. "You're the mother of my heart." I don't know what makes me say it, but when she meets my gaze, her eyes are wet.

"And you're as much mine as if I had brought you wailing into the world."

"Not that I care, but you're going to miss the ceremony, and I put in a lot of my valuable time to make you look halfway presentable," drawls Lida, just as Heath hisses, "Andi!"

I turn from Sasha in time to see two red-uniformed Enforcers—sent from the Federation specifically to administer the Invitation—pushing through the crowd.

"Age?" the one in front barks at me.

"Nineteen. I was just going," I say, gesturing toward the red-and-white bedecked platform which has been temporarily erected beneath our wheel monument.

"Clearly a plain face doesn't equal brains," snarls the second Enforcer, who is nearly a head shorter than I am. He latches on to my arm and propels me toward the platform.

I pull my arm from his grip. "And clearly being a shrimp doesn't stop a person from being a bully."

His hand connects with my cheek so hard that my head whips sideways. I feel something trickling down my cheek and lift my hand to my face, my fingertips coming away scarlet. The Enforcer twirls the heavy ring on his middle finger back into position, his pale blue eyes fixed insolently on my face. "In the East, we value girls with wide hips and receptive wombs. Not smart mouths."

Disgust shivers through me as his fingers close around my arm again. He only lets go of me when we reach the stairs leading to the stage. "Wipe your face, love. You're going to be on camera."

I jerk away from him, mounting the stairs quickly. My foot catches in my hem on the last step, and I stumble onto the stage, knocking into a girl who pushes me away from her.

"What are you doing? And what happened to your face?"

I catch sight of myself on the jumbotron next to the stage. Head and shoulders taller than every single one of the other fifty girls on the stage. Angular face with blood streaking my left cheek from a nick below my eye. My hand moves to cover my face, and I turn helplessly, not knowing where to go or how to get the cameras away from me.

"Psst. You! Skyscraper!" A plump, pretty redhead beckons to me and I hurry gratefully to where she is waving other girls aside to create a space in the line for me. "What did you do to your face, girl?" She clicks her tongue against her teeth, and without waiting for an answer, fishes inside her décolletage. "Here."

"I'll ruin it," I say, staring at the scrap of lace she's forced into my hand.

"What are handkerchiefs for?" She waves impatiently. "Come on. You don't want to look like you came straight from a street fight to the Invitation."

"People of Cinq." A technologically magnified voice booms out over the speakers, and the girl flaps her hands at me, still motioning to my face. I scrub the lacy scrap against my cheek as words that I've heard three other times in my life echo halfway between reality and memory.

"Behold your daughters. Your true treasures. Your future. And ours. One of these young women will become a connection, a stepping stone in the path linking our futures. Five of these lovely ladies will have the honor of bearing children to rebuild the ravaged population of the Federation while at the same time sending aid to support and comfort the families they leave behind. And one of your daughters will have a chance to become the next Consort of the Federation, providing the heirs who will one day rule the most powerful nation on this continent."

I school my features to hold back a cynical smile. *A nation so powerful it would have gone extinct without the buying of young women from another country.*

The voice of Lothar Grimsby, chief advisor to the Xavier family, drones on, detailing all the benefits that the city-states of Cinq receive as a result of the treaty: the Watchdogs that patrol our harbors, ambulances, the cruise ships that go to Paradise, sprinkler systems for our fields, and enough morphine to support our medical needs. I glance toward my family and see that Heath is huddled behind Sasha, his narrowed eyes fixed on his mother and sisters. Sasha's face is serene as always, but when she feels my gaze, her eyes meet mine and for an instant, I see a lost expression on her face. Lida's eyebrows are scrunched together, indicative of her hatred of crowds.

"And now comes the moment you have all been waiting for." My eyes lift to the screen which has been projecting Lothar Grimsby sitting at his desk in the Situation Room in the White House complex. "First, let us select our candidate from Seattle's eligible maidens." He taps the small square device lying on the desk in front of him, and the jumbotron goes black. Then, slowly, letters begin to emerge on the screen, forming dozens of tiny names, swirling in a circle, moving faster and faster as each new name appears. Every girl over eighteen in Cinq whose blood passed the initial fertility testing has an entry. The Feds claim that each young woman has an equal shot at being chosen. I don't trust anything they tell us. But right now, I hope it's true. In a random selection, my odds of being selected are next to nothing.

Jasmine.

Delilah.

Zuri.

Seraphina.

Margaret Rose.

The names are swirling so quickly that looking at them is beginning to make me feel sick. I close my eyes. Then, I hear a collective gasp from the crowd. My eyes open to see the name "Zuri Pendleton" filling the screen in flashing golden letters. The screen goes black before flipping to an image of the red-and-white decked stage in Seattle at the foot of their city's strange needle-like monument. The camera zooms in on a brunette with a pixie cut and dark blue eyes. A silver sheath dress encases her fairylike figure. For an instant, her eyes stare into the camera, black lashes fluttering. Then, her lips curve into a small smile, and she steps toward the edge of the stage and begins to wave to the crowd as the girls behind her applaud politely.

"Congratulations, Zuri! We look forward to seeing you in DC," says Lothar Grimsby's voice as the feed cuts back to him. "And now to Vancouver."

I look past the jumbotron screen, fixing my eyes on a rusty red seat attached to our spinning wheel. The white flurry of names on the black screen in the corner of my eye reminds me of the one and only time in my short life that I saw snow fall, on a mid-December day in my fifteenth year.

"Clotilde Katzmiller." My gaze goes to the screen, to the buxom girl in the pink-checked gingham, her blonde hair wound in a crown around her head. The freckles on her cheeks stand out in sharp relief as her face blanches. She buries her face in her hands, shoulders shaking with sobs. Before the feed cuts out, I see the girls on either side of

Clotilde with hands on her shoulders—whether to comfort her or force her toward the front of the stage, I am unsure.

"Would you look at that? Your new husband will certainly cry tears of joy when he sees you too, Clotilde." Anger spikes through me at the sneering tone of Lothar's voice, followed by a surge of dread.

Imagine having to live in the same complex as that man.

The names begin to flash again. In the silence, a child whimpers before being quickly hushed. Just as I am beginning to wonder whether the connection has shorted out, Grimsby says slowly, "Bella Solantis."

And her face fills the screen. It's a face I have seen before, splashed across the jumbotrons on Sunday nights during the weekly newscast along with scrolling headlines that read:

Mayor of Florence Chooses to Raise Child After Wife's Death.

Solantis Daughter Held Back Twice in Elementary School.

Bella Solantis Causes a Sensation by Singing Comic Songs During State Dinner.

Will Solantis Daughter Bella Take Part in the Invitation?

The girl now smiling sweetly into the camera has a round face and large green eyes. Blonde ringlets brush her cheeks as she walks slowly to the front of the stage, her movements bouncy. The dress she wears is like a princess gown from a storybook; light pink with a golden, lace-up bodice and skirts so long and flowy that she has to pick them up in both hands as she walks.

"Daddy!" she calls, and for the first time that day the camera pans out onto the crowd. Mayor Solantis, in a white and gold outfit clearly designed to match his daughter's, gazes up at the stage, his face slack with horror. "Daddy, they picked me! I got picked!"

Her father blinks rapidly and then, with visible effort, lifts his hands and begins to clap. The camera returns to Bella, her smile so wide it lights up her entire face, as the crowd follows her father's lead and applauds her.

"Congratulations, Bella." Grimsby's smile does not quite reach his eyes. "And on to San Francisco!"

For an instant, anger flares inside me at his lack of enthusiasm. Then I remind myself I have nothing to do with this girl. I will watch news reports about her competing in the Gauntlets and getting married in a lavish ceremony. My eyes travel to the horizon.

As soon as this is over, I'm going to take Heath to play on the beach.

"Andromache Kanoska."

What?

"No!" Sasha is always cool and collected. That cannot be her voice.

But then I look out into the crowd and see that Lida has her arms around my aunt. Lida doesn't comfort people. Heath's head is buried in Sasha's hip. His shoulders are heaving. Heath doesn't cry.

"Andromache Kanoska," Lothar Grimsby repeats, and I see myself appear on the screen above the stage, mouth open in shock.

"It's you!" The red-haired girl is yelling in my ear, her hands pushing at my shoulder. "Smile! You could be the next Consort!"

I walk to the edge of the stage, my steps slow and careful. My face on the jumbotron is contorted in a painful smile, scrunching the barely congealed scab visible on my left cheekbone.

"Well, we clearly have one candidate who won't have a problem looking the Ascendant in the eye." The strangeness of the tone in which the remark is uttered barely registers as my eyes find my family again. A single tear is making its way down Sasha's cheek. Lida's eyes are full of despair and reproach. Heath kneels on the ground beside them, broken.

"I need my stylists." I don't know how my voice rings out above the applause, but the clapping dies. The screen flickers away from Grimsby and back to me as silence settles over the crowd. I turn to where the Eastern cohort is standing. "My stylists," I say again, pointing out into the crowd. "I can't go East without them."

The Eastern cohort glances at each other, clearly without any idea of what to do. Then Grimsby's voice rings out, and his face reappears on the screen.

"Of course a girl needs her stylists!" His smile is patronizing, but relief floods through me nonetheless. "Have them join you on the stage!"

I beckon Lida forward, gesturing that she should bring Heath as well. Sasha's eyes find mine, and she gives the faintest shake of her head.

The ache that started in my heart as I watched Bella's father applaud her is growing larger, a fungus threatening to eat out the very core of my being. But I know that she is right.

Sasha is needed in San Francisco. But Lida and Heath are in danger here.

They are struggling through the crowd toward me, and I force myself to smile wider, extending my hand like a game show hostess of long ago. "Ladies and gentlemen, I give you Lida Paige and Heath Insley!"

Jez's expression is livid as she watches her son join me on the stage.

I stare her down, keeping my smile firmly in place.

The only good thing about this moment is that I'm taking your son where neither you nor his father will ever be able to hurt him again.

Try to stop me, Jez. I dare you.

CHAPTER 4

"What did I tell you?" Lida mumbles in my ear as we climb the metal steps leading to the door of the giant titanium bird. The fans mounted beneath its wings are whipping my hair into a rats' nest. "I told you you'd be getting on a plane."

"You said I'd be leaving you," I respond, clutching Heath's hand to keep him from racing off to explore. "Seriously, buddy, you have to calm down or it's going to be a very long trip."

"Can I have a seat by a window? Please, Andi?"

"Sure. Let's sit."

Heath drops my hand and darts into the first row.

"Gotta keep moving, miss," a voice says behind me. I turn to see a tall, rangy man dressed in the white and red of the Federation smiling at me. "I'm afraid we have to keep these seats up front for the gals we're picking up later. Makes the boarding process easier."

I like his deep, kind voice. "Second to last row, okay?"

"Reserved 'specially for you and your stylists, missy." He turns to smile at Lida, who glowers at him.

"You look like you could use a stylist yourself."

"Lida!"

The man's smile only widens. "This your usual tactic for getting clients, ma'am? Insulting them?"

Lida tosses her scraggly gray curls. "I'm not in the habit of taking on hopeless causes."

I turn to gape at Heath, but he is too busy trying to raise the small shade on the window to have noticed Lida's rudeness.

"There's a reason she's a stylist rather than an etiquette tutor," I say apologetically to the flight attendant. He laughs, eyes fixed on Lida as she walks forward and plops into the seat next to the aisle. She doesn't look back, but a smirk twists the corner of her mouth.

"Hey," I say, shepherding Heath into the row and then sitting down next to her. She doesn't deign to look up from the electronic pad perched on her knee, which she must have pulled out of the holder on the back of the seat in front of her. "Hey!" I say again, placing my palm over the screen.

"Oi! Fingerprints!"

"Lida!"

"What?" She finally turns to look at me.

"What was that?" I ask.

"I don't know what you're talking about."

"Lida, listen." She turns away from me, and something inside snaps. "Armageddon, Lida! You can't treat people like that. Not where we're going." The plane has begun to move, faster and faster, and she's still staring out the opposite window, watching the ground slide away as we lift into the sky. "You do realize that you were about to go to Paradise?" My voice is sharp with the remembered pain of the look on Sasha's face as she stood outside the glass barrier on the airstrip, watching me walk away. "I vouched for you. I made sure you came East. If you alienate everyone around you, it's not just your neck on the line, Lida. It's mine."

Her shoulders slump further with every word I utter. "It's official." I have to lean forward to catch her words. "I'm no better at flirting than at anything else."

Flirting.

She was flirting with him.

I sit back in my seat. Lida's moment of banter with the flight attendant was probably the last glimpse of romance I will ever get to see.

Because in a nation where brides are a commodity, the chances of finding love are as remote as those of an Infertile girl ever reaching Paradise.

CHAPTER 5

"Hello!"

I open my eyes. The gunk of hours sleeping on an airplane coats my eyelashes. A face peers over the back of the seat in front of me. It is a face with a snub nose and wide green eyes, surrounded by golden curls and wreathed in a wide smile.

"Hi." I sit up. A glance around shows me that Heath and Lida are both still asleep. "Bella, right?"

"That's right!" Bella's grin stretches even wider. Then her face falls. "But I don't remember your name."

"That's okay," I say, stifling a yawn. "It's Andromache. Andi for short."

"Who's that?" Bella points at Lida's slumped form.

"She's my stylist."

"This is my stylist, Francine." Bella gently pats the shoulder of a dark-haired woman who is sleeping in the seat next to her. "I think Daddy was happy she was going with me so that I wouldn't be alone. But he still felt very sad. He cried all last night. Did your daddy cry when you left?"

"My dad is dead. My aunt, Sasha, raised me."

"I'm so sorry." Bella's eyes crinkle in misery and, on impulse, I reach out a hand to her. For a moment, she stares at my outstretched palm before putting her soft hand into my rough one.

"It's okay," I say. "I don't remember my dad at all. He died when I was a baby. My mom too. I miss Sasha though."

"My mommy died too." Bella squeezes my hand. "She died when I was born. My daddy says that some people thought he would die too. That he couldn't keep going without her. But he says that he had a good reason to keep living. Me," she adds unnecessarily.

There is no right response. "Do you know where we are?" I ask abruptly.

"We stopped once already to pick her up," Bella says, gesturing to the row in front of her. I glimpse blonde braids. "The pilot said we have one more stop before we go East."

Seattle. Then East. I glance behind me. A pair of hostile dark eyes look back, and I face quickly forward again. I was too preoccupied to pay attention when Los Angeles's candidate was announced, so I have no idea who this girl is.

"Are you excited?" Bella's voice pulls my attention back to her. In my mind's eye, I see again the tremor in her father's hands before he brought them together in applause. This innocent, trusting young woman will be in more danger than any of the rest of us. If a certain kind of man buys her, her life will be a waking nightmare.

Stop it, Andi.

The voice that has helped to keep me and those I love safe for as long as I can remember sounds in my mind.

You already need to keep Heath and Lida safe.

You can't protect her too.

"I'm tired. Could you stop talking?" My closing eyes block out the hurt on her face but cannot erase the guilt gnawing my gut.

CHAPTER 6

"Andi!"

Heath's hiss wakes me. The cabin of the aircraft is dark, broken only by a circle of light from the window beside us.

"What? Are you okay?"

"Look!" His nose is glued to the window. "There's green grass! And the buildings! They're...whole."

I lean with him to look at the ground drawing nearer.

What he's saying wouldn't make sense to someone who hasn't grown up in one of the five remaining Western cities. But as someone whose existence was hemmed in by rubble and dead vegetation and bombed-out buildings, I understand his wonder.

The buildings circling up to meet us are pure white. Not a smoke stain in sight. The grass is so green I am sure that the Xaviers and their cronies must have invented some sort of grass-color enhancer, with a robot to spread it around. Bodies of water shine blue, reflecting a sky unobscured by smog.

"That weird pointy thing looks like it could spear this entire airplane!" Heath exclaims, just as I say, "There are no people."

"That's why they need you, obviously." Lida stretches her bony arms high above her head in a painful-looking stretch. "Though what good you—"

Heath lets out a sudden yell. Every head in the hold whips toward him. "Sorry," Heath says chirpily. "I thought I saw a robot."

"Is it just me?" A drawling voice slides through the cabin. "Or does everyone really believe that midget is a stylist?"

Heath stiffens next to me. I click my seatbelt open and push to my feet, looking for the speaker.

"Zuri, is it?" I say. "Yeah, it's just you."

Zuri rises to face me. She looks impossibly put-together for just having spent ten hours on a plane. Her scarlet pantsuit is smooth, and not a hair is out of place in her styled pixie cut.

"'Skyscraper', is it?" The nickname which sounded endearing coming from the redhead in San Francisco is now an insult. "I think your appearance provides all the evidence we need as to the efficacy of your 'stylists'."

"Well, you wanna know what I think?" Heath bursts out, heedless of the tightening of my fingers on his shoulder. "I think the Elector would choose Andi over you if she was wearing a burlap bag!"

Lida's snort combines with a trill of laughter from Bella as a faint pink flush creeps up Zuri's cheeks. Before she can speak, Bella turns to Heath, her shoulders shaking with laughter. "You're funny," she gets out.

Zuri's lips thin with disdain. "Keep your menagerie away from me," she says with a gesture that encompasses Heath, Lida, and Bella. She sits back down.

"Please remain seated with your seatbelts fastened as we land." The voice coming from the speakers is crisp, free from the crackling static I associate with audio technology. For some reason, this tiny fact brings the reality home to me that I am about to be in a place where technology is an art, and where science is pursued and revered with an almost religious fervor. For the first time since I saw my name flashing above the ruins of Golden Gate Park, the tightness in my chest eases.

"Andi!" Heath tugs on my hand. I drop into my seat and fumble for my seatbelt.

"I owe you one," I say under my breath.

A dimple pops into Heath's cheek. "You can pay in the form of a limitless supply of honey-flavored shaved ice when you're Consort."

"You know, I bet they have something better than shaved ice here."

The plane's wheels bounce onto the landing strip, and the engine's roar becomes momentarily deafening. A bony hand pinches my wrist, and I turn toward Lida.

"It won't happen again."

"What was that? Did you say 'I'm sorry'?"

Her lips pinch as she glares at me. "It won't happen again!"

"It's too loud! I keep hearing you apologizing!"

Lida reaches across and grabs the unopened bag of pretzels I was saving in case Heath needed it later out of my cup holder and tears it open. Before her, I never knew that eating pretzels could be a passive aggressive act, but every snap and crunch sends a clear message.

Smirking, I am about to lean across Heath to look out at the airport again when a voice arrests me. "What did she mean that I'm your menagerie?"

Bella peers over the back of the seat at me. "Don't worry about her," I say, making no effort to keep my voice down. "She's not worth bothering about."

"Why isn't she worth bothering about?"

"Because she's..."

Lida's voice fills in my pause. "An arrogant, bitter little cardinal who should know more than any of us about being someone's pampered pet."

Bella's laughter rings out again, mingled with Heath's, and I am about to join in when my eyes connect with Zuri's. She looks away almost immediately, but there was something in her expression that I didn't expect.

Suddenly, I wonder if Lida's jab about being someone's pet struck a little too close to home.

Is anyone at home weeping for Zuri? Like Bella's father and Sasha are weeping for us? Or are they celebrating the fact that all their careful training finally paid off?

CHAPTER 7

"T hose who brought their own stylists will be shown directly to their rooms to begin preparing for tonight's dinner. Those who did not will be assigned a Barbara."

Clotilde's hand creeps into the air. "A what?"

"A Barbara." The crisp voice of the silver humanoid standing before us is not unpleasant, but the lack of volume and tone variation is jarring. "A droid designed as an expert in ideal human appearance. Custodia 835 and Custodia 671 will guide you and the other maiden with no stylist to our salon."

Two humanoids with bodies made of some white material I've never seen before come forward. They halt before Clotilde and the candidate from Los Angeles.

"Clotilde Katzmiller," the first one intones. "I am Custodia 835, your protector and guide. Please prepare to follow."

"Raquelle Mortimer," says the second, its voice the first male timbre I have heard in an automaton. "I am Custodia 671, your protector and guide. Please prepare to follow."

Raquelle runs one hand through her auburn hair in an exaggerated motion. "All prepared," she says. "Lead on, Todi."

I bite my lip to keep from smiling. Custodia 671 has no ability to alter his facial expression, but if he did, I am certain his eyebrows would be scrunched in confusion. "My name is Custodia 671," he says.

"Ah, but Todi suits you so much better." Raquelle's eyes are wide and innocent.

"But my name—"

"I know your name." Raquelle's melodious voice sharpens. "And because *my* name appeared on a screen, I'm here to act as the unpaid surrogate for some excuse for a human who won't care what my name is as long as my fertile years are long. Now, are you leading the way or shall I?"

In the silence that follows, I stare at the back of Raquelle's head, admiration for her mingling with disgust for myself. Every word she just said expresses my feelings exactly. But I won't ever join her in slinging cutting truths. Because of Heath and Lida. And because I don't have the guts.

Todi starts toward a door at the far end of the hall with Raquelle following, when the silver droid speaks. "Raquelle Mortimer." Raquelle stops walking. "Stand by for a transmission," the silver automaton intones, tapping a finger against the center of her chest. A crack appears in the silver, and the droid's chest divides, the halves pulling apart and back like a beetle's wings. Where in a human, a fist-sized red orb would rest, sits a miniature screen.

As we watch, the image of Lothar Grimsby's smiling face appears. "Raquelle, my dear, how nice to get a little glimpse into your personality."

A muscle twitches in Raquelle's jaw.

"However." The voice over the speakers is crystal clear, and a shiver creeps up my spine at the icy menace in the next words. "Here in the Federation, speaking of marriage or childbearing in a disparaging manner is an offense meriting the strictest punishments under the law." Heath's arm trembles against my side. "I am aware that you have not yet had the opportunity to become acquainted with our laws." Grimsby's voice is honeyed once more. "Patricia 003, just a slight reprimand to remind Raquelle of basic civility."

I glance over my shoulder, unsure who he is speaking to. A grunt draws my eyes forward in time to see the silver humanoid withdrawing her fingers from around Raquelle's wrist. A bracelet-like band of rosy welts remains imprinted into the skin.

"Ladies." Swallowing, I look back at the tiny screen. "We look forward to meeting you at the welcoming banquet tonight. Go and make yourselves beautiful."

"The green makes you look seasick." Lida studies me critically. The contents of my suite's closet are strewn on the furniture around us. She gestures to another gown draped over the back of the couch. "The red exudes confidence.

And it shows off your legs. If I had mile-long legs, I'd want to show them off."

I run my fingers along the silky skirt of the green dress. "What do you think, Heath?" When he doesn't answer, I turn to see him huddled in the salon chair, lips tightly compressed as though he's afraid he's going to be sick. "Heath?" I move toward him, squatting next to the chair to put our faces at the same level. "Buddy, what's wrong?"

Small fingers worm their way into mine. He leans forward, his curls brushing my face as his breath fills my ear. "What if there are more cameras?"

"More cameras?"

"Like the ones they used to see that girl. When she was talking bad about marrying one of the Feds."

I study the room for any sign of cameras or suspicious wiring. I don't yet know enough about Eastern technology to be sure how Raquelle's words were overheard. "I think," I say very quietly, pretending to rest my hand on Heath's forehead as though checking for a temperature, "that the recording device was in the robot—Patricia 003. But you're right that we have to be careful, Heath. We have to act as though everything we say might be overheard."

I barely catch his next words, even with our faces inches apart. "I don't want Patricia 003 to burn me, Andi. My dad already did that once." His hand twitches in mine, and I glance down to see a raised pink circle of skin in the center of his palm that I had never noticed before. "I was staying at his place once, and he got drunk and started beating his girlfriend. I grabbed on to his leg to try to stop him, and when he tried to shake me off, I bit him right above the knee. His girlfriend raced to the door and got away. But my dad grabbed me before I could follow her and he...he...held me down and pushed the burning end of his cigar against my hand. He said if I ever tried a trick like that again, he'd lock me in the house and burn it down with me inside it."

I grip his shoulders. "Listen to me," I say. "Have I ever let anyone hurt you?" He shakes his head. "Here is no different than home," I say. "No one is going to hurt you. Not while I'm around."

"But as soon as you get married, you won't be around." Out of the corner of my eye, I can see Lida with a perfume bottle clutched in her hands, straining to hear my answer.

My anger morphs into determination. "Then I'll become the Consort," I say. "When I have the Elector's ear, you'll all be protected. I promise."

CHAPTER 8

*T*his must be the entire adult human population of the
Federation.

Here.

In this room.

I fidget with the sparkly golden skirt of the dress that
Heath picked out for me. He was so distraught at the punishment inflicted on Raquelle that I didn't have the heart to
reject his suggestion. The dress is so tight that my thighs
are sticking together, and the sequins lining the slit ending
just above my knee cause my skin to tingle and itch.

In an effort to distract myself, I scan the expansive room.
Men. So many men. Federation soldiers, dressed in their
distinctive red-and-white uniforms. Nobles dressed in suits
of every conceivable color—lime green, sunset orange,
cough-medicine blue. The few women I see are dressed

much more conservatively than their male counterparts, their black, silver, and white apparel causing them to blend in with the floor, walls, and tablecloths. Only about two hundred people in all.

Across the table, a throne-like platinum chair sits vacant. Two chairs sit on each side of it, waiting for the four noble sons who will be lucky enough to obtain a Western bride. But I don't care about the men who will sit in those chairs. I have my sights set on the man who, if I can somehow make him choose me, will be able to protect those I love.

A second table runs parallel to ours. At it sit three middle-aged couples and one woman alone. The women are dressed in matching cream-colored evening gowns. The men wear suits even more extravagant than the rest of the hall. A platinum seat identical to the one at our table sits vacant, as does the smaller silver seat beside it.

A throbbing drumroll begins close by, swelling over the banquet hall. It grows louder and louder until it is vibrating in my chest cavity. I look around for the source but see nothing.

Silence abruptly falls. Then applause breaks out. It takes a moment for me to realize that every person in the banquet hall has risen to their feet. I scramble to follow their example, and the heel of my stiletto catches on the hem of my dress. A ripping sound fills my ears. I glance down, and my heart drops at the sight of my black slip peeking through the slit which now extends to my waist.

"Gentlemen! And ladies." My fingers clutch at the material of my dress in a fruitless attempt to close the extended slit as I look up to find Lothar Grimsby—in the flesh—standing on a small revolving platform that has miraculously appeared between the tables below the dais. As I watch, the metallic arms supporting the platform extend, slowly rising until Grimsby is looking down upon the crowd, even at those of us seated at the high table. "First, I must bring you sorrowful tidings. The Elector is feeling unwell this evening. He and the Consort will not be joining us."

He allows a respectful pause before continuing. "Later this evening, you will all get the chance to marvel at the beauty and class of the five young women selected from the daughters of our ally, Cinq, to compete for the honor of becoming the Federation's seventh Western-born Consort. But now let me present to the ladies themselves, our five most eligible bachelors!"

Applause rises from the tables below us, and Grimsby pauses, an indulgent smile curling his lips. To my left and right, Zuri and Clotilde are applauding politely, but I am too scared of releasing the material of my dress to join them. My eyes catch on Bella, sitting on the far side of Clotilde. Her curly blonde hair is arranged in an elegant twist, and she is wearing a princess-style blue dress that brings out the color of her eyes. She is not clapping either, but staring around the hall, her expression one of delighted wonder.

"Alden Fenwick!" Grimsby's voice booms out above us, and I turn, taking in the young man striding out onto the edge of the dais. His dark hair is buzzed short on the sides with a slightly longer top. A pure-white suit with a light-blue shirt beneath accentuates the tan of his skin, and as he moves purposefully to the edge of the dais, I notice how his suit coat strains against his shoulders and the bulge of his thighs in his dress pants. An athlete?

Alden Fenwick bows slightly to the crowd, then turns sharply and strides to the chair at the far end of the table, across from Bella, who gives him her signature guileless smile. "I'm Bella!" she says.

"That suits you," he responds, the words genuine rather than flattering.

Bella's reply is drowned as Grimsby's voice booms out again. "Nicholas Pendell!"

The man striding toward us is handsomer than Alden. And he knows it. His extravagant scarlet suit gleams with traces of silvery embroidery. His blond hair is pulled into a ponytail at the base of his neck, highlighting his sharp chin and high, angular cheekbones. His bow is exactly what I would have expected—long and full of unnecessary flourishes. When he finally approaches the table, he takes the seat at the opposite end from Alden, across from Raquelle. She ignores him, staring out sightlessly over the crowd, her hands folded in the lap of her long-sleeved black dress.

"Barek Montego!" This man is short and stocky, but the bulge of his muscles could compete with Alden's. Curly red hair frizzes around his face, matching his bristling beard. As he reaches the edge of the stage, he raises his arms in acceptance of the crowd's adulation, but for some reason the gesture bothers me far less than Nicholas's flourishes. As he pulls out the seat across from Clotilde, my heart rate begins to pick up.

Only one more before *him*.

"They say you shouldn't have favorites." Grimsby's voice is more jocular than I've ever heard it. "But the next bachelor is mine. Meet my youngest son, Hugh Grimsby!"

I know the short man striding across the stage, clad in the red-and-white uniform of an Enforcer. I recognize the arrogant face. The short dark hair. The ring glinting on his middle finger.

Wipe your face, love. You're about to be on camera.

He saunters to the edge of the dais, raising one hand in lazy acknowledgement of the tumultuous applause. As he turns toward the table, his eyes find mine, and a smile spreads slowly across his face.

"Well, if It Isn't the smart-mouthed girl," he says softly as he sinks into the chair opposite Zuri. Unpleasant heat fills me as his gaze traces the exposed skin of my collarbone and follows the descending line of my single-shoulder dress.

I sit back in my chair. "Well, if it isn't the bullying shrimp," I say.

"Careful, sweetheart." Hugh's voice is so low that I must lean closer to catch the words. "You might want to remember that I have the ability to buy you. And that there are no laws here to prevent a man from making his possession's life a living hell."

"It might do you good to remember that if I marry the Elector, I will have the power to not only make your life a living hell, but to end it entirely. I'm sure scarring the Consort is frowned upon here."

I gesture to the pale-pink nick barely visible on my cheekbone. Hugh opens his mouth, his face twisting, but just then the applause begins again. It continues to surge, accompanied by the stamping of hundreds of feet, growing louder and louder until the dishes on the tables are rattling with the sound. Hugh stands, rearranging his features into a smile. Carefully, I rise to my feet, wincing inwardly as I hear another few stitches tear. Feeling Hugh's gaze, I twist to present the undamaged side of my dress to his perusal as I join in the applause. For now, the torn side of my dress is facing a blank stretch of wall.

"And it's the one we've all been waiting for!" Grimsby's magnified voice projects above the tumultuous applause. "Ladies, I give you the most eligible bachelor of them all, who will be choosing one of you to rule the entire Eastern Federation by his side, His Excellency...Denzel Marcellus Xavier!"

What a pretentious name, I think as I look toward the back of the stage.

Though in all fairness, that is rich coming from someone named Andromache.

And then he appears, walking straight past me, shoulders back and head held high, causing all my thoughts to dry up except for one.

All of this would have been easier if you were short and ugly.

CHAPTER 9

I f anyone had asked me, I would have said that there wasn't a man on the planet who could pull off a pink tuxedo.

But Denzel Xavier can.

His mahogany skin contrasts perfectly with the light rose of his suit. And that isn't all.

He's wearing an earring. A single diamond stud in his left ear. He's pulling that off too.

And with barely a hair on his head, he's clearly taller than I am. By a good six inches.

Denzel Xavier reaches the edge of the platform and pauses. I stare at his rigid back, wondering if he is making some sign to the crowd that I cannot see.

"Still think you have a chance of becoming Consort, smart girl?" whispers Hugh.

"Maybe he wants a girl who can look him in the eye without getting a crick in her neck," I say without turning my head.

As the Elector's son turns toward the table, Hugh flashes a broad smile at him. The Ascendant's expression does not change. He strides to the table, lifts one of the platinum arms of his chair, and sinks down, fingers flying over the keypad on the other arm.

A soft humming noise reaches my ears just as Grimsby says, "No one wants to watch festivities on an empty stomach. Please place your orders now!"

A babble of talk fills the hall as I glance surreptitiously to either side. Clotilde is tapping the silver rectangle in front of her, which I had taken to be a plate. Zuri, however, leans forward, the curled black lines of her eyeliner scrunching slightly as she smiles at Denzel Xavier.

"My name is Zuri, Your Excellency," she says, her clear voice cutting through the noise around us.

Xavier turns to look at her. Then, without a word, he withdraws from his pockets two small black objects that he slips into his ears.

Hugh has the grace to look mildly embarrassed. "Clearly, he's not feeling social tonight," he says to Zuri. "Denzel?" He nudges the future Elector's shoulder. When nothing happens, except that Xavier continues to tap on the screen in front of him, Hugh reaches out and removes the black object from Xavier's ear.

The Ascendant of the Federation turns his head slowly and stares at Hugh, still saying nothing. Then he holds out a hand, palm up.

"Denzel, you can't act like this." Hugh's voice is barely audible.

"Correct me if I'm wrong, Hugh, but these girls are all dying to marry me and not one of them cares how charming I am." His voice is like dark chocolate, smooth and rich with a slight edge.

"Denzel, your father..."

"His happiness has been at the bottom of my priority list for quite some time."

"These girls have traveled thousands of miles. You could at least be civil."

"Civility doesn't produce heirs. Which is their entire purpose."

"You know, I've always been in favor of castration for males who can't produce children." I had thought I wouldn't be fool enough to follow in Raquelle's footsteps. But after everything I've been through over the last twenty-four hours, the Ascendant's indifference and arrogance are suddenly too much. The silence that settles around the table following my words is so thick I could cut it with a knife.

"Skyscraper, was it?"

"I didn't think names concerned you."

"Yours certainly doesn't," Xavier says, leaning back in his chair and crossing his arms over his chest. "Tell me more about this castration agenda of yours."

I give him a smile that is all teeth. "Why, yes. It seems only fair to me since fertility is such a valuable trait here."

"And what should be done to the infertile women? Given your all-consuming desire for fairness?"

I can't help it. I laugh. "I thought intelligence was the other valuable trait."

Hugh leans toward me, eyes narrowing as his mouth opens. Xavier's arm catches him in the chest, pushing him back. "I fail to see the problem with wanting your population to be as physically strong and mentally robust as possible."

Anger causes my words to come out too quickly, tripping over each other. "You fail to see a problem with 'pruning' anyone who fails to meet your mental and physical standard? Do you even know your own history? That kind of thinking led to the near extinction of your population through abortion."

"Abortion is no longer practiced here, Miss Kanoska. The practice bears the strictest penalties under our laws."

You knew my name all along.

"Oh, well done. You don't kill children in the womb. You just kill the females outside it who, due to inability or age, can't produce a baby."

Xavier surveys me with a faintly amused expression. "I'll make sure our honeymoon suite is booked in the closed ward, love. Less for my dimwittedness and more for my wife's paranoia."

I can see the boat full of women exploding, fire shooting into the sky. I remember waiting every month for years for blood to streak the insides of my underwear, my sense of being broken growing with each absent cycle. I remember seeing each new baby in Jez's arms as Sasha collected blood samples to mark with my name, and jealousy ate at my heart.

Lida and Heath and any thought of safety is swept under in the tide of my fury as I plant both hands on the table, pushing myself to my feet. There is a tugging resistance as I rise, but the mild opposition only angers me more, and I yank upward. Over the thunder in my ears, I hear the rending sound of sequined fabric.

And I am too slow to grab my dress as it slides off my shoulder. It pools into a puddle of gold streaming off the table, held down by the single shoulder strap still looped around my wrist.

"Andromache Kanoska, thank you!" Grimsby's voice rings out. "Everyone, please welcome the first of our contestants to give her greeting speech!"

CHAPTER 10

On any other night, the Andi who is smart and quiet and safe would have asked for a moment. A moment to go and make herself presentable. A moment to collect herself.

But after my conversation with Denzel Xavier?

I am no longer clever Andi.

The sequined gold dress falls to the ground as I lift my hand from the tabletop. I stride toward Lothar Grimsby on his little pedestal, which is lowering to receive me. His eyes widen as he takes in my stilettos paired with the opaque black slip that stops mid-thigh.

I've heard the recorded versions of the greeting speeches from the last Consort contestants. Speeches explaining how much they would do for the Federation. Speeches talking about the wonders of this technological empire. Speeches drooling over Denzel Xavier's father, Cronus.

Grimsby hands me an amplification device as I mount the platform. "People of the Federation," I say. The buzz of conversation softens but does not fade completely. "I am Andromache Kanoska, a native of Cinq, born and raised in the city of San Francisco on the Pacific Ocean." The platform continues to descend, probably on Grimsby's signal, to keep everyone in the hall from staring up my slip. Soon I can no longer see Denzel Xavier or any of the girls from the West.

"I spent my growing up years playing hide-and-seek in the rubble, eating eggs because there was nothing else, and listening to the Pacific roar me to sleep at night. Before I went to bed, I would tinker with chemical experiments, hoping to one day invent some amazing product that would ease the lives of those around me. It was work that I loved. But the work I loved more was helping to deliver babies. Because no matter how broken and scarred was the world into which they were entering, I knew that these children were the future. They were the light in the darkness surrounding all of us."

I stare at the muttering crowd, their looks of incomprehension and amusement stoking my anger. "Cinq is my country," I say into the microphone. "Its people are my people. Everything I do is to benefit my people. And nothing that happens here will ever change that."

I turn and push the device back at Grimsby. After a moment, the platform begins to rise again. As soon as it is level with the dais, I jump off, staggering slightly in my high heels. In the silence, I walk to my empty seat and scoop the folds of the ruined dress into my arms. Xavier's eyes seem to magnetically attract my gaze, and I meet his look, unable to read the expression on his face.

"Thank you"—sarcasm drips from my words—"for an *unforgettable* evening. I'm afraid I'm a little tired. If you will excuse me."

The river of emotion that had control of me is already draining away as I make my way toward the exit at the back of the dais. As the door clicks shut behind me, only a trickle remains. And by the time I pause next to a window in an abandoned corridor, a pit of fear is forming in my stomach.

What was I thinking? And what will my actions mean for Heath and Lida?

I sink against the window frame and stare out into the dark night, barely registering the fact that the horizon is moving in gentle waves.

Civility doesn't produce heirs. Which is their entire purpose.

My fingernails dig into my elbows as a tiny sliver of my previous fury pierces through my fear.

That arrogant, self-centered jerk. Sitting there with his earplugs in, not even pretending to be polite to girls who had just been ripped away from their homes and families for the sole purpose of marrying him and his cronies.

Memory surfaces of being thirteen years old and Sasha telling me that I would most likely never have a baby. She told me then that being infertile didn't make me less of a woman.

But a part of me has never believed her. Because the ability to bear children is so quintessentially female that the lack of it makes me feel irreparably broken.

Xavier's words pick at that old, scabbed-over wound, prodding at the buried belief that I am damaged goods.

A beeping noise makes me turn as my arms clutch protectively around my torso, trying automatically to add to the scantiness of my outfit. I expect to see an automaton of some kind, but the hallway is empty.

"Hello?"

The beeping is growing louder, and I do not want to be found alone in a hallway, clad in nothing but my undergarments. I wriggle out of my stilettos and, holding them in one hand, run silently down the hallway in the opposite direction from the beeping.

As I round a corner and the sound dies away behind me, I slow, realizing that I am running with no idea how to get back to my suite. For lack of a better plan, I continue to walk down the new hallway, looking around. The walls are a pristine white, hung with images in shiny golden frames. My walk slows as I examine the pictures, which are like nothing I have ever seen before.

One is of a girl in a voluminous pink dress and a tiny hat suspended by ropes above a lush green garden. Another shows swirling balls of yellow light above a dark, sleepy town. Then there is a long one of a man at a table surrounded by other men, all whispering and staring at him.

My steps come to a halt, and I turn on the spot, staring in wonder at the art on the walls. In the cities of the West, people are too concerned about where their next meal is going to come from to worry about creating beauty. Occasionally, crude graffiti appears on some undamaged wall if a street urchin gets his hands on a can of spray paint. But nothing like this.

After what feels like a long time, I begin to walk again. As I reach the end of the corridor lined with paintings, I realize, with a start, that the grief and anger and fear have all eased, calmed by the beauty of the paintings into something close to peace.

At the end of the hall, there is a landing with one staircase curving up and another down. I begin to climb up, since I know that the metal box that took me to the banqueting hall went down. On the next landing, I push open a door. It only takes a glance for me to be sure that it is not the hallway containing my bedroom, but just as I am turning away, something catches my eye, and I turn back.

Directly to the left of the staircase is a wall of glass. And through it, I see something even more amazing than the paintings.

I make my way to the windows and peer in, careful not to leave smudges on the glass. The room beyond stretches almost the entire length of the hallway and is impossibly clean, with gleaming white floors and shining steel tables. On some of the tables, there are vials and jars of different solutions, all neatly labeled. In the space beneath the tables are rows of shelves, stocked with scientific instruments, most of which I have never seen before. The back wall of the room is lined with machines—refrigerators, some sort of washing apparatus, and several computers.

There is an electronic scanner on the wall beside the entrance, but the door is ajar. Whoever was last in the room failed to close it properly.

I glance around. The hallway is empty. All the human citizens of the Federation are down in the banqueting hall. I could get caught by a patrolling robot though.

On the other hand, no one actually said that I couldn't look around. If anyone finds me, I can honestly say that I am lost.

I hover for a few moments, weighing the risks.

Finally, with a glance over my shoulder, I slip into the lab.

I had planned to only stay for a moment, but as the hallway outside remains empty, I find it difficult to tear myself away from equipment the likes of which I have only dreamed of. I walk between the tables, examining vials and instruments, trying with a kind of delighted hopelessness to guess what they are for. I think of my garage at home, my scribblings on scrap paper, and my concoctions in old mason jars, and jealousy prickles to life.

How much more could I have helped Sasha and the mothers and infants of San Francisco if I had access to equipment like this?

My initial feelings toward Denzel Xavier grow stronger with every step.

He could do so much good. He could send the kind of aid to the West that would save hundreds, if not thousands, of lives. But no.

The measly aid he does send requires payment in the form of some girl he will make miserable for the rest of her life so that she can produce heirs for him.

The sound of the door opening makes me drop instinctively to the ground before realizing how suspicious such behavior seems. From the farthest corner of the room, where I had been examining a set of blue vials labeled with the cryptic annotation "Long. Ser.", I peek through the metal legs of the tables. I catch a glimpse of a pair of legs clad in light-pink pants before I curl into a ball against the wall, holding my breath.

"Thank the First Cause that's over." Denzel Xavier's mumble rumbles through the silent room. There is the sound of footsteps, then the thump of him settling into a chair, followed by a clicking sound.

I am just debating whether to try to see what he is doing when sound explodes through the laboratory. I think it must be music, but like the paintings in the hall, it's like nothing I've ever experienced before. For one thing, the volume is so loud that I almost cover my ears. For another, there is a drumming, swishing sound throughout that I can feel throbbing in my chest like a second heartbeat. And I am just deciding that this is exactly the sort of music Denzel Xavier would listen to when I begin to catch the lyrics.

The song is about a couple who are so poor they're scared that they won't make it. But the fact they're together means that every trial they face is worth it. In spite of the volume and the drumming and the screaming, it is impossible to escape the fact that Denzel Xavier is listening to a love song.

The music keeps playing as I huddle on the cold laboratory floor.

There is a song about the end of the world.

One about a tiger's eyes.

Another about not forgetting the person you love.

The style of the music is mostly the same, loud and heavy, but I get so caught up in listening to the lyrics that I lose track of time. When quiet finally descends over the laboratory again, I almost miss the pulsing beat. But the next moment, footsteps approach the table I'm crouched behind.

Denzel Xavier pauses on the opposite side of the metal table. "What the—" he mutters, and I tense, certain that he is about to call me out.

But there is only a clinking noise, followed by the sound of receding footsteps. The laboratory light clicks. I stay still for a while before getting up and sneaking toward the door. As I reach for the door handle, the horrible thought that Xavier might have remembered to lock the door this time flashes across my mind. Then I notice the sliver of light along the doorframe. Relief floods through me as I open it and slip out into the hallway. However, I haven't made it more than three steps from the lab when a voice speaks behind me.

"Your suite is upstairs, Miss Kanoska."

I turn, knowing from the automated voice that I will not see a human. The silver humanoid, Patricia 003, stands before me.

"I left the banquet early and got lost. Could you show me the way?"

Patricia 003 nods once. "Come," she says. I follow her as she leads me back to the staircase and up two more flights of steps. As we make our way down the hallway, I study every door and window and light sconce intently, determined to start learning my way around this place.

Patricia 003 stops outside my door. "Goodnight, Miss Kanoska."

"Goodnight, Patricia 003," I say. "Thank you."

"Administration is my purpose," the automated voice responds coolly, and the silver humanoid turns and glides away. For a moment, I stare after her before opening the door of the suite and creeping inside. In my room, I pull on a loose-fitting shirt and pair of pants. Then I fall into bed, my eyes closing before I hit the pillow.

Nightmares haunt me. Tiny black bugs swarm out of the bedclothes and into my pajamas, nipping and clawing at my skin. The more I thrash and scream, trying to escape them, the more they seem to multiply. Finally, I sink back in despair, allowing the creatures to swarm every inch of my body, horror as thick as mud coating my tongue.

The next morning, I wake to Heath perched on the edge of my bed, his eyes crinkled with concern as he peers down at me. "I just wanted to check on you," he says. "You were moaning half the night."

"Nightmares," I start to say, leaning down to scratch my ankle. Then I pull up the leg of my pajamas and stare at my skin, which is pockmarked with thousands of red welts, like bites from innumerable miniature jaws.

CHAPTER 11

"You did *what!*"

I had found a game on the electronic pad from my bedside table and sent Heath to play it on his bed before showing Lida the sores covering my body. Then, I reluctantly explained what happened at the banquet the night before.

"Andi, are you crazy?" The mixture of disappointment and horror on Lida's face makes me squirm as I scratch nervously at the bites on my wrists. She slaps furiously at my hands, glaring at me. "Do you want scars to help you remember this debacle?"

"I messed up, okay? You didn't hear him, Lida."

"I don't care if he said that every woman on the face of the planet should be put in a sack and dropped into the Atlantic Ocean! Did you expect him to be Prince Charming out of a fairy tale—some perfect gentleman? Of course he's an evil, arrogant megalomaniac, Andi! If you marry him, then yes, you will be signing up for a loveless marriage. But if you can win him over, then you will be able to protect those who are unable to protect themselves. Across two nations."

The weight of her words settles over me. I thought I had dismissed the hope of a fairy-tale romance long ago, after watching years of misery and suffering play out around me in San Francisco. But clearly the hope for something else has lingered.

I could settle for trying to win one of the other bachelors. Alden and Barek both appeared decent at first glance. But, like Lida says, it is Denzel Xavier who holds the power of change. Of protection for the powerless. Denzel Xavier and whichever woman sits beside him as his Consort.

"You're right," I say. "I was a fool yesterday. But it won't happen again. Consort material. That's what I'll be. Beautiful. Irresistible. And untouchable. Nothing anyone says or does will get to me."

Something shifts in her eyes. Then she says, "Given your—ahem—*minimal* attire last night and the bites, I have just the outfit for you."

"A little bit of a seesaw on the fashion front, aren't we?" Zuri's mocking voice cuts through the breakfast suite, causing every head, including those of the serving droids, to turn toward me.

I smile benignly at Zuri, resisting the urge to fiddle with the black lace mitts Lida used to cover the bites on my hands. "Just thought I'd go on the safe side. To avoid a repeat of last night."

Before Zuri can retort, Bella bounds toward me. "I think you look wonderful, Andi! So striking!"

"Striking" is a good word for the olive-green romper with flowing legs and sleeves. Lida cinched it tightly around my waist with a broad black belt and added a jade necklace and a pair of high-heeled leather boots to finish the look. A much thicker layer of makeup than I would usually wear covers the bites on my face, and my hair is braided into a loose, chunky French braid.

"You look nice too," I say, allowing Bella to seize my hand and drag me to the seat next to her. "That dress is adorable. And the brown complements your skin tone."

"Did you mean to rip off your dress last night?" Bella asks me as soon as we are seated.

I feel heat rising up my face and take a deep breath, hoping that the thick layer of foundation on my cheeks will keep them from turning red. Before I can respond, Bella continues, "I heard the Ascendant telling his friend that you just did it to get attention, but that that kind of stunt wouldn't work on him."

"My dress tearing was an accident," I say levelly, forcing myself to focus on Bella's face and ignore the mocking stares I can feel coming from Zuri and Raquelle.

"That's what I thought," Bella says cheerfully, reaching across the table to add some grapes to her plate. "You seemed really upset about it, so I was sure it couldn't be on purpose."

I fight the urge to turn away from her and engage someone else in conversation.

She's so tactless. I'm already a laughingstock without her help.

But she's honest, whispers a tiny voice inside. *Everyone else here, including you, is lying. Playing a part. But not her.*

"What did you think of the bachelors?" I say, following her example and adding fruit to my plate.

Bella glances up at me, and a faint blush colors her cheeks. "Alden was really nice to me. He said my name suits me. Bella means 'beautiful' in French. Did you know that?"

"I didn't know that. Do you think you'll see him again today?"

Before Bella can answer, the automated voice of Patricia 003 fills the room. "Ladies, I hope you are enjoying your breakfast. If you need anything, simply relay your desire to one of the Custodias and they will assist you." She pauses, and I marvel inwardly at the programming that keeps her monotone voice from running on without a break until the entirety of her message is finished. "As you all know, you ladies are here to compete for the honor of becoming Consort of the Federation and wife to our Ascendant, Denzel Xavier. In six months' time, on the birthday of the Federation's very first Western Consort, Elvira Xavier, her great-great-great-great-grandson will choose a bride from among the five of you."

She pauses again. "In the first two months, your objective will be to show the prince your prowess as a hostess. Each of you will plan an event, to be held at the end of that time period. The Ascendant, in conjunction with the Elector, the current Consort, and a Council consisting of the parents of the other four suitors, will evaluate each event based on its enjoyableness and networking potential, to get an idea which of you would be most adept at forging and maintaining ties between the royal family and its allies."

Plan a party. Check.

"The second two months will be devoted to physical strength. The Consort of the Federation must be a paragon of fitness and health, fully prepared to assist her husband in all aspects of ruling, and unencumbered by physical ailments. Her capabilities in bearing children will also be greatly enhanced by a strong body. At the end of the fourth month, all five contestants will compete in an obstacle course designed to push the contestants to the limits of their strength and endurance."

Obstacle course. Check?

"The third and final test will be of your ingenuity and technological skill. The Federation was sustained in its darkest days by my kind, under the administration of the first ruler of this nation. The Federation is no longer teetering on the brink of collapse, but even now, it is its technology that has made this country a world power and the dominating force on this continent. Any Consort of the Federation must be able to contribute to this noble tradition that has sustained us throughout our history. You may work on your inventions during all six months, and on the last day of the sixth month, you will present your creation to Denzel Xavier and the Council of nobles."

Invention. Now that might be something I'll actually enjoy doing.

"How is the Federation the most powerful nation on this continent?" Every head turns toward Raquelle, who hasn't bothered to raise her hand but is staring aggressively at Patricia 003. "Why didn't Canada or Mexico attack while this place was 'teetering on the brink of collapse'?"

"Due to the shifting of tectonic plates following the devastating 2156 earthquake, the country of Mexico is no longer a part of this continent." Patricia 003's monotone exhibits no change in response to Raquelle's tone. "The land masses separated such that it is now the northernmost part of the continent of South America. And climate change resulting from the atmospheric shifts following the nuclear battles of the twenty-third century has led to excessive melting in the polar ice caps, which has caused much of northern Canada to be submerged by the rising oceans. This natural disaster prevented them from being strong enough to mount an offensive against us, while the border wall that was built along the northern edge of the United States in 2097 prevented an influx of refugees."

I have never heard any of this before. The schools in Cinq were barely equipped to teach basic math and language arts.

"If there are no further questions, I will go over the schedule," intones Patricia 003. "Your days will be structured as follows. You will remain in your rooms until breakfast, which will be served at 8:00 a.m. every morning. As soon as breakfast is finished, you will have a tête-à-tête with the suitor who is assigned to you. Lunch will be served here at eleven thirty, after which time, you will proceed to a classroom on the ground floor to participate in a mandatory class covering the history and government of the Federation. From two thirty until dinner at six, you will have free time, during which you may participate in a variety of approved activities, including visits to the library or laboratories, spa treatments, gym time, social activities, games in the grounds, or alone time in your suites. There will be a variety of mandatory political and social events in the evenings throughout the week, but whatever evenings are free may be spent as you choose as long as you are in the White House compound and in your suites by curfew at 11:00 p.m. Saturday mornings will be spent in mandatory fitness classes in the morning and spa time in the afternoon, and Sundays may be spent however you choose. Do you have any questions?"

Zuri's hand rises into the air. "Today's suitor assignments?" she asks.

"Suitor assignments will be as follows. Alden and Clotilde. Nicholas and Zuri. Barek and Bella."

Please. Maker of this blue planet. Not—

"Hugh and Raquelle. His Excellency Denzel and Andromache."

CHAPTER 12

"**S**kyscraper?"

I tense against the balcony's railing, my fingernails digging into the painted wood. Then I turn slowly to look at the young man leaning against the doorframe behind me.

"That's me," I say, smiling blandly. "My chief purpose in life before coming here was reaching items on top shelves for my aunt."

"Your uncle was a dwarf?"

Every word that comes out of his mouth sets my teeth on edge. "Sasha wasn't married."

"And you hoped to follow in her footsteps."

"I hoped to be allowed to live out my days happily and usefully, whether married or single."

"You're giving me a toothache, Kanoska."

"What?"

"After last night, I expected to avoid the nauseous necessity of listening to saccharine platitudes from you. Brazen come-ons, maybe. Syrupy clichés, not so much."

The bites on my hands are beginning to itch beneath my lace mitts, and a wave of anger is building in my chest that threatens to obliterate my common sense for the second time in two days.

Heath.

Lida.

Every other unwanted outcast in Cinq.

I force my mind's eye to focus on their images swimming before me, obscuring for an instant the arrogant visage in front of me. "Last night was not indicative of my personality in general, Your Excellency."

One of Xavier's eyebrows creeps up. "Really."

"Really, Your Excellency."

He pushes off the doorframe, stepping closer. I feel a strong urge to back away, but the balcony railing at my back prevents me from going anywhere. Instead, I pull myself to my full height and meet his eyes.

"That's strange. If I were a betting man, I would bet"—he pauses, eyes boring into mine—"every one of the years we *won't* be spending together, that you're itching to send me on a quick headfirst trip into that fountain."

My smile feels closer to a grimace. "I thought Patricia 003 mentioned something about activities being planned for these little morning tête-à-têtes."

"You aren't enjoying this?"

"Oh, I'm enjoying it exactly as much as you mean me to, Your Excellency."

His eyes widen. Then he turns abruptly and strides back out into the hallway without a word. We follow stairway after stairway down, and from what I can see of Xavier's profile, he has become again the surly man of the night before.

Just as my calves are beginning to protest, the stairs end, and Xavier pushes the door at the bottom, holding it open with the tips of his fingers just long enough for me to slip inside after him.

I look around, trying to make sense of the scene before me. The room is divided into a carpeted section with puffy chairs and couches scattered around, and a gleaming wooden area, which is in turn divided by small, evenly spaced gullies into long peninsulas of flooring. At the end of each peninsula sits a configuration of white objects shaped like chicken drumsticks.

"Well, is this a satisfactory activity?" Xavier's cold question arrests my attention. He is standing next to a short table with a lip, full of brightly colored, heavy-looking balls.

"Of course," I say haughtily, striding over to join him and glancing down at the large balls, each of which has three holes arranged in a triangular configuration.

Xavier scoops up a maroon-colored ball before reaching down to fiddle with a pad affixed to the front of the short table. A screen high on the wall above the wooden peninsulas flickers to life, and as Xavier continues to tap at the keyboard, the names Xavier and Kanoska appear, with ten empty spaces and a zero at the far side of the screen.

"Do you call all girls by their last names?"

His back is to me. "Only girls whose names I can't spell," he says, and there is something in his voice that triggers a mad impulse to tell him to call me Andi. Then he says stiffly, "Besides, first names denote friendship," and I reach down to choose a ball of my own, wishing that wisdom didn't prohibit me from "accidentally" losing my grip on it directly above his toes.

As if in answer to my thought, he wriggles out of the blue-green lace-ups he was wearing and reaches down to slip out of his socks, bunching them into his discarded shoes. Then he strides forward and flings his ball down the wooden peninsula. The wooden drumsticks explode outward, ricocheting off the walls of their enclosure. A small "x" and a number ten appear next to Xavier's name. Wordlessly, he turns and gestures me toward the peninsula.

"What, no celebration dance?" I ask.

"You know what I like about bowling?" he responds.

"What is that, Excellency?"

"The sound of balls rolling and knocking over pins makes talking *unnecessary*."

I fiddle with the balls, lifting each to feel the weight before selecting one with a swirling, galactic pattern. Refusing to look at Xavier, I walk awkwardly up to the wooden peninsula and throw my ball. With a clunk, it hits the waxed wood of the peninsula and begins to roll, curving toward the gulley on the left side. I watch the gulley funnel it away, every white drumstick gleaming mockingly upright.

I turn and move to step out of the way for Xavier. "What are you doing?" he snaps.

Unable to help myself, I glare at him. "I was under the impression that in most games, you take turns."

One of his eyebrows flickers. "You've never bowled before."

"Where I come from, trying not to die of starvation or disease takes precedence over game playing, *Your Excellency*."

For a long moment, we stare at each other. Then he lets out a gruff laugh. "I was wondering how long it would take."

"How long what would take?"

"How long it would take for the 'blandly polite' facade to crack."

I scoop up my ball, which has magically reappeared on the little table, and stride forward, flinging it with all my might. It rolls straight into the forest of white drumsticks, and they topple, knocking into each other until not one remains standing.

"Yes!" I fling my arms into the air, my hands coming together in a resounding clap above my head. My hips begin to sway as my arms pull circles in the air in front of me. "Yes!"

I don't care that Denzel Xavier is standing there gaping at me as I shimmy and punch the air. He doesn't want to like me. And I have an inkling that trying to force the Ascendant of the Federation to do anything he doesn't want to do is going to be next to impossible.

Happy dance concluded, I step aside, gesturing toward the wooden peninsula. For a moment, Xavier continues to stare at me, an unreadable expression on his face. Then he opens his mouth.

"Remember what you like about bowling, Your Excellency?"

Xavier's lips snap together. Then a slow smile spreads across his face, teeth flashing, as dimples appear in his cheeks. My heart gives a weird bump as our eyes meet. The Ascendant of the Federation turns away from me and reaches for his maroon ball, leaving one thought beating against the bars of my brain.

Would it be too much to ask you to refrain from smiling at me?

CHAPTER 13

I should have been more specific. Denzel Xavier needs to refrain from smiling at all.

At dinner, it's not me he's smiling at. It's not Zuri either, even though the one she is leveling at him is so wide her back molars are visible.

The girl who is on the other end of his heart-stopping grin isn't even looking at him. She is talking to Patricia 003, her light brown hair obscuring her face as she taps on a pad. Xavier's eyes follow her movements as the hand not holding the device rises to tuck her hair behind her ear, exposing an earring composed of a cascading mix of red stones and golden loops.

"Who's that talking to Patricia 003?" I quietly ask Nicholas, who is seated next to me, taking careful bites of his herb-roasted salmon and vegetables.

He spares a glance over his shoulder before saying languidly, "Oh, that's Evangeline Langley. Chief Jeweler of the Federation." His voice gains slightly more animation as he pulls back the collar of his dress shirt, exposing a thin chain alternating bits of amber with slightly larger fragments of obsidian. "I commissioned this from her. Exquisite, isn't it?"

I make an appreciative noise in my throat. Xavier's eyes are still fixed on Evangeline Langley, clearly willing her to turn and meet his gaze. But she makes a final note on her clipboard and leaves the room without so much as glancing toward the table.

As I watch Xavier's face fall into hard, set lines again, the thought occurs to me that Evangeline is just as difficult to spell as Andromache.

When I push open the door to the gymnasium, my hopes that I will be working out alone are dashed. Even though there is only an hour until curfew, there are thumps and grunts coming from the back corner of the room. The sounds pause for an instant when the door bangs behind me, then resume with renewed vigor.

After surveying the various different machines scattered around the space, I walk toward the one which Patricia 003 had described as a "treadmill" during the free time activity tour.

Raquelle Mortimer comes into view, strands of auburn hair stuck to her face with sweat as she pummels the large red bag hanging from the ceiling. Her fists and feet fly in a strange dance, striking the leather again and again in a deadly, practiced sequence.

I don't realize how long I've been staring, mesmerized, until an angry voice demands, "Can I help you?"

"Where did you learn to do that?"

Raquelle swipes a bead of sweat from her cheek with her wrist. "As a girl living alone on the streets of LA, you need to be able to beat anyone who attacks you so thoroughly that they'll spread the word to all their worthless buddies to leave you alone."

"But what you were doing just now," I say. "It looked—this probably isn't the right word—choreographed. Like dancing."

Raquelle stares at me for such a long time that I know she is debating how much to tell me. Finally, she says, "When I was sixteen, I took up with a guy who boxed in several of the big nightclubs. He taught me."

"Can you teach me?" I'm not sure why I bother asking. Of all my fellow prospective brides, Raquelle is by far the most off-putting. I expect her to laugh in my face or else turn away without bothering to answer.

"Why?"

I pause before approaching her and drawing back the sleeve of the polyester shirt I'm wearing. She whistles through her teeth at the sight of the scabs speckling the inside of my forearm.

"Something tells me this place isn't much safer than the streets of LA," I say.

Raquelle gestures toward the bag. "Hit it."

I stare at her. "What?"

"Hit. It."

I open my mouth again, but at the sight of the look on her face, I haul back and sock the bag. It barely quivers.

Raquelle rolls her eyes. "Have you never hit anything before? I've seen six-year-olds who punch better than you."

"There's a reason I asked for lessons," I say, fighting to keep irritation out of my tone.

"Well, there's no way you'll have any power with your feet like that. What's your dominant leg?"

"Uh..."

Raquelle's lips move silently, as though in supplication. "Kick me."

"What?"

"If you say 'what' one more time, I'm going to kick you. And trust me, I know which is my dominant leg."

Not needing to be told twice, I aim a weak kick at her thigh. Raquelle's hands close around my ankle, yanking me around so that I crash onto the mat beneath us.

"Right leg dominant," she says calmly as I gawk at her from the floor. "Get up."

"What...in tarnation," I splutter.

"You said you wanted to learn to fight. Want to know how you learn to fight? By fighting. And that starts by spending a lot of time on your butt. The people who become the best fighters are just the ones who refuse to stay there. Get up."

I am limping away from the gymnasium an hour later, inwardly cursing Raquelle and her the-best-fighters-spend-a-lot-of-time-on-their-butts training strategy, when I hear voices coming down the hall from the opposite direction. One of them belongs to the last person I want to meet looking like I just got thrashed.

A half-open door into a darkened room catches my eye. I hobble across to it and slip inside, cracking the door wide enough to be able to peer into the hall outside.

"Langley, listen."

"Denz, stop. You're just making this harder for both of us."

"I'll abdicate."

"In favor of whom, Denz? You have one younger sister."

"In favor of Hugh. The Grimsbys have been in positions of power just as long as the Xaviers."

They are in view now. For some reason, they come to a stop right outside the room in which I'm hiding. Xavier has hold of Evangeline Langley's hand, and as I watch, he pulls her toward him and wraps his arms around her. Her shoulders begin to heave.

"Don't cry, Langley." His voice is unlike I've ever heard it, gentle and without an edge.

"I've always known I couldn't have you." Her words are muffled. "I'm such a fool."

"Loving me makes you a fool. Ouch."

"Stop it." She pushes out of his arms, burying her face in her hands. "You're not abdicating in favor of that weasel Hugh. Not because of me."

"Langley, I know you don't like Hugh, but—"

"I'm getting married."

When Xavier speaks, his voice is unrecognizable. "When?"

"In a week."

"To whom?"

"Achilles Pendell. Nicholas's younger brother."

"Well, that's fortuitous." Xavier's tone is so cold it sends a chill up my spine. "You can keep that little peacock decked in rings and cravat pins for the rest of his life."

Through the slit in the door, I see Evangeline Langley's face tighten. "Well, your wedding night should be a riot if you pick Andromache Kanoska. Just try to make sure she keeps her clothes on the rest of the time."

"At least she's honest!" Xavier's roar reverberates through the silent hall. "Regardless of what she was wearing at the time, she got up and told the entire Federation what her priorities are. I know exactly what matters to Andromache Kanoska. But you? For five years—FIVE YEARS, Langley—you've known how I felt about you. You told me you felt the same way. You listened to every secret I told you. And then, at the last minute, when the rubber meets the road, when we actually need to sacrifice in order to be together, you give up!"

Tears drip down her face. "The Federation needs you, Denz," she whispers. "I'm doing what's best for our country."

"Don't lie to me." He isn't shouting anymore. "Tell me you don't care. Tell me forging a new life in the Midwest would be too hard. Tell me you can't leave your jewelry business. But don't give me any crap about our country, Langley. For once in your life, have the guts to tell me the truth."

"The truth? The truth that both our hearts are broken now? The truth that we'll never be free of each other until the day we die? Is that the truth you want, Denzel Xavier?"

I hear feet running and realize that I've unconsciously closed my eyes as if to ward off a blow. When I open them again, Denzel Xavier is standing alone in the hallway, head bent so that I can't see his face. Then he turns and strides away.

My hand is on the door, about to push it open, when a voice speaks from the shadows behind me. "Love is pain, smart girl. Denzel isn't fool enough to make that mistake twice."

CHAPTER 14

I turn around so fast that I stumble, catching the door-frame to steady myself. The room floods with light.

It isn't Hugh Grimsby sitting in the throne-like leather armchair behind the desk at the back of the room. The hands that are closing the silver computer on the desk's surface are thicker-knuckled than Hugh's, and the expression on the stranger's face is calmly detached rather than smugly arrogant. But something is familiar about that face.

"That isn't what your son calls me, Your Excellency," I say, and the man behind the desk smiles, wrinkles forming behind the glasses perched on his nose.

"No." He doesn't elaborate, and I wonder whether his use of Hugh Grimsby's name for me was a coincidence.

"If I were smart," I say, "wouldn't I set my sights on marrying one of the others who hasn't given up on the idea of love?"

"Whether that would be smart depends on what you want. What do you want, smart girl?"

I hesitate.

"You need have no fear of me relaying your words to my son," the Elector says. "He does not come to me for advice."

"Is your estrangement a result of your son's attachment to Miss Langley, Your Excellency?"

"Call me Cronus. You would be surprised how much of your personality appears to dissolve when you have a title."

"You know, I don't even call your son by his first name."

"Ah, but you don't like my son, Miss Kanoska."

I study his features, which are more rugged but just as handsome as those of the young man who was outside a moment ago. "Why do you say that?"

Cronus's smile widens. "There is very little that goes on in this complex that I do not know. But you have not answered my question. What do you want?"

I ponder my response. "I want influence," I say. "The power to bring about change."

"Then I would certainly not pursue love. Liking is no necessity for a successful marriage."

"Supposing that I was willing to concede that," I say, "it would still be necessary for the other party to like me enough to want to marry me."

Cronus's eyes crinkle again. "But you are in luck, Miss Kanoska. My son fancies himself brokenhearted. He won't be looking for love, or even liking. He'll be looking for the girl who will be happy to walk by his side, bask in the power of a Consort, assist—or at least not hinder—him in his royal duties. He will be looking for the girl who asks only for a strong arm to lean on, an able father for her children, a respectful partner through life. But nothing more. If you can make my son believe that you have no interest in making him fall in love with you, then I would put my money on you becoming the last Western Consort of the Federation."

Our eyes meet. "Last Western Consort?"

It is clear that Cronus is debating whether to confide in me. After a moment, he gives a little laugh and says, "Did I say last? A slip of the tongue. The *next* Western Consort."

Cronus rises, and I see with a shock that he is extremely short, the top of his head barely level with my shoulder. His smile stretches as he takes in the question in my gaze. "The elevated platform that Lothar used for the opening banquet? He invented the first prototype for my wedding so that I would be able to look Denzel's mother in the eye."

"Zuri might need to borrow that if Denzel chooses her."

"You mustn't think like that," Cronus says. "Concentrate on throwing a party like this nation has never seen before, and there will be no question of Denzel choosing that little prima donna over you."

He moves out from behind his desk and pulls the door open, clearly dismissing me. But on the threshold, I pause, looking down at the small, regal man whose face reminds me so irresistibly of his son's. "Forgive the impertinence," I say, "but why me?"

Cronus's eyes crinkle again. "I have a weakness for tall girls," he says.

I am almost out the door when I turn back. "One more thing. Any good party ideas?"

Cronus throws back his head and laughs. When he is finally capable of speech, he says, "Smart girl, remember? You'll figure it out."

CHAPTER 15

"Don't go to the lab again," whines Heath, latching on to my arm as I make for the door at the beginning of free period a week later.

"Yes, aren't you supposed to be planning a spectacular bash so that Ascendant Denzel will fall madly in love with you and spare all your unworthy friends?" Lida asks caustically.

"Why not, brat?" I say to Heath, ignoring Lida.

"Because I've been stuck in here with her since we got here." Lida doesn't deign to look up from the solitaire game she is playing on an electronic pad. "I'm this close"—he holds up two fingers an inch apart—"to going insane, Andi. If you don't get me out of here, I'm going to have to set Lida's hair on fire, just to see if Patricia 003 can spray water out of her chest cavity."

Guilt twinges inside as I stare around the cramped living area of our suite, realizing that I hadn't given a thought to how Heath and Lida were occupying themselves during my packed days. I had now gone out with each of the bachelors once and with Alden twice. Of the five, I liked him the best, with his serious demeanor and kind eyes. Nicholas was exactly the peacock I had taken him for at our first meeting, while Barek had turned out to be the most boisterous of the bunch, roaring in alternate jubilation and despair at the bot fight he took me to see on our tête-à-tête. Surprisingly, my time spent with Hugh was almost pleasant, since he took me to a private screening of an old movie and we did very little talking. But underneath the amicable ambiance, tension pulsed, and I couldn't wait for our allotted time to end.

Despite Lida's rudeness, her words also pinch my conscience. Clotilde and Bella are telling anyone who will listen about plans for their parties—a masquerade for Clotilde and a carnival for Bella. Zuri has had closed meetings with event staff every day. But the truth is that I've never been to a party. And with Cronus's words about throwing a party like this nation has never seen before in my ears, I don't want to ask any of the droids or humans around the palace about their party experiences. My event has to be original. And I've been responding to that pressure in the unhealthiest way possible—by ignoring it.

"Andi, let's go see a bot fight!" Heath is still tugging on my hand. "That sounded really fun."

I shake my head. "Heath, Barek arranged for a special showing of the fight I saw in the middle of the day. Most bot fights happen at night in the White House's club."

"Let's go tonight, then."

"I have curfew, buddy."

"Blow it off."

"I can't, Heath."

"Yes, you can, Andi! Or better yet, let's sneak out into the city. Running around the streets at night—it would be just like old times." His impish smile is wide and real, but I can't return it. I've only just been able to start wearing short-sleeved outfits again.

"No." The word comes out harsher than I mean it to. As his face falls, I reach for his arm, but he shrugs me off. "We can do anything you want inside the White House complex or the grounds, Heath, but we can't go out into the city. We can go to the gym, and I'll show you some of the kickboxing moves Raquelle's teaching me. We can go to the bowling alley. We can play hide-and-seek in the maze—"

"Why are you like this now?" The words are brittle, and I break off abruptly.

"Like what?"

"Like the selfish, snotty princess they want. Like a person who's really trying to win the approval of one of those idiots."

His words are like a slap. "I brought you here to save you from your worthless father and a mother who never wanted you. I saved you from a life of poverty and misery. And this is the gratitude I get? One of us is definitely excelling at being selfish and snotty, but it's not me, Heath!"

"If this is saving, I don't want it!" he yells at me. "You just put me in a cage, Andi! A fancy, frilly"—he gestures furiously, struggling with his seven-year-old vocabulary—"frou-frou cage! And since you haven't spent more than five minutes with me in the last ten days, you clearly don't want me much more than my parents ever did!"

The accusation pierces deep. Memories flood over me. I see him, sneaking into my garage at all hours of the night. In my mind's eye, I watch him jump between piles of rubble, light on his feet like an alley cat. I see him digging through dumpsters for food and books. I watch him huddle on the windowsill of an abandoned building, peering down at the gang members whom he had taunted, chuckling to himself.

And I see us, playing endless rounds of a game I don't even know the name of, with a tattered pack of playing cards and a wooden board with holes for miniscule pegs. I see us, sprawled on the dusty floor of my garage, me helping him to sound out words in a dog-eared copy of an ancient book called "The Bible." I see us racing along the beach and dancing through the waves of the Pacific with the stars sparkling high above.

The life he lived in Cinq was hard. Dangerous. Unpredictable. But he was free as the gulls scuttling along the sand and taking off into the endless sky if anyone got too close.

"I'm sorry." Heath's shoulders slump. "You're right. All of this—trying to impress the bachelors, trying to fit in—it was supposed to be for you, brat. For you and Lida. For everyone like us back home. But I lost sight of that. I'm sorry."

Wordlessly, he slips his small arms around my waist, his head leaning into my side. I run my fingers through his hair, still subconsciously expecting to feel the grit of the streets rather than the softness of freshly washed curls. For a moment, we stay there, and as I look across and meet Lida's eyes, I know that she realizes my apology wasn't just meant for Heath.

When he finally lifts his head to look up at me, I see familiar mischief glinting in his eyes. "So about sneaking out tonight...?"

"Think again." I give his hair a final tousle before pushing him toward his bedroom. "Lose the pajamas. We're going out."

"Where are we going?" He pauses with his hand on the doorframe. "I don't want to do any of the boring things you've been doing, Andi. No lawn parties. No small talk."

"I'm not telling you where we're going," I say, and the corners of his mouth tip up, the promise of the unknown tugging at his adventurous little soul. He darts into his room, and before the door fully closes, I raise my voice. "Remember that lifetime supply of honey shaved ice you wanted? This is infinitely better."

If we're caught, there will be another nightmare tonight.

But the look on Heath's face makes the possibility seem as trivial as the possibility of being pulled out to sea by a riptide when you're dancing in ocean waves. His cheeks are smeared brown and green from the ice cream cone I bought him at the cart in the street just outside the complex. Alden took me here during one of our tête-à-têtes and bought me a bowl of the brown-flecked, green treat that he called mint chocolate chip ice cream. While we were out, he showed me the small door carefully camouflaged in the ground at the corner of the maze that grants access to the city beyond.

"It's the worst-kept secret in the palace," he had said.

"Why don't they block it off?" I asked, looking up at the top of the towering green walls. I could see the faint shimmer of a force field, which Patricia 003 pointed out to us during our first tour. She had said that the rectangular force field surrounding the entire grounds of the White House complex—with only one exit in the floor of the main foyer, requiring a fingerprint, a security card, and a passcode—was an almost impenetrable defense to protect the few remaining humans from the Federation's enemies.

That was when I first realized that what was once a nation's capital is now a ghost town. The White House is three times the size it was when the United States crumbled, and every single human in the Federation lives in the complex, which is also equipped with a hospital, a school, and innumerable forms of entertainment. Patricia 003 was right. Such defenses would be close to impossible to breach. But as I stared at the shimmering mirage for the first time, I didn't see defense. I saw an escape-proof cage.

Alden leaned close, his words a whisper. "It's Cronus's. So he can go into the city at night. Without Boadicea knowing. He had it put in the week of their honeymoon."

"He comes out to find"—I swallowed as an image of Jez surrounded by children, not one of whom had the same father, rose in my mind—"ladies of the night?"

Alden gave a short laugh. "The only humans in this city outside the White House are the faculty of St. Juno's. From the gossip I hear, our sovereign was quite taken with a nurse he met there when he was quarantined with an unknown virus shortly before the ladies from Cinq arrived. But he hasn't used the gate in years. All his subsequent conquests have been nobility." My disgust must have been evident on my face because Alden said, "Not all arranged marriages end that way, Andi. Denzel isn't like that. And neither am I."

Looking into his serious eyes, I believed his words about himself. But in my mind, I saw Xavier's hands on Evangeline Langley's waist as he pleaded with her and heard his father's voice echoing in my head, "Liking is no necessity for a successful marriage."

Of course it isn't. If you can find the companionship you crave in the arms of everyone besides your spouse.

"This is"—*slurp*—"the best thing"—*slurp*—"I've ever eaten."

I turn and raise my eyebrows at Heath, whose bright eyes meet mine as he crunches down on the point of his cone. "Ever heard of keeping your mouth closed while eating, brat?"

He shakes his head, clearly unconcerned, and begins licking his fingers. I glance around the empty street. St. Juno's tall brick facade casts everything in shadow, but there is no sign of life in any of the windows. Only the most severe injuries and illnesses are treated at the hospital, which is apparently located outside the White House grounds in case another deadly virus should ever surface in the Federation. The robotic ice cream cart was a gift from Cronus to the bored hospital staff.

A crew of cleaning bots moves slowly up the street, inhaling the few leaves that have fallen from the trees and hosing nonexistent dust off the asphalt. A tall white android with a red stripe running from hip to ankle along her left leg strides purposefully past, a palace messenger headed to St. Juno's. Overhead, planes and hovercraft soar, perhaps bringing in oranges from the plantations in Florida or halibut from the coast of Maine.

An eerie feeling prickles along my spine as I think about the fact that Heath and I are the only two human beings on the streets of a city that once was home to three-quarters of a million people. But as I turn to tell him that it's time to go back, my eyes catch on something.

I was wrong. We are not the only human beings on DC's streets.

A tall young man has just emerged from the alleyway next to St. Juno's, his hands deep in the pockets of the scarlet jeans he wears. Despite the warmth of the day, he is sporting a leather jacket over his white T-shirt. I see the glint of a chain disappearing into his neckline. It probably holds an exquisite pendant wrought by the Chief Jeweler of the Federation. White glints in his ears. Briefly, I wonder whether he is listening to a love song or one about the end of the world today.

His eyes are covered by dark glasses, but his face is turned toward us. Trying to stifle sudden panic, I glance down at Heath, who is staring raptly at a disc that has just rounded a corner, skimming a few feet above the ground. Xavier remains motionless in the hospital's shadow. As I watch, his eyebrows rise slowly from behind his sunglasses.

Reaching down, I grab Heath's sticky little hand and make my way across the street toward him. "What are you doing out here?"

Even in my ears, the words sound needlessly aggressive, and the slight smirk that curves his lips confirms my perception. But he doesn't answer the question. Instead, he says, "What's your name?"

"You know my name. Just because you refuse to use—"

"Heath Insley." I break off and glance down at Heath, who is studying Xavier with a guarded expression.

"Denzel Xavier." A large hand brushes my arm as it reaches to enfold Heath's small, sticky paw. Electricity tingles from my elbow to my shoulder.

"I've heard a lot about you," Heath says, his demeanor so self-assured, the fact that his face is stained with mint ice cream seems irrelevant.

"Oh? What does she say about me?"

"Who says she says anything?" demands Heath, crossing his arms. I feel Xavier's gaze but refuse to look at him.

"You know, it's a crime to be outside the grounds as non-citizens."

Heath stiffens next to me, and I cut in before he can do or say anything foolish. "I know," I say innocently, "but we were playing in the maze and when we heard the ice cream truck outside, Heath wanted to try some so badly that I didn't think it would hurt to just slip outside for a second."

Xavier slowly removes his sunglasses. "You know what I hate?" he says. I lock gazes with him, thanking whatever First Cause determined my genetics that I don't have to crane my neck. "I hate people lying to me," Xavier says quietly, and I hear his voice echoing through my mind:

"For once in your life, have the guts to tell me the truth!"

"You know what I hate?" I say, just as quietly. "I hate living in a world where you have to choose between honesty and safety."

His eyes crinkle in confusion. Then his forehead smooths. "Ah, the alleged killing of infertile women."

Anger, a familiar emotion in his presence, sparks to life. "Alleged?"

"You forget that I am the Federation's heir, Kanoska. If our government or military were killing Cinq's infertile women, I would know, because I would be in charge of giving the order to do so."

"You're not Elector yet."

"You're accusing my father?"

"It's in the agreement between Cinq and the Federation," I say, fighting to keep my voice calm.

"The amendment to the original treaty which you are referencing stipulates that women whose blood test fails to provide the desired FSH reading will be sent to Paradise, the islands of Hawaii."

"Let's suppose that you're right and that's where they're going," I say, my voice beginning to tremble in spite of my efforts. "What gives the Federation—or Cinq, for that matter—the right to exile women who can't bear children?"

Xavier blows out a breath, whether in frustration or contemplation, I can't tell. "Listen, Kanoska," he says. "A society is only as strong as its citizens. Weakness breeds weakness and strength breeds strength. As the history of this nation proves, weakness, if left unchecked, will run rampant, to the point that it could bring about a nation's destruction. A government that chooses to segregate those who are weak, sick, or damaged in some other way is only doing so to promote the health of the society as a whole."

He watches me, clearly waiting for my response.

My anger has crumbled away into ash, leaving a pale coldness, deeper than any fury could be. "You're more dangerous than all the rest of them." My voice sounds far away in my own ears. "You use those words—those smooth, rational-sounding words—to mask the truth, to make yourself believe that you are doing something noble, important, for the greater good. You don't want to come face-to-face with the presumption, the selfishness, the arrogance that makes you write off the value of human life. You label weakness a fatal flaw, forgetting that every human comes into the world completely helpless and dependent, and that even those who were strong once end their lives weak and dependent once more, no matter how many grand deeds marked their existence. And you call reproduction the ultimate female purpose, labeling those unable to produce children as damaged goods without a second thought, without pausing to consider that it takes far more strength to nurture life than to produce it, and forgetting that the arms of many whose wombs are barren have become a refuge for the children abandoned and neglected by the women—and men—responsible for their births."

I take Heath's hand and turn away from him. As we begin to walk toward the passageway into the gardens of the White House, Heath suddenly stops and tugs his hand from mine. He glares at Denzel Xavier.

"My mom didn't want me," he says. "Because I wasn't a girl, which meant I wasn't useful to her. She left me on the beach to die. Andi found me on her morning run. She took care of me. And protected me. When I was no use to anyone. I ran away when I found out she wasn't my 'real' mom. But now I know that I was an idiot. Because someone who loves you when you can't do anything to repay them? They're the realest of all."

His hand slips back into mine, dragging me away from theAscendant of the Federation, back toward our gilded cage.

CHAPTER 16

"**A**ndi!"

For a mad second, I think that Xavier has followed Heath and me through the maze and back into the grounds of the complex. Then the pitch of the voice and the use of my first name register.

"Bella." I wish there was a way to communicate to her without words that I'm not really in a chatty mood.

"Andi, there's going to be a fire eater at my party! Custodia 065 just told me that they'd be able to make it."

Before I can respond, Heath interjects, "You should have the ice cream truck come to your party."

"That's a great idea!" Bella reaches into one of her bell-shaped pink sleeves and pulls out a tiny notebook and a pencil stub. She begins to scrawl on a blank sheet.

"What, no electronic pad?" I say without thinking.

Bella glances up. "I don't understand how to use them." Her face lights up. "Could you teach me?"

Between tête-à-têtes, lab time, kickboxing lessons, and trying not to completely abandon Heath and Lida, I've got about as much as I can handle on my plate right now.

"I'm a little busy at the moment," I say as gently as possible. "I'm still trying to come up with a good party idea."

"I could help you!" Bella looks delighted. "Come here!" She grabs my hand and drags me toward a bench situated next to a pond with a tiny pagoda on the island in the middle. "Sit down."

She plops down next to me and flips to a clean page in her notebook. Out of the corner of my eye, I see Heath drift down to the pond's edge and begin gathering stones. "What do you miss most about home?"

Of all the questions she could have asked, this was probably the one I least expected.

"I miss the ocean," I say slowly. "I used to run along the beach every morning. And our apartment was only a block from the Pacific, so I would fall asleep every night to the sound of the waves. I miss the sand and the smell of salt. I miss looking for shells and glass and cool rocks—the treasures the sea tosses carelessly out onto the shore." Bella has her tongue between her teeth and is scribbling as I talk. I have no idea whether she is writing down my words in some kind of shorthand or party ideas or something else entirely. "I miss the babies."

Some sort of dam seems to have broken inside me. Words come pouring out as I struggle to articulate the feelings I haven't had time to examine since coming here. "There are a few kids here, but I've hardly seen any babies, and at home, I used to hold them every day. I helped bring them into the world. Watched their first moments of life and then their first milestones and growth when their moms would bring them back for us to do checkups. I miss the smell of newborns and the looks on—well, some—of the mothers' faces when they got to see the humans they had grown inside themselves for the past nine months."

A breath pauses the flow of words. Then I say, so quietly I'm not sure that Bella will even hear me, "I miss Sasha. All the time. I used to see her every day. Some days she was my favorite person on earth. Other days I felt like I couldn't stand her. We had normal days and good days and horrible days and, in a way, it didn't matter which was which because I always thought I'd have more days with her. More time together."

The only sound is the continuous scratching of Bella's pencil. I stare out over the pond, watching Heath attempting to skip stones. I feel drained, but also strangely at peace.

"You should have your party on a boat." Bella's voice pulls me back to the moment.

"What?"

Bella gives me a look that clearly says, *Catch up.* "You should have your party on a boat. In the harbor. And you can invite Sasha. It only took us a day to get here. She could come for the party and be back home in a weekend."

"Bella."

"Yes?"

"You're a genius," I say, pulling her into a hug that surprises even me. As her arms come around me in response, guilt washes over me for the second time today. I realize that deep down, I've been viewing her as an inconvenience. A liability. As somehow less.

You don't want to come face-to-face with the presumption, the selfishness, the arrogance that makes you write off the value of human life.

My own words to Xavier echo in my mind. "What do *you* miss most about home?" I say.

"My daddy," she says immediately.

"I could invite him to my party too," I say.

"I would love that!" Then her smile fades the slightest bit, a shadow of doubt marring her pure happiness. "I would especially like that because I'm not going to go back home. Even if they would let me."

The way she glances down and away denotes a shyness that is completely un-Bella-like. "Is there someone you would stay for?" I ask slowly.

"How did you know?"

"I don't know much about love, Bella. But it always leaves a mark."

Her teeth dig into her lower lip before she says, "It's Alden, Andi."

Relief floods through me. Of all the suitors, he is the one who might actually love Bella. Protect her. Treasure her for who she is. "He's a good man, Bells."

"Why would he want to marry me?" she asks suddenly. "I'm different. Everyone says so. Some people say worse things."

I squeeze her hand, searching for words that are true but not cliché. "You might be different," I say, "but you're also one of the happiest people I've ever known. You radiate joy and light. You're kind. When I said I didn't know what to do for my party, you immediately offered to help me. And you're perceptive. You took random facts that I told you about myself and used them to create an idea that is perfect for me."

"What if he picks someone else? And I have to marry one of the others, knowing I love him? Would that be wrong?"

I watch yet another of Heath's skipping attempts strike the surface of the pond and sink slowly to the bottom. "Everything about this is wrong," I say heavily. We are both quiet. Then I say, "What do you like about Alden?"

"He's funny," she says. "Our first tête-à-tête, he took me to a room in the complex where you make things by throwing paint onto a tile stuck to a spinning wheel. While I was making mine, he suddenly said, 'Oh look, your tile's slipping!' I looked down, and his finger came up and brushed blue paint on my nose." Bella laughs at the memory, and I can't help but join in even though the story isn't nearly as funny to me as it is to her. "He's brave too. He volunteered to join the Federation's army when it looked like England might attack a few years ago. And he's handsome. Really handsome."

Her frankness is endearing. But as she rambles on about Alden, I think of the young man I hope to marry. As I ask myself the same question I just asked Bella, a terrifying blank fills my mind.

He's arrogant.

And coldhearted.

Heedless of the feelings of others.

Friends with a man who delights in cruelty.

There isn't a single thing I like about Denzel Xavier.

Oh, wait.

I guess he's handsome.

CHAPTER 17

That night, when I am walking down the corridor toward the gymnasium for a boxing lesson from Raquelle, I hear a sound that stops me in my tracks.

"Please." The word is hoarse, but recognition of the voice sends my heart thundering. "Stop. Please don't."

I creep toward the glass door of the gymnasium and push it silently open. I peer inside.

Raquelle is backed against the wall next to the punching bags. Standing in front of her is Hugh Grimsby, with his back to me. As I watch, transfixed with horror, his fingers trail along the sweaty skin just above her collar, tracing up her neck to her chin where they clamp down hard.

"Oh, but I don't want to stop." He brings his mouth down on hers with a ferocity that causes bile to rise in my throat. Her eyes squeeze shut, and her fingers curl into fists, but to my shock, she doesn't even try to fight him off. She is limp under his hands, already defeated.

It is when I see a single tear course from under her closed eyelid that I can't take it anymore. I reach out and bang the glass door as though I had just entered the room.

"I just came for my boxing lesson with Raquelle," I say, fighting to sound casual. At the sound of the door, Hugh steps back from Raquelle so quickly that he catches his foot on one of the exercise mats and stumbles. Now he turns toward me, eyes blazing with a look equal parts lust and fury. Then his expression clears, and he steps back toward her, running a finger softly down her cheek before leaning down to plant a lingering kiss.

"Until next time, love."

As he passes me on his way to the door, his fingers close around my ponytail so aggressively and unexpectedly that I stagger as he yanks my ear toward his mouth.

"If you say anything about what you think you saw to anyone," he breathes, "it'll be her body that's covered with bites. Again. Pretty soon she'll be so scarred that even *I* will find her repulsive."

He releases me. The door bangs, and I turn to look at Raquelle. The blankness in her eyes stabs at my heart. I move toward her, pushing down the voice that whispers I'm caring again.

"Raquelle—"

"Don't."

"What? Raquelle—"

"Hit the bag."

Images of what I just witnessed flash sickeningly through my mind. "Raquelle, I can't just—"

"Hit the bag. Or I'll hit you."

I spread my hands. "Hit me. If it will make you feel better."

The dead look in her eyes morphs into one of helpless fury. Then her fist darts out, embedding itself in my side. As I double up, gasping, and stumble backward, her fists drop. My wheezing breaths are becoming stronger by the time she crumples and curls into a fetal position on the exercise mat at my feet.

"That didn't make it better," she whispers and begins to sob.

I sink down beside her, my hand hovering uncertainly for a minute before coming to rest on her shoulder. "Why?" The word is hard to get out. "You could have obliterated him. Why did you let him do that to you?"

More tears leak down her pale cheeks. "I hit him once," she says, her voice monotone. "That night they came. The fire snakes. Slithering all over my body. I thought it was a nightmare. Until I woke up covered with burns." She lifts the hem of her shirt, and I see a peeling, crusty pink line etched into the skin of her abdomen. "That day I had to go on a tête-à-tête with him."

Her jaw clenches. "He said that he is commander of the Department of Correction, a position bestowed by Elector Cronus. He told me that if I resisted him, he would marry me and torture me for the rest of my life." She chokes on a sob. "But he's making my life hell now. I despise myself more every time I let him touch me. Every time I listen to his poisonous words about how I'm ugly and damaged and not worth any man's time without knocking his teeth out."

I open my mouth to say that she should tell someone and then close it again. Hugh is acting on the orders of

Cronus Xavier. The image of the little man with crows' feet and glasses rises before me, and I feel sick. I liked him. He was funny. And quirky. He flattered me. Seemed to see my potential.

Now I know that not only did he create a specific outlet to allow him to cheat on his wife, but he sanctions the torture of his people to ensure their compliance. He's a monster. A monster concealed in a pleasing, benign shell.

"What are you going to do?" My question comes out creaky with the weight of my emotion.

The expression in Raquelle's eyes is chilling. "I'll tell you what I'm not going to do," she says. "I am not going to marry that swine. I'll slit my own wrists first."

"Don't say that." I grab her shoulder. "Raquelle, you can't let him force you into taking your own life."

She wrenches away from me. "I won't marry him," she says again.

"You won't have to."

She gives a derisive laugh. "Oh, well, since you say so…"

"You won't have to," I repeat, digging my fingers into her shoulder so that she meets my gaze. "I promise you, Raquelle. I give you my word. I'll find a way out of this."

The cynicism is gone from her face, replaced by weariness. "What if you can't?"

"Give me time," I say. "There are still over five months until the Ascension. If I haven't found another way for you not to marry Hugh Grimsby by the night of the second Gauntlet, then you'll have to figure it out yourself."

After a pause, Raquelle shrugs. "You can try," she says indifferently. She pulls her arm from my now limp grasp, and pushes to her feet. "I don't think I have a lesson in me tonight."

"I wouldn't either," I say as she leaves.

After she is gone, I pull my knees to my forehead and bury my face in them. Already, the flame of desperation that prompted me to promise my help to Raquelle is fading, leaving a cold stillness in its wake.

All my life I've played it safe. I've lived in the shadows. I've closed off my heart to almost everyone, knowing that caring would threaten my highest priority—staying alive. I allowed chinks in my armor to let Sasha, Heath, and Lida slip inside. For nineteen years, I've avoided caring about anyone else, determined to focus on my own safety and allow others to do the same.

But in the two weeks since coming here, more chinks have formed against my will, allowing not only Bella, but also Raquelle, to worm inside. And I know that if this keeps going, this nonsensical practice of caring, then eventually my walls are going to crumble into dust, and I won't be able to hide anymore. Caring will force me out of the shadows, force me to speak out against the destruction of the lives of those I love.

I want to putty up the chinks. To go back to the safety of survival being the highest good. But as I remember the blankness in Raquelle's eyes, and Hugh's repulsive words, the burns and bites she and I have both suffered, inflicted at the Xaviers' command, and the door in the maze representing the greatest possible human betrayal, I can't.

I stay huddled on the exercise mat, immobilized between the terror of going forward and the inability to pull back, until the tension threatens to snap something inside of me.

I get up, knowing that I have barely any time left before curfew but needing the comfort that only one place in this accursed complex provides.

I push open the door to the lab, balling up all emotion and shoving it into a dim, inaccessible corner of my mind. I move over to the table I have staked out as my own and run a finger down the cool glass of one of the vials perched on a stand. Reaching under the table, I pull out a drawer and rummage for a lab coat and goggles, two things I hadn't even heard of before coming here. My fingers graze the electronic pad at the bottom of the drawer, and I pause before grabbing a notebook and shutting the drawer. Tonight, I want as few reminders as possible of where I am and my inability to escape the nightmare I'm living.

Flipping through the notebook to a clean page, I jot the date at the top and then pause, drumming the end of my pencil against my teeth. My serum is almost ready to begin trials, but I want to make sure I haven't forgotten anything obvious that could drastically alter the outcome.

I rifle back through my notebook to the beginning of last week and stare down at the list of ingredients. Propylene glycol. Human growth hormone. Cortisol. Lymphoblasts. All combining to promote super-immunity in humans.

This was the project I had been working on for the past two years back at home before I was taken. It was supposed to be a formula for premature infants, to promote immunity without introducing pathogens into their already frail bodies. The only good thing about coming to the Federation is that this is no longer a pipe dream. There is technology here that could allow my formula to become a reality, changing the lives of thousands.

I bite my lip, staring at the ratios of the ingredients, then reach down to erase a decimal point, making a minor adjustment.

"Planning to blow off curfew?"

Shock makes me back into the wall, my pencil held like a spear. Denzel Xavier is standing barely a foot away, close enough to have been looking over my shoulder a second before. I have no idea how he got so close without me hearing him. The corner of his mouth tips as he studies me. "Well, that should leave a scar."

It takes me a moment to look down and see the pencil clutched in my fingers. I know that he is joking, but the word scar conjures memories of a girl's abdomen, marred by a peeling, pink, snake-like line. I see her, crouched on an exercise mat, her strength broken, contemplating taking her own life because of the invisible wounds inflicted on her. Scars? If she lives long enough, she will be covered in them. Mostly inflicted by the best friend of the man standing in front of me.

You want to survive, a tiny voice whispers in my mind. *Don't do it.*

But I can't stand here, pretending everything is normal, speaking politely to this man who is responsible for so much suffering. I stuff my supplies back into my drawer and push past him, heading toward the laboratory door.

"Wait!"

I don't stop. Until I am forced to, as he passes me and stops in front of the lab door, blocking my way. "Is this about earlier?"

"Get out of my way."

"Kanoska." He is exasperated, but the expression in his eyes is open, a look I don't understand. "It doesn't have to be this way. Just because we disagree on some policy issues—"

"Policy issues?" I can't get enough air into my lungs. "You monster."

His eyes widen, but his voice is still level when he says, "Is this because of what happened to your friend? Heath? His mother chose that, Kanoska. This government is in no way responsible—"

"Your government grades the value of human life!" I am shouting now. "Your price tag for young, fertile women explains which lives you think are worthwhile quite plainly. Can you blame his mother for carrying your idea to its logical conclusion when she already had eleven mouths to feed? Heath couldn't do anything for her. So she got rid of him."

"Your government entered into this treaty freely. And just because young women are scarce, making us value them highly, doesn't mean we don't value young men. No one is killing boy babies here."

"You don't value all young women."

Xavier sighs. "Kanoska. What use are infertile—" Then he pauses, and his eyes find mine. "Not helping my case, am I?" His next words are hesitant. "Why do you care so much?"

Because I'm one of them. Someone you brand useless. Undesirable. Worthless.

A part of me wants to tell him everything, to leave the shadows behind, but I can't get the words out. Even if he doesn't kill me on the spot for what I am, I'll be disqualified from the competition. Sasha will be punished for helping me to lie. Heath and Lida will be sent back to the miserable lives they tried to escape by coming with me. And Lida and I will both end up on the next boat to Paradise.

"I watched a friend board one of those boats you say go to Hawaii," I say. "I wanted to make sure she would be all right, so I followed the boat. As soon as it was out of sight of the shore, Federation bombers attacked. They sent the boat, with my friend on it and fifty other 'useless' women, straight to the bottom of the Pacific."

"How do you know they were Federation planes?"

"Oh, I don't know. Maybe because the treaty states that 'all control of aircraft capable of inflicting aggressive action must remain in the hands of the Federation'."

"It doesn't make any sense." He's talking to himself now. "How could I not know about this?"

"There seems to be a lot of things that you don't know." The words are out before I can stop myself.

Xavier's eyes narrow. "Like what?"

I hear Hugh's whisper. *"If you say anything to anyone, it'll be her body that's covered with bites. Again."* Besides, it is the Xaviers who made the Grimsbys the disciplinary executives. For all I know, Denzel Xavier might have ordered the punishments meted out on Raquelle and me.

My shoulder rises and falls in a noncommittal shrug.

"I'm dying to hear all these things I don't know, Kanoska." His voice is silky, but there is an edge to it.

"Well, I don't trust you." The words are ashy gray, the last defiant vestiges of my fury. "I don't trust you not to use whatever I say as a weapon to hurt more people."

For a long moment, Denzel Xavier stares into my eyes. "I'm going to prove you wrong," he says finally. "I'm going to find out whatever you're hiding from me, and I will bring whoever is responsible to justice."

A tiny flame of hope flickers to life. "If you do that," I say, needing to lighten the mood to keep my hopes from getting too high, "I promise to let you play whatever loud, obnoxious music you want to at my party."

A smile spreads across his face, a real smile that makes my heart stagger. "Loud, obnoxious music like this?"

Before I realize what is happening, he pulls one of the white things out of his left ear and slips it into mine. His fingers barely brush my neck as his hand drops away. His eyes widen, and his smile slips. The air suddenly feels too thick in my lungs. Music fills my ear, a ballad-like song about how someone you love can bridge the troubled waters of life. It isn't anything like the music I heard him playing my first night in the Federation. This song is rippling and heartfelt, conjuring images of the Pacific pounding the beach during a thunderstorm and making me ache for Sasha's calming presence.

His hand fumbles in my ear, withdrawing the earpiece, and as his fingers brush my ear and down the side of my neck again, I jerk away from him. "I...I guess you could play that," I stammer, inwardly cursing myself.

His eyes have narrowed again and before I can back further away, he closes the distance between us, one large hand scooping beneath my hair to cup around the back of my neck. His thumb runs along the skin behind my ear as I stand frozen with shock, desperately praying that he will not try to kiss me, because no matter what physical sensations his touch elicits, I still despise him for the passivity that has allowed people around him to be hurt when he could have put a stop to it.

"What is this?" he says, and I suddenly realize that his thumb is not caressing the skin behind my ear but probing at the raised, scabbed lump of one of the last remaining bites, a result of infection due to my constant scratching.

I pull back, and his hand drops away, but he continues to glower down at me, clearly waiting for a response. "Someone wasn't happy about my speech at the welcome banquet," I say. "My punishment was waiting for me when I went to bed."

"What punishment?"

"Prove me wrong." My voice is flat and stale. "I'd love some justice." Then I brush past him and peer through the glass door of the lab to check that the hallway beyond is empty. When I leave, he doesn't stop me.

CHAPTER 18

"To better understand the third stage of the selection process, during which the contestants must display technological prowess and innovation, we will have a guest speaker today."

Patricia 003's monotone voice drones in my ears, making little impression, as I surreptitiously study Raquelle, who is sitting at the desk diagonally in front of me. It has been a little over a week since I saw Hugh forcing himself on her in the gymnasium. Since then, she has become steadily pricklier and more reserved, refusing all attempts at conversation beyond what is strictly necessary. During our boxing lessons, she pushes me relentlessly so that there is no time for chatting, and when I watch her attack the punching bag herself, I see a pent-up fury so savage that it is almost frightening to watch.

"Greetings, ladies." The familiarity of the voice brings my eyes to the front of the room, where they unexpectedly land on a stranger. But when the woman smiles, I know exactly who she is and why I recognize her voice. "I am Boadicea, mother of the Ascendant, Denzel Xavier."

I remember Cronus's quip about having a weakness for tall girls as I study Denzel's mother. Unlike my gangly frame, Boadicea's physique is that of a queen, curving and robust. Her silver-streaked black hair is knotted into a soft chignon at the base of her neck with a slender circlet of copper resting on her head. Her smile is as devastatingly beautiful as her son's, and as I watch her move to the side of the room, I understand exactly why she was Cronus Xavier's choice.

Then I remember the door in the maze. There is nothing in Boadicea's beautiful, serene face that hints at years of infidelity, but that is likely due to the fact that she has had years of practice hiding her pain from a watching world.

"I remember the day I was chosen to come here." Boadicea's voice is barely raised and yet clearly audible in the silent room. "I was excited. Like you. I was frightened. Like you. But when I stood in the foyer of the White House and Patricia 003 told us that one of our Gauntlets would be to invent something to benefit the Federation, any eagerness I had felt was drowned in terror. I was eighteen years old, and I had only attended school until the sixth grade. Already, in my brief time in the Federation, I had seen technology beyond my wildest dreams. What could I, the daughter of a divorced seamstress, possibly invent that would benefit this great nation?

"Weeks passed. I lost weight as I fretted continually over what I could possibly create. At the end of the second month, I threw my party." Her lips curve in a slight smile. "I'm not going to tell you what it was, since I want you all to come up with your own ideas, but it was a smashing success. The Ascendant began to pay me marked attention. The other girls began to say that I would certainly be picked as the next Consort. Their words only added to my stress. I still had no idea what to create. In an attempt to alleviate my tension, I asked for sewing materials and began to make myself and my fellow Westerners clothing items.

"One night, a friend stopped by my room and found me working on a suit that one of the other girls had requested in anticipation of the obstacle course in the second Gauntlet. He asked me why I was so frazzled, and when I confided that I had no idea what to make as an invention, he told me that I was thinking about things all wrong. 'The Federation needs new ideas,' he told me. 'Don't look around and think that you couldn't make any of the things they currently have. That's the whole point. Think about what you're good at. That's your starting point.'"

Boadicea looks around the room. "I realized that he was right," she says. "And it wasn't hard for me to figure out where my skill lay. I began to examine my ability to make clothes, questioning what purposes they could be used for beyond being aesthetically pleasing." Her hand rises, an elegant, slow-motion gesture, and a hologram forms in the air before us. "As you all are doubtless aware, the commanding division of our military is pitifully small. We have been fortunate to avoid becoming embroiled in a military conflict up until this point, but one is almost certain to come eventually. At that time, it will be imperative that the humans commanding our droid forces be protected to the highest degree."

Her hand moves in a swirling motion, and I catch a glimpse of a tiny remote in her hand as the hologram revolves slowly before us. "I designed this suit to make the wearer virtually invincible. The polyester is interwoven with threads of tungsten, the strongest metal in the world, which renders it bulletproof. A thin coating of PTFE protects from acid. A reflective layer on top deflects most lasers." She clicks a button on her remote and a thicker suit appears, outlining the first. "The outer layer is not only fire-resistant, but"—she clicks the remote again and the image zooms in, focusing on the row of buttons down the front of the coat—"the middle layer inflates the coat when pressed, providing protection against impact and doubling as a floatation device."

A final click and the hologram flickers and fades. "My advice to you is the same advice that was given to me," Boadicea says. "Focus on what you already know. Focus on the strengths you already have. Half a year is not much time. Make friends who excel in the areas where you are weak. Do you have any questions?"

Zuri's hand rises. "I just want to say how amazing your design is, Excellency. Truly original."

Boadicea smiles graciously. "What is your name, dear?"

"Zuri, Your Excellency."

"Thank you, Zuri. I look forward to seeing what you come up with. Anyone else?"

Silence stretches. Raquelle is staring out the classroom's only window. Bella is holding up her notebook to admire a sketch she has just completed, clearly oblivious to social conventions. Clotilde's hands are folded in her lap, her usually serene smile a little strained as she waits for someone else to break the awkward stillness.

"What is the hardest thing about being Consort?"

I'm not sure what makes me ask. Maybe I just want to divert Boadicea's notice from the inattentiveness in the room. Maybe looking into the face of the woman who has succeeded—as much as success is possible—at being a Western Consort of the Eastern empire makes me think that the possibility of a happy ending exists for me as well. If I can anticipate the pitfalls along the way.

Boadicea's eyes meet mine, and in their depths, I see agony that makes me want to withdraw the question. Then the expression is gone and she says stoically, "The betrayals. When you receive a position of power, there will always be those who seek to use and manipulate you. Over the years, I have learned that the less emotionally invested you become in any given situation, the less vulnerable you are."

And there it is. The philosophy that has guided me all my life.

Look out for yourself. Put up walls. Don't care.

My eyes find the back of Raquelle's head. Bella turns in her chair to smile at me, brandishing a sketch of a long, flowing ball gown. I look back up into Boadicea's eyes, and there is a knowing expression there.

"Does that make sense, Andromache?"

"Yes, Excellency," I say quietly. "Thank you."

CHAPTER 19

"**W**ow." Heath turns open-mouthed to Lida. "Were you *really* a stylist before you gave up and decided to live on the beach?"

Lida cuts her eyes at him while stepping close enough to spritz some perfume along my neck. She sniffs and then spritzes again. "It'll take a lot of this to keep you from smelling like a sweaty gym mat."

"I took a shower," I protest before seeing the twinkle in her eyes. "Even if I did smell like a sweaty gym mat, being able to trounce Feds who try any funny business would be worth it," I say. "And Heath's right." I study myself in the floor-length mirror standing in the corner of my bedroom. "We've found your calling."

My dress is the deep orange of a tiger lily, falling in a soft cascade of chiffon to hide my bare feet. The bodice and skirt are both scattered with the embroidered silver out-lines of flowers, butterflies, and birds that create sparkling illuminations wherever the light catches them. My face is mostly free of makeup, but silver dust shimmers on my eyelids and coral lipstick outlines my mouth. I touch the earrings dangling from my earlobes—progressively small-er gold and silver leaves layered up to a single tourmaline. A matching necklace rests against the bare skin below my collarbone.

"Please let me bring the shrug," I say, and Lida's brows draw down as she pulls a mesh-like slipover away from my clutching hands.

"Absolutely not."

"I already have a reputation for wearing too little cloth-ing."

"This is a ball gown. It's different. And I don't intend to be known as the stylist whose protégé was a wallflower during the first Gauntlet. Here." She places something small and hard into my hands. I look down at an orange half-mask bordered with pearls, with a cluster of silver tiger lilies pinned above the right eyebrow. "You can cover up with that."

I place the mask on my face before reaching back to settle the elastic string in a comfortable position among the cascading curls of my hairdo. "I'll freeze."

"Find someone with a pink suit jacket to drape around your shoulders."

"Pink and orange clash."

"I guess you'll just have to freeze, then."

A deep, resonant gong vibrates through the complex. "You're late!" Lida sounds more flustered than I've ever heard her. "Go, go, go."

"Late is fashionable," Heath says as Lida bustles me toward the door. "Bet you're the prettiest one there, Andi."

"Wish I had you to dance with," I say, turning to give him a tight smile before Lida pushes me out of the suite and the door clicks shut behind me.

I'm not a good dancer. Not real dancing, like this. If I could just stand in the shadows for the entire evening and watch the beautiful aristocracy of the Federation whirling past me, I think I could enjoy this party. But Lida would kill me.

"I was afraid you weren't coming."

I continue to stare out over the swirling couples as I say, "If Lida hadn't shoved me bodily out the door in a ball gown, I wouldn't have."

"What would you be doing instead?" His breath brushes my ear, and I am suddenly very aware of him standing behind me, whatever-color suit jacket he is wearing skimming my bare shoulder.

I step away and turn to look at him. His dark purple ensemble is patterned with swirling black-and-silver DNA helices. On anyone else it would look ridiculous. But somehow he pulls it off. Just like everything else he wears. "Not having a pointless conversation," I say, because I don't know why he's sought me out, and I hate the draw I feel toward him.

He promised he'd give me justice. But every time I've seen him since that night, he's been with Hugh.

"Less talk, more action, huh?" His hand extends toward me, palm up, and I glance involuntarily over my shoulder just to make sure he isn't asking someone else to dance.

My eyes catch on Evangeline Langley, her hair pulled up in an elegant twist, the silvery blue folds of the sheath-like dress she wears accentuating her curves as she dances gracefully past in the arms of a haughty-looking man with white-blond hair. My heart drops as I turn back to Xavier, whose extended fingers have curled into a fist.

I imagine telling him that I'm not going to be his way of getting back at another woman before walking away. But then I remember the door in the hedge and the look in Boadicea's eyes as she spoke of betrayal, and I know that unless I want to walk away from a chance to protect everyone I care about, a dance will be the least I have to accept from this man.

"I'm not a very good dancer."

"Neither am I. That's why I have to wear the scintillating suits. So that hopefully my partners will be dazzled and won't notice me stepping on their feet."

I cock an eyebrow at him. "Oh, I'll notice." I lift my skirt to reveal my bare feet.

"Where are your shoes?"

"Have you ever tried running away from someone in high heels?"

"Who exactly do you anticipate having to run away from tonight?"

I stare at him through the holes in my mask. "In this entire room, there are only two people I trust. I like being prepared."

He steps closer. I can barely see his eyes through the holes in his eggplant mask, but for a moment, I wonder if he's going to ask what it would take to bump the two up to three. Instead, he says, "Dance with me, Kanoska."

"Is that an order?" I say.

He smiles again, and I look away, because if I see it too much, I might get addicted to making Denzel Xavier smile at me. "Yes," he says. "But it's the only order I'll ever give you."

The music slows as he leads me onto the dance floor. With a sudden movement, he pulls me close. I try to draw back, to put a little more space between us, but his arms tighten as his feet begin a rudimentary version of a three-step.

"Xavier—" I start.

"Shh," he murmurs, and his cheek finds mine. The music swells around us and couples begin to spin faster.

"You were right." The words are so quiet that for a moment I am not sure that I really heard them. I want to pull back and look into his face, but that would destroy the entire image he has been building up to allow us to talk privately without appearing to do so. "I found footage. Of the airstrikes. And records. Of a secret government department. The Department of Correction. I'm sorry." His breath brushes my ear. "Kanoska, I didn't know. I swear to you. I would have put a stop to it if I had. I will put a stop to it now."

His feet slow, pulling me to a stop as lights suddenly blaze, illuminating the previously dim dance floor. Stunned, I watch a phalanx of armor-plated droids carrying stun guns glide through the double doors of the ballroom. People scramble out of their way as they move inexorably toward the far side of the room. A spotlight flares, pinning Lothar Grimsby with a cup of some scarlet liquid clenched in his fist as he watches the droids bearing down on him.

The lead droid speaks, its deep, measured voice ringing out across the silent room. "Lothar Grimsby, you are under arrest for crimes against the citizens of the Federation and unauthorized attacks against our allies."

"On whose charge?" His voice is still the voice of an announcer.

"On mine." Xavier steps forward, and the spotlight swivels to find him, catching me in the edge of its glow. I try to inch sideways, but the light follows, and I freeze, thankful for my mask before realizing that my height alone is a dead giveaway of my identity.

Grimsby's face pales. The hand holding the glass tightens convulsively, and for a moment I think he is going to hurl it at Xavier. But instead, he places the flute on a small table before sinking into a low bow. "Excellency."

Xavier motions, and the droids converge on Grimsby. I can't see what they are doing, but after a moment, the droids move back into formation with Lothar Grimsby walking unshackled in the middle. His suit coat is gone, and his shirtsleeves have been rolled up. As he passes, I catch a glimpse of a black string of numbers imprinted on his left forearm before the ballroom doors swing shut.

"I apologize for this disturbance of tonight's festivities." Xavier's voice rings across the silent crowd. "Special apologies to our lovely hostess." A spotlight finds Clotilde. A blush suffuses her cheeks below her navy-blue mask. "Let the revels resume!"

Music ripples through the room, and a few couples begin to dance again, but the majority of the assembly is huddled together in twos and threes, whispering animatedly. Xavier turns to me. "I'm tired of you stepping on my feet. Come on."

Normally, I would laugh. Not only is he funny, but he kept his word. He promised me justice, and justice was served. Just not to everyone. "What about Hugh?"

His lips tighten, and I know I should have expressed some sort of gratitude before blurting out more accusations. "Hugh has nothing to do with this. When I told him, he was just as surprised as I was."

I open my mouth, then close it again. Hugh is his best friend. My word will hold no weight against his unless I can bring proof. And the only proof I can bring would involve breaking my word to Raquelle and putting her in more danger of retribution.

"Denz?" We both turn. Evangeline Langley is standing beside us, effortlessly lovely. "I mean, Your Excellency." Tear tracks swirl through the smudged makeup on her cheeks. "Could we...talk? Just for a minute?"

Xavier's shoulders have gone stiff. "All right."

Without a backward glance, he follows her off the dance floor, leaving me with a feeling similar to receiving a punching bag straight in the stomach. A feeling that is only increased by the low, familiar voice that whispers in my ear, "Not your brightest move, smart girl."

When I turn, I see Hugh Grimsby spinning away through the crowd with Raquelle held too tightly in his arms.

CHAPTER 20

S asha will be here soon.

Over and over, as the next three weeks plod past, I tell myself this, trying to ignore the mounting pressure of too many secrets and my inability to do anything. Raquelle barely speaks anymore. I am certain that Hugh has just as much access as his father ever did to the "tools" in the Department of Correction, but I still have no idea how to broach the subject with Xavier of his best friend's duplicity. The two of them are together constantly. And Xavier always looks happy. Uncharacteristically relaxed.

But I've been unable to relax since the night of Clotilde's ball. Because Nicholas Pendell has, for some unfathomable reason, decided he's in love with me. After Xavier disappeared with Evangeline Langley-Pendell, Nicholas asked me to dance. As we fox-trotted around the ballroom, he dished up the dirt on every single person we passed. This one was a famous singer, but the rumor was that she had an addiction to nirvana pills. That one had paid thirty million euroyens for a bride price. This one was so afraid of gaining more weight if she had another child that after her second she commissioned a robot that would attend to all her husband's "needs" so she wouldn't risk getting pregnant again.

I had listened in sick fascination to his lurid stories, with no idea how to redirect the conversation. After the dance, I had excused myself and headed toward the doors leading out onto the terraces but was brought up short by the sight of Denzel Xavier with his arms wrapped around Evangeline Pendell. As I froze, I heard Nicholas's voice at my shoulder.

"Well, well. Someone really should tell Achilles. But it's not going to be me. My brother is a self-obsessed prick who could give Narcissus a run for his money. That poor girl deserves to find happiness somewhere."

And what about Xavier's soon-to-be wife, Nicholas? Where will she find happiness as she has to watch her husband with his former lover?

Desperate to get away, I asked Nicholas if he'd like to get a drink with me. As we headed for the open bar in the corner of the room, he prattled on about his younger brother's obsession with virtual reality. "He's not here tonight because he never goes anywhere. Sleeps, eats, and sits in his VR room. Horrendously in debt because he can never resist new technology. But he is notoriously touchy about his money issues. I heard he forbade Evangeline from making jewelry since he says they don't have the money for supplies and he doesn't want people thinking his wife is selling jewelry to make ends meet."

"I thought she was the regime's jeweler," I said, shocked out of my preoccupied silence.

"Not anymore. Her assistant's taken over the position."

Somehow, we ended up spending the rest of the evening together. I really didn't want to dance anymore, so I sat with Nicholas, allowing his continuous flow of talk to wash over me, occasionally putting in a "mm" or "I see" while letting my thoughts wander.

Unfortunately, the ability to sit silently while he talks seems to be high among Nicholas's criteria for an ideal wife. He has been following me ever since, attempting to switch tête-à-têtes with the other bachelors, appearing in the gymnasium to pedal languidly on a stationary bike while watching my kickboxing lessons with Raquelle, and taking the chair next to me at every meal.

The only place he doesn't follow me into is the lab. So that is where I am lurking during this afternoon's free period, curled up in a desk chair because for once I don't feel like working on the immunity serum. I am reading on my electronic pad. The Federation used to have a library within the White House complex until a few years ago, when Cronus decided that the space was needed and destroyed all physical books, instead setting up a digital library which all citizens can access from their electronic pads.

I am reading the Bible, trying to imagine myself back in my dusty garage helping Heath to sound out the words. The story I am reading, which I picked at random out of the middle, tells of a beautiful young woman who becomes queen just in time to save her people from being massacred by one of the king's friends. It gives me the strangest feeling of déjà vu, even though I don't think Heath and I ever got that far during our garage reading sessions.

The sound of the door opening behind me causes me to silently draw my feet up, tucking them carefully under me, as I pray that Nicholas has not found my last retreat.

"You still haven't shown me what you've been so busy working on lately." The deep voice causes my heart to skip a beat.

"It's not finished." That voice sends chills up and down my back. "I've hit something of a snag."

"Having someone to bounce ideas off of usually helps with that."

After a beat, Hugh says, "Fine. But you can't tell anyone, all right? This could get me the Einstein at next year's science showcase."

"The Einstein? Boy, are we confident."

"It's genius, Denz. I've found an enzyme that, when injected into a human subject, adheres to the telomeres on the ends of cells, effectively halting aging. If cells don't die, we don't die."

"Immortality," Xavier says quietly.

In my mind's eye, I can see Hugh's small, satisfied smile as he nods, and the cold in my bones seems to deepen.

"But not true immortality." Hugh's fingers drum on the metal countertop.

"Because people could still be killed?"

"It's not murder I'm worried about. We've nearly reached the point technologically where our generals will be able to control all of our armies without leaving the safety of the complex. Disease, on the other hand...well, it almost wiped us out once. I need to find a way to not only halt aging, but to fortify the human body to a superhuman level of immunity."

I feel Xavier's words coming before they leave his lips. "You know, one of the girls is working on an immunity serum for her invention."

I hold my breath.

"Really?" Hugh's voice is filled with the forced calm necessary to cover wild excitement. "Which girl?" I pray desperately that Xavier won't answer before realizing that if he doesn't, Hugh will almost certainly try to torture the information out of Raquelle. Xavier hesitates. "You know you can tell me anything, Denz. Haven't I always kept your secrets?"

"It's not exactly my secret."

"What do you think I'd do? Steal the formula?"

Yes. I think that's exactly what you'd do.

Xavier remains silent.

"Suit yourself," Hugh says. "But speaking of the girls, we've had three parties—the masquerade, the carnival, and the bot fight. Getting any ideas about whom you might pick? Or whom you won't?"

"Don't worry. I won't steal your beautiful boxer." There is a smile in Xavier's voice, and I know that he thinks he is just teasing his best friend about a crush, but the words conjure before me Raquelle's pale, set face and her dead eyes. My stomach twists.

"Much appreciated." Hugh's airy tone makes me want to jump out of the desk chair and box him into a pulp. "Come on, Denz. I know you're still pining after Langley, but in four months, you'll have to pick someone. Any ideas?"

I lean back in my chair, listening. "There's only one of them that I could kiss without turning into a hunchback."

"You fancy Kanoska?" Hugh's voice is carefully measured.

It is hard to analyze Xavier's tone when he speaks. "She was the one who tipped me off about the unauthorized bombings and civilian punishments. She's sharp as a syringe."

Oh no.

He's still speaking. "And I never know what she's going to say or do next. At the very least, life with her won't be boring." After a beat, he snaps, "What?"

"Nothing." Hugh's voice is still neutral. "I just would have thought a man recovering from a broken heart might prefer boring. A nice, predictable wife like Zuri Pendleton who throws twelve-course dinner parties would be the model Consort."

"What do you have against Kanoska, Hugh?"

Hugh laughs. "Relax, Denz. I just want you to be happy. All I'm saying is that you went with exciting once, and it didn't turn out. But if that's your type, go for it. After all, drama adds spice to life."

"I'll definitely consider my life a failure if my suits are the most exciting part of it." There is amusement in Xavier's voice now. "Come on. We need to get ready for the banquet."

The door clicks open, then shut, and I peer around the edge of the chair before stretching my cramped legs. I need to get ready for Zuri's party too. As soon as I'm able to stand, I leave the lab and set off for my rooms. In the hall outside my suite, I meet Nicholas.

"Andromache! I'm so glad I caught you before you got dressed." He rotates in front of me, holding out the edges of his golden suit jacket. "I want to escort you to dinner, but it would be uncomfortable if our outfits clashed."

I'm relieved at the idea of sitting with him. After overhearing Xavier's conversation with Hugh, my thoughts and emotions are in an uproar. Sitting next to someone with the gift of holding a completely one-sided conversation will be almost relaxing.

"I'll make sure not to wear peach," I say.

CHAPTER 21

I didn't expect a crack the size of the San Andreas Fault to splinter my heart upon seeing Sasha walking down the airplane steps. I expected to feel happy. To feel whole again.

But seeing her makes me remember nights playing cards in front of our old gas stove.

I remember us on either side of a straining, sobbing mother, promising her that the pain was about to be replaced by the miracle of life. I remember her work-hardened hands smoothing my forehead when she thought I was sleeping. I remember her running into the Pacific fully clad, after ten-year-old me had accused her of being no fun.

She is dressed exactly the same as I remember, with a beige T-shirt and pants hanging loosely around her slender frame and her gray-streaked hair pulled into a knot at the base of her neck.

She stops in front of me. "You clean up good," she says, and the lump I've been trying to swallow ever since my first glimpse of her rises, choking me. She stands on tiptoe, placing her hands on either side of my face.

"No further delay is possible." Patricia 003's crisp, official voice breaks the moment. Over Sasha's shoulder, I see Bella and her father. Bella's face is streaked with happy tears, and Mayor Solantis's smile is so wide I am sure that his cheeks will hurt for days.

"Sasha Denton," Sasha says, nodding to them. "I'm Andi's aunt."

"This is my daddy," Bella says, looking adoringly up at her father.

"Indeed I am." Mayor Solantis's voice is gravelly, but the edge is softened by his evident affection for his daughter. "However, most people call me Gavin."

"It's a pleasure to meet you."

"It sounds like we should head back to the complex," Sasha says, casting a glance at Patricia 003. "Which is good, since I need to clean up for your party tonight."

"The White House is not our destination," Patricia 003 says. "A luxury vehicle will be arriving shortly to take us to the bay."

Sasha turns to me, her calm ruffled for the first time. "Andi?"

I give an apologetic half-shrug. "Apparently, party host-esses are supposed to arrive at events four hours early." I put an arm around Sasha and steer her toward the self-dri-ving limousine that has just pulled up. "But don't worry. The staterooms on this boat are bigger than our house. And Heath and Lida will be there to help make you presentable."

"Nice suit," Sasha murmurs next to me as we watch Denzel Xavier stride up the illuminated gangway toward us.

"He looks exactly like he did the first time I saw him." But that's not entirely true. The pink tux is the same. The diamond stud glints in his left ear. The smile, though? That wasn't there my first night.

"He doesn't look like he minds that your outfits clash." Sasha eyes my sparkling blue and gold sheath. When she asked on the ride over if any of the suitors struck my fancy, I avoided the question by regaling her with stories of Nicholas's infatuation.

"Do you mind?" I hiss, and she smirks at me as Xavier comes to a stop in front of us.

"Your Excellency," I say, swiping my hand from my forehead to my chest and then from shoulder to shoulder. In Federation history class, Patricia 003 told us that this used to be a religious symbol but that now it symbolizes willingness to be drawn and quartered if a subject ever shows disloyalty to the Elector.

"Not planning to run tonight?" he says, and I look down at the strappy, high-heeled sandals Heath insisted on.

"Take a look around. Tonight's environment isn't exactly conducive to running."

A ramp leads up to the top deck of the ship, which is set with round tables draped in blue and gold like the flag of the Commonwealth that Cinq still uses. On each table, candles flicker, illuminating place settings of crystal and porcelain. Overhead, twinkle lights sparkle like miniature stars. Droids stand around the perimeter, holding trays filled with hors d'oeuvres and glasses filled with a variety of hot and cold beverages. At the front of the boat, a small stage has been erected, and a man sits at a grand piano playing soft, lilting music.

"Once the boat takes off, running away would involve a very long, cold swim," I tell Xavier. His smile widens, and I look away. My eyes fall on the man standing behind him.

"And who's this?" Hugh says smoothly, gesturing to Sasha.

"My aunt." I know I sound stiff, and my heart sinks as I catch sight of Cronus Xavier, arm-in-arm with Boadicea, standing behind Denzel and Hugh.

"Sasha Denton," Sasha says, nodding to both young men before her.

"A pleasure," says Hugh. "Your niece is an absolute delight, Miss Denton. As clever as she is beautiful. Eh, Denzel?"

The sight of Xavier's expression gives me the same feeling of weightlessness that I used to get when running along the beach. But all he says is, "I hope your flight was pleasant, Miss Denton."

Hugh shrugs expressively at Sasha before following Xavier up onto the ship, and she smiles in return. The sight makes my stomach twist. I need to tell her what Hugh is really like. But by the time the last guest has boarded, three automatons stand at silent attention behind me waiting for instructions, and when I've finally resolved the issues enough to get the party into full swing, Sasha has disappeared.

The bathroom door swings closed, and I lean against the sink, blowing out my breath. Upstairs on the main deck, the Federation's most famous singer—whom Xavier connected me with—is performing, and my guests sit quietly around their candlelit tables, replete with a gourmet dinner and spellbound by the music.

My shoulders are starting to relax for the first time today when a choked sob makes me whip around. "Hello?"

No one answers, but a gasp sounds from the end stall. Heart sinking, I walk to the end stall and pause outside. "Raquelle?"

Again, there is no answer. I hesitate before placing my hand on the door, which moves inward. "Raquelle?"

She is there, huddled on top of the commode. When I reach to touch her shoulder, she jerks convulsively away, raising her head. There are nail marks in her cheeks, as though she has been gripping them frantically, and crying has caused her eyeliner to run into the shape of long black tears. "Go away." The words are hysterical, barely louder than a whisper.

"Raquelle, what did he do?"

"You promised to help me." Her breathing is fast and shallow. I have no idea what she might be capable of in this state. "But you're full of it, just like everyone else here. As long as you're safe, you don't give a euroyen about what happens to me or anyone else."

"That's not true." I try to channel Sasha's calm bedside manner into my voice. "I am trying. I was the one who got Lothar Grimsby arrested."

"Lothar isn't the one who's making my life a living hell!"

"I know." The words come out defeated, and I scramble to continue. "I'm just waiting for the right moment—"

"There won't *be* any right moment!" Her voice echoes around the bathroom. "Because you won't do anything to endanger your chances of becoming Consort."

"Raquelle, you don't understand—"

She pushes up off the toilet. Her dress shows more skin than it hides, with a plunging neckline, slits in the short, tight skirt, and a back scooped nearly to her waist. "I understand plenty." She's no longer shouting. "I understand that unless something drastically changes, Denzel Xavier prefers you above all the rest of us. I understand that in a few months' time, you'll have the chance to marry a man who is decent, who won't torture you just to show that he can, who won't use words to flay away every shred of self-respect you ever had, who won't force you to go out in public dressed like a common streetwalker. And I understand that it would be lunacy to throw away your chance of a safe, comfortable, secure life by accusing the Elector's best friend to protect a girl who is already damaged goods."

"Don't say that." I get to my feet. "It's not true."

"What do you know about it?"

I wrestle with the self-preservation instincts shouting at me that to confide in her would be madness. But that is exactly what she expects of me. That I will protect myself regardless of who else is harmed in the process. And maybe choosing to trust her with this secret that could be my ruin will convince her to trust me as I wait for the right opportunity to expose Hugh Grimsby.

"I know all about being damaged goods. In this society's eyes, it is impossible to be more damaged than I am."

"What are you talking about?"

I glance toward the ceiling for recording devices before remembering that cruise ships are used so infrequently now that most of them don't contain up-to-date technology.

"I'm infertile," I say, and inexplicably, a lump rises in my throat, choking off any more words. I remember the last time I held a baby. Heath's little sister, tiny and pink and perfect with her rosebud mouth and thick black hair. Never will I hold a child that is my own, the product of my body.

"What about the tests? The fertility tests?"

"I sent in someone else's blood."

"But they'll find out." At first I think Raquelle is threatening me before she says, "When you don't get pregnant in a few years."

"Don't you get it? I've been living on borrowed time for most of my adult life. Either I'll find another way to save myself or I won't. But don't act like you're the only one who's ever struggled to survive. I know exactly how awful it is to spend your life looking over your shoulder. When I say I'm going to save you, I mean it."

Her body sags. At length, she nods without saying anything.

"There's a stateroom down the hall," I say. "You can lock the door and spend the rest of the evening there. I'm the only one who has a key."

After showing her to the stateroom, I walk slowly up the stairs to the upper deck. Already, I regret confiding in the furious, cynical girl I am leaving behind. I care about Raquelle. But I'm not sure how she feels about me. And now I've placed a knife in her hands which she could choose, at any moment, to plunge into my back.

As I step onto the upper deck, I hear the singer. Every eye is fixed on her as she sends music soaring out over the water surrounding the boat, so no one notices me slip into a dark corner next to the railing. My eyes sweep the audience again, and I notice two people who are not fully engaged in the performance.

Hugh Grimsby is beside the railing across from me. He leans down to speak to Sasha, and whatever he says makes her smile. Her expression becomes serious again, and she says something that makes Hugh's eyes narrow in concentration. He glances around, and I quickly draw back into the shadows, turning to stare out at the sparse lights of the city that was once the capital of a global superpower.

"When you said I could pick the music," a voice says in my ear, "I thought it was implied that you actually had to stay and listen to my choice." When I don't answer, Denzel Xavier says, "Andromache?"

"You never call me by my first name."

"A slip of the tongue, I assure you."

I can't banter with him. Not after my conversation with Raquelle. I turn away again. Let him think me rude.

An arm in a pink sleeve slips around my waist. Shock tangles my vocal cords, and I stand stock-still as warmth begins to expand in my chest, tingling down to the tip of every finger and toe.

"Relax, Kanoska." He pulls me more tightly against him, and I lean on his shoulder. His cheek moves against the top of my head. "Your hair is so soft."

"Not sure how it can be, with all the hairspray Lida put in."

"We're on a boat in the middle of a glassy bay. There's a full moon. And twinkly lights. And the most romantic singer this side of the continent. Just take the compliment, Kanoska."

"I don't have much practice taking compliments," I say.

"I can fix that," he whispers, and it's as though his voice and his nearness and the memory of his smile are moonshine, rising to my head and making me tipsy. But then Evangeline Langley is striding through my mind, popping the joyful bubbles until the golden haze dissipates into nothing.

"Because you have lots of practice?"

The brittleness of my voice makes his arms fall away. "Why do you say that?"

I am suddenly intensely grateful that I can't see his face. "I know about Evangeline Langley."

"And?"

His tone nettles me. "And you wanted to run away and marry her!"

The air around us seems to grow colder with every second that passes. Finally, Xavier says, "I don't ask about whatever boy is back in San Francisco eating his heart out over you. My past is my affair. Not yours."

Applause breaks out, and I push past him without a word, plastering on my hostess smile as I walk to the front to thank the singer.

And if you pick me, Xavier? Is it still not my affair then? Am I destined to become your mother, betrayed and left brokenhearted by a man who asked her unwavering allegiance without a speck of loyalty in return?

CHAPTER 22

A t least the first Gauntlet is over.

This is the thought uppermost in my mind as I sit down at my desk a week after my party. The past seven days have been rubbish, but since Raquelle's party happened last night, at least I can throw myself into training for the second Gauntlet, which won't require smiling or making small talk or wearing shoes that leave you limping for days afterward.

Sasha's flight home left at six a.m. the day after my party. I had no idea. So instead of soaking up our one precious night, I had returned to my suite at midnight and fallen into bed. She shook me awake at five to tell me goodbye.

"What?" My sleep-fogged brain failed to comprehend the situation. "You can't leave yet!"

"They don't want me distracting you. Or causing you to miss your old life."

"I miss my old life every day as it is! Having you here makes it better, not worse!"

"I have to go, Andi." The words are final, but the lack of emotion in them doesn't fool me. This is her parting gift, a clean break without hysteria to make it harder for both of us.

Since her departure, I've been haunted by fears of how much she told Hugh Grimsby. I tell myself I am imagining things, but every time we are in the same space, it feels as though his eyes are on me constantly, filled with an expression that leaves me unsettled and jumpy.

I've managed to almost completely avoid Xavier since the night on the ship. Group meal times and Raquelle's party have been the only exceptions, since a meeting with his father caused him to reschedule our last tête-à-tête to this afternoon. The thought of spending hours in his society is making me even more jumpy than Hugh's constant scrutiny. Questions have started to creep into my mind about the wisdom of trying to marry the Elector, fueled by Raquelle's inquiries about what will happen to me if I fail to produce a child a few years into our marriage.

There is a possibility—albeit a slim one—that if I marry a nobleman and never get pregnant, the fact will get chalked up to bad luck or an issue with my husband and will be overlooked, especially if there are a lot of other noble children produced by the remaining Western brides. But if I marry the Elector, failure to get pregnant will be failure to produce an heir. And there is no way that will be overlooked. Inquiries and fertility tests will result, and even if my previous trickery is not discovered, my marriage will still be annulled, and I will be sent West to join the next shipment to Paradise.

But the way Xavier makes me feel scares me even more than the possibility of exposure. If he marries me only to begin, or continue, an affair with Evangeline Langley, I know I will never allow another person close enough to touch my heart again.

Perhaps it would be better to just marry Nicholas. That would be the best bet for a safe, comfortable existence, undisturbed by any feelings toward my husband beyond indifferent tolerance.

"Good afternoon, ladies." Patricia 003's mechanical voice breaks into my reverie, and I focus on the automaton standing at the front of the room. "The first phase of the Espousal is complete. Here are your rankings, assigned to you by the nine parents of your prospective husbands. Ordinarily, there would have been ten judges, but due to unforeseen circumstances, Lothar Grimsby has been deemed unfit and disqualified."

Bella swivels in her chair to look at me, but I only shrug. This is the first I've heard of rankings. Patricia 003 taps her chest, and a hologram appears in the air beside her, revolving slowly. I recognize Cronus's features before the image opens his mouth and sound fills the classroom.

"Ladies, I wish, first and foremost, to thank you for your efforts in this first stage of our competition. The events which you curated were, for the most part, unique and enjoyable. However, certain ones stood out while others were below the general standard. It is for this reason that my fellow judges and I have ranked your five parties in the following order, going from the least to most well executed. Scores in the first round are distributed in increments of eleven points.

In last place, with a current score of eleven points, is Raquelle Mortimer. Next, with a score of twenty-two points, is Clotilde Katmiller. In third place, we have Bella Solantis, with a score of thirty-three points."

I hadn't realized there was such a structured grading system, but being in the top two places can't be bad, right?

"In second place, with a score of forty-four points"—the hologram of Cronus pauses dramatically—"is Zuri Pendle-ton."

I applaud politely along with the other girls. Zuri smiles, but the expression is strained.

"Which means that the reigning champion, with a total of fifty-five points, is—as you will have surmised—Andro-mache Kanoska!" The hologram freezes, then flickers before disappearing.

"Yay, Andi!" Bella's excitement for me is so genuine that it is impossible not to smile.

"I'd never have had the idea of a boat if it wasn't for you, Bells. I owe you one."

Patricia 003's dispassionate voice drifts through the classroom. "If your current standings are unsatisfactory to you, be reassured. This was the easiest, and therefore, the lowest scoring of the three Gauntlets. In the next Gauntlet, the scores will be awarded in increments of forty-three. Your inventions will be awarded points in increments of ninety-seven. This will allow even those of you who per-formed poorly in this first Gauntlet a shot at the top two spots, which will be the only ones from which Ascendant Denzel Xavier will be allowed to choose a bride."

"What!" I expect the exclamation to come from Zuri, but the voice is Raquelle's.

There is no change in the inflection of Patricia 003's voice. "This information is not provided initially, in order to reduce the stress upon the contestants during their first weeks in a new environment."

Zuri's expression remains unconcerned, but her hand shakes slightly as she raises it. "Just to clarify, it is *impossible* for Denzel Xavier to choose a contestant who is not ranked in one of the top two places at the end of the three Gauntlets?"

"That is correct." Patricia 003 taps a rhythm on her chest, and a series of pings sounds through the classroom. "I have just sent a link to each of your devices, which will allow you to check your standing should you need to refresh your memory. This rule is in place to protect the Federation from the unchecked passion of a single man. By allowing the Ascendant to choose between two candidates, his freedom of decision making is preserved, while at the same time, the culling of the pool of candidates by a panel of unbiased judges ensures that a fit Consort will be selected. Are there any questions?"

Zuri speaks again. "I understand that our next challenge involves completing an obstacle course. Will we be allowed to practice on the course before the second Gauntlet?"

"No contestant will be allowed to use the obstacle course before the competition date. However, I have been instructed to end this class early to allow you to familiarize yourselves with your new training facility. Follow me."

I put my pad in my bag and hurry to join the other girls in Patricia 003's wake as she lock-steps toward the class-room door. Down the hall, we all squash into the elevator. Unfortunately, I end up in a corner next to Zuri.

"Bet that was a nasty shock. To learn that sucking up to Xavier isn't enough to get you picked as Consort."

Said without a hint of irony.

"You know, I would actually have felt worse if I had spent over half of my party budget on a professional planner and still was runner-up."

Patches of pink appear on her cheekbones. "You think you're so smart."

"I don't actually," I say. "But I do think that I'd rather not get picked as Consort if I knew that the girl Xavier really wanted was the one he just couldn't have because of an ordinance imposed on him by others."

Not true, a voice whispers in my mind, and I see him standing on the balcony with his arms around Evangeline Langley. *That was the girl he really wanted.*

The silver doors of the elevator slide apart. My uncomfortable thoughts are banished for the moment by what I see outside.

We are on the roof of the complex. The entire space is enclosed in a clear material that looks like glass, but the monkey bars and climbing ropes suspended from the ceiling make me certain that it cannot be the kind of glass I am used to. A ditch runs around the entire perimeter of the room, filled with an odd, tar-like substance and rocks spaced at various intervals. Inside the ditch, one half of the room is taken up by an enormous pool with a ropes course dangling above it. The other side consists of dozens of trampolines with padded partitions of varying heights rising between them.

"Come," says Patricia 003, stepping out of the elevator onto a narrow band of no-man's-land that runs the entire width of the room, dividing the two halves. The other girls follow her, and I am barely able to make it out of the elevator before the doors slide shut.

"This, in addition to the gymnasium downstairs, will be your training ground for the next two months before the second Gauntlet," the automaton intones. "The substance filling the gully surrounding the perimeter is known as 'boue.' Due to its unique chemical makeup, it hardens around any object that enters it for a full sixty seconds, then becomes liquid again for a mere five seconds. The water in the pool is regulated to remain at thirty-four degrees, making it unpleasant to fall into. Should any injury result from utilizing the variety of climbing apparatus which you see throughout the training arena, there is a panic button located at the center of this bridge which will alert medical personnel to the incident. Are there any questions?"

For a moment, there is silence as we take in the space around us. Then I raise my hand. "Are there set hours during which we may use the training arena?"

"As long as you continue to attend meals, your classes, your outings with the suitors, and are in your rooms by eleven o'clock, you may use the training center any time you wish."

CHAPTER 23

I am lying on my bed, working on a training plan, when a knock sounds on my suite's outer door. Before I can power down my electronic pad, I hear a creak and then the sound of Heath's voice, followed by the low rumble of Xavier's.

Rolling onto my back, I stare at the ceiling. I still haven't decided what to do about Xavier. I don't know whether I should keep competing for the position of Consort.

Lida's nasally laugh sounds outside, mingled with Xavier's deep chuckle. I am suddenly irrationally angry that Denzel Xavier has the nerve to hang out in my suite, with my friends, laughing at jokes in which I have no part.

I stride over to the door and yank it open. Lida and Xavier both turn to stare at me. "What's so funny?"

"Your face." Heath snorts with laughter, and I see Xavier choke a little as the seven-year-old that I am going to throw in the freezing pool in the training center at the first opportunity disappears into his bedroom.

"I was just telling His Excellency about how at six years old you refused to dance with any of the boys on Ratification Day because you said none of them were tall enough," Lida chimes in.

"You'll have to tell me more about that, Kanoska," drawls Xavier, as I stare daggers at Lida.

Lida smirks at me, mouthing, "He's handsome."

"We were *actually* talking about the time my younger sister bet I couldn't keep one finger against the force field in the garden for a full minute," Xavier says. "I did it, but completely forgot that I was supposed to be playing 'Für Elise' on the piano for visiting dignitaries from Germany that afternoon. The burn was so bad that I just skipped all the notes I was supposed to play with that finger. Afterward, I heard one of the visitors congratulating my father on my compositional skills. Apparently Beethoven with a third of the notes missing isn't recognizable."

I don't know what to say. The story makes him more human. More likable. That is the last thing I need right now. "What should I wear? For our outing?"

"No skirts. And something you don't mind getting wet."

"Wow. This—wow." Heath steps out of the elevator into the training center, his eyes and mouth comically round.

Before I can stop him, he takes a flying leap off the central metal strip onto one of the trampolines, his body sailing into the air as his feet meet the elastic surface. He twirls and then pulls his knees into his chest, managing to turn a three-quarter flip before splatting down onto his back. His twinkling black eyes find my face, then Xavier's. "This place is awesome!"

"Let's see if Kanoska can land a flip." Xavier follows him onto the trampolines, bouncing Heath into the air.

"Why do you call her that?" Heath asks between giggles as his body finally stops bouncing.

"Because I've called her that so long, anything else would feel strange." A thread of warmth slips through a chink in my heart's walls. "Come on, Kanoska. Let's see it."

I join them on the trampolines. I've never done a flip before, and I would have preferred not to have my first attempt be in front of the Federation's Ascendant. I jump in place, each bounce throwing me higher into the air. A few times I almost make up my mind to try the flip, but at the last second, my body remains rigid and I can't bring myself to do it.

"Come on, Kanoska!" yells Heath. "Don't be a chicken!"

I make a face at him and continue jumping as Xavier says, "My name, boy."

"Fine. Andi, you're going to hit the ceiling! Come on!"

He's right. I have to try. Launching myself into the air, I wheel my arms before tucking them into my body and curling forward. The air leaves my lungs with a whoosh as I land on my back, my body bouncing helplessly to a stop. Heath's and Xavier's faces appear above me.

"Smooth landing, Kanoska."

"You okay, Andi?"

"I'm fine," I wheeze, ignoring Xavier's extended hand and scrambling clumsily to my feet.

"That's why you shouldn't bounce so much—you fall from higher up," Heath says. He takes three bouncing steps and curls into a flip, staggering as he lands but managing to stay upright. "Yes!"

"Let's see your upper body strength." Xavier jerks his chin toward the knotted rope dangling above one of the scattered partitions.

I take a running start and manage to scramble ungracefully to the top of the partition. Then I grab the end of the rope and hoist myself up, pulling until I can get my thighs around the bottom knot. "I wouldn't stand anywhere close unless you're interested in being squashed flat when I fall off this."

I shimmy up the rope, surprised at how manageable it is. Apparently kickboxing with Raquelle has really helped my overall fitness. I am about halfway to the ceiling when Heath lets out a yell that nearly causes me to let go of the rope.

Twisting around, I catch a glimpse of Xavier kneeling next to Heath, whose leg is embedded knee-deep in the boue trench. By the time I manage to make it back to the ground, Heath's leg is free, and he is exclaiming over the boue. As he prods it experimentally with a finger, I draw Xavier to the side.

"Is he supposed to be in here?" I ask quietly.

"He's not hurt, Kanoska."

"That's not what I meant." My voice sinks lower. "Does he need to keep it a secret that he came in here?"

"I don't actually know what the official policy is."

"Then I'll just tell him not to say anything. He's good at keeping secrets."

For some reason, his expression hardens. "I suppose he learned from the best."

"You're not going to guilt me into telling you anything, Xavier."

"And if I pick you?" He glances around, but Heath is out of earshot, jumping from rock to rock in the boue trench. "Would you still keep secrets from me then?"

Yes.

"You're saying that I should be so grateful for the 'honor' of your hand that I start spilling my guts?"

"Armageddon, Kanoska. You know I didn't choose to land in this situation any more than you did."

"But you're still here! In your home. Where you grew up. With everything and everyone you love. And if you're not satisfied after our marriage, there's nothing to stop you trysting with your old flame all over the complex, is there?"

His face twists and he turns away from me, running his hand along his scalp. "Is this how it's going to be?" he says at last. "Hot, then cold? Over and over and over again? Acting as though you like me, then attacking me with groundless accusations? I listened to you. I had the father of my best friend arrested because of what he did to your nation and mine." He jerks his head in Heath's direction. "And it's not that I don't like kids, but I don't normally hang out with seven-year-olds."

He's right. I need to decide. Neither of us can keep going like this. But even if I decide that it would be safest for me to be chosen as Consort, I don't think I'm going to tell him the whole truth. Because I still don't trust him enough to place my life in his hands.

"Tonight," I say. "Let's meet up somewhere quiet. One hour before curfew. We'll talk."

"The private basketball courts," he says. "We'll play. Loser talks." I open my mouth, but he keeps going. "And we have to meet after curfew. I have a meeting with my father and Hugh at nine."

"What if we get caught?"

"It'll just make everyone sure who their next Consort will be." He starts to walk toward Heath, then turns back to me. "Oh, and it'll break poor little Nicholas Pendell's heart. Shame."

CHAPTER 24

"The date is set for a week after the wedding. We'll have had time to tidy everything up by the time Denzel returns from his honeymoon."

The words, drifting out of a door to my left, cause me to freeze. It is ten minutes until midnight, and the halls of the complex are dark. There is no light streaming out from beneath the door, and I imagine Hugh Grimsby sitting in the pitch darkness, his eyes glowing like some wild beast of the night. A chill skitters down my spine. *What is he talking about? And who is he talking to?*

"Did you find the formula?"

Cronus.

"No." Hugh's voice is terse. After I overheard Xavier talking to Hugh in the lab, I moved my formulas and equations into a password-protected file on my personal pad and destroyed all the physical evidence. "But it doesn't matter. Whoever the girl is will be required to show her work at the third Gauntlet. And we'll have plenty of time after the first inoculation to boost everyone's immunity. The important thing is that Denzel is gone during the airstrikes and that we make it look like the attack came from China."

"Why not tell Denzel? At your insistence, we've hidden this entire plan from him for four years. But secrets undermine a nation quicker than anything else, boy."

"Do you know your own son?" Hugh's voice drips scorn in a way that surprises me in someone addressing the Elector.

"If we tell him before he becomes Elector and he reacts badly, then we have the chance to put up an alternative candidate before the crowning ceremony. If he finds out after the power is in his hands, you and I will spend our immortal days rotting in solitary confinement or else learning exactly how well immunity works against a cocktail of every virus and pathogen under the sun."

"If we tell him before the plan is executed, we lose control. He could pretend to go along with us and then sabotage everything. It has taken my father his entire life and me half of mine to develop this formula. If it is destroyed, it might take another lifetime to redevelop it. You know as well as I do that the Federation's coffers have been drained just to produce enough enzyme for our current population. If Denzel were to tamper with what we have, the entire plan would implode."

Pieces of information are spiraling in my mind, coming together into an incomplete, yet sinister, picture.

Something tickles in my nose. I draw in air as slowly and quietly as I can through my mouth, trying to swallow the sneeze rising up my throat.

For a moment, it feels like I have succeeded. Then the sneeze explodes out of my mouth.

I run.

Behind me, the door flies open. I sprint toward the staircase, praying to whatever First Cause is out there in the void, that my dark clothing and the lack of light will keep Hugh from recognizing my fleeing form.

I manage to calm my breathing by the time I walk out onto the private basketball court.

"Practicing? No fair," I say to Xavier's back as he swishes a ball from the three-point line.

"Do I look like I need it?" he responds as the ball bounces back to him. He tosses it lightly from palm to palm.

"Do you really want an answer to that?" I dart forward, snatching the ball from his loose grip, and dribble toward the hoop, feeling the cold rim beneath my fingers as I leap and slam the ball through the mesh.

His laughter rings out, and I catch a glimpse of moonlight reflecting off his diamond as he comes at me. I turn my body, pushing into him as he reaches around me, trying to steal the ball. Dribbling acts as a stalling tactic before I get around him and shoot again. The ball clangs against the headboard and straight back. Xavier and I both leap, but his hands close around the ball above my head.

"Too small," he snarks as I vibrate in front of him, blocking his attempts to shoot.

"Yeah, people tell me all the time what a pixie I am."

"I think you mean 'imp'," he counters, finally sending the ball over my head and through the hoop. "All right, start talking."

"I got the first point and you didn't say anything."

"What if I say the game hadn't started yet?" I can see now why he picked this as our meeting place—not only far from listening ears and cameras, but a place so dim that we will be able to share our deepest secrets without blazing lights illuminating every look on our faces.

"Fine." His voice becomes serious. "What do you want to know?"

"What did Evangeline Langley want? At Clotilde's party?"

The ball drops from Xavier's left hand and bounces up into his right. Another bounce and it is back in his left. For a space, there is quiet, broken only by the rhythmic thumping of the ball. Then he says, "Who told you about us?"

I hold out my hand wordlessly, and he tosses me the ball. I bounce it, my eyes following its trajectory to avoid looking at his face. "I heard you talking to her," I say. "About a week after I got here. You said that the two of you should run away together to the Midwest. And she told you that she was going to marry Achilles Pendell instead."

I bounce the ball in his direction. He catches it. "I had tutors growing up, so I didn't go to school with the rest of the White House children. I met her at a wedding when I was fifteen. We began seeing each other shortly thereafter. I would have done anything to be with her. But she always valued her own safety above anything else. I should have realized that wouldn't change."

The words are emotionless and factual. Nonetheless, they sting. "Do you still want to be with her?"

He makes an incredulous sound. "She agreed to marry a pompous little ninny and didn't even have the guts to tell me until a week before the wedding. Even if her husband died tomorrow, I wouldn't want to marry her."

"What if you could have her without marrying her?" The darkness makes me bold. "I know why that door was put into the maze."

When he speaks, his voice is no longer emotionless. "My father broke my mother's heart. He was crazy about her when he married her, but where women are concerned, he has always had the attention span of a gnat. I remember the night of my tenth birthday, lying in bed, hearing her sobbing, begging him not to leave. You've seen my mother. She isn't the type to cry. And I never heard her shed another tear over him. But she became what she is now. Hard. Unreachable."

He lets the ball drop from his hands and catches it again, the single thump ringing out over the silent grounds. "Making promises to a woman and then leaving her to eat her heart out over you is a coward's way. Not mine."

I'm glad you can't see my face.

He still hasn't fully answered the question. "What about at the masquerade?"

"She's miserable." Xavier's answer holds the ring of truth. "She's stuck with a man she doesn't love who only emerges from his fantasy world in order to take his pleasure with her. She can't even lose herself in her work anymore. There's nothing between us now, but I cared about her for a long time. And I'm sorry to see her like this, even though she brought it on herself."

I hold out my hands, and he tosses the ball to me. "Your turn." I clench the leather sphere. After what he's just said, I owe him honesty. But I'm still not sure whether I can give it to him.

"Why do you care so much about what happens to infertile women?"

You ask the right questions, Xavier.

"Because." I swallow, my mouth dry and sandpapery. I try again. "Because..." I need to be brave. But even he doesn't call me Andi. Because that's not who I really am. "Because I believe all human lives have value." The words are cliché. Just true enough. But also utterly false.

"Why?"

Not the question I expected. "Before I came here," I say, "I helped my aunt deliver babies in the slums of San Francisco. Dozens of babies. And even in all that squalor and darkness, each time I held a newborn baby and looked into their face, I saw a work of art. A uniquely designed masterpiece that Someone had poured their heart into. Whoever that Someone is, I am sure they wouldn't want their works of art to destroy each other."

"You miss it." The words are a statement, and a lump rises in my throat. After a pause, he asks, "Is there someone? Back in San Francisco?"

"What?"

"You heard me, Kanoska."

"You have to make more baskets to get more questions." His only answer is to tug the ball from my hands and send it spinning in a perfect arc through the net. "Fine. Yes, there's someone."

"Tell me about him."

"Him?" My voice is innocent. "Sasha's someone."

"You little…"

My laughter explodes out, and I dart away from him, wanting to get the ball before he can. His hands close on my waist, spinning me around. The moon chooses that moment to break free of the clouds, and I can see every detail of his face—his dimples, the straight line of his nose, and something in his eyes that makes me turn my head sharply to the side so that his kiss lands on my cheek.

I can still feel the warmth of his lips as I pull away from him and grab the ball. My shot is bad, but after rattling around in the rim for what feels like an eternity, it thumps to the ground. "What would you do if I told you that one of the suitors was molesting a contestant?"

Clouds slip across the moon's face again, casting the court in shadow, but I hear his sharp intake of breath. "Kanoska, I didn't mean to cross a line—"

"Not you, Xavier." The devastation in his voice makes me reach for his hand. "I…I'm just not ready."

Not after I lied to you.

"Then I'll wait for you to kiss me. Just know that if you take too long, I'm going to start eating my feelings. Gallons and gallons of ice cream's worth of feelings"

I laugh, unable to stop myself. He gently tugs on my hand, and I walk into his arms. I am so distracted that it takes me a moment to understand what he means when he says, "They'd end their days in a sterile cell, being injected with test products, until the day some experiment fails."

"You...you actually do that here?"

"Death is an easy sentence, Kanoska." His voice is so cold that it is hard to believe that a moment ago, he was flirting with me. "Here we believe in repaying debts."

Would he really sentence his best friend to that?

"I assume your original question wasn't rhetorical." He lets go of me.

"No." I remember the dead look in Raquelle's eyes. Hugh has made her life a nightmare. Him getting a taste of the same would be justice. Pure and simple. "But I'm not going to tell you who it is," I say. "You would have no guarantee that I wasn't making it up out of spite. I have to *show* you."

"If you can show me proof of this, the perpetrator will pay. You know you can trust me to get you justice, Kanoska. I've done it before."

CHAPTER 25

I've never been weak.

Genetics gifted me a strong, tall physique and in my Cinq days, running added a hint of muscle to my lean frame. But there is something about feeling your strength grow daily—in leaps and bounds—that is almost intoxicating.

Three weeks into training I've established a routine. Stretching and core strengthening exercises first thing after I wake up. A light breakfast, followed by running or biking for an hour in the gymnasium. A break for my tête-à-tête, which, if it involves Xavier, is usually spent in the training center scaling ropes, practicing flips, hopscotching across the rocks in the boue pit, or swimming laps in the frigid water of the pool. After my tête-à-tête, I either head to the training center if I haven't been there already, or go to the gymnasium and lift weights between alternating sets of pull-ups and push-ups. During the last hour of free time, I hang out with Heath and Lida and, more often than not, Xavier. After dinner, there are often diplomatic or social events, which I escape from as soon as possible to fall into bed, utterly exhausted.

I would still be making time for kickboxing, but when I showed up at the gymnasium the night after the initial scores were announced, Raquelle wasn't there. My imagination kicked into overdrive, and I raced to her room and pounded on the door.

When it opened, Raquelle looked no different than she had over the past weeks. "What do you want?" she asked brusquely.

"Kickboxing?"

She laughed then. "How the tables turn."

"What on this spinning blue planet are you talking about? Is this because of Hugh? Because I talked to Xavier last night, and all we need to do is find a way to make sure he sees Hugh abusing you—"

"So that he'll think I'm damaged goods and kick me out of the competition, thus upping your chances of winning? I don't think so."

"What is wrong with you? I'm trying to help you, Raquelle."

"Oh, drop the altruistic act, Andi. You want to win. You want to save your own hide, just as much as I want to save mine. Xavier is a means to an end for both of us."

My insides flooded with ice. I had told her my deepest, darkest secret, believing that in some strange way, we were friends. If she chose to reveal the truth to anyone, I would be doomed, and she would be one step closer to her goal of winning.

But my anger kept me from pleading with her not to sell me out. I strode away, knowing that my only slim hope lay in telling Xavier the truth. I was starting to believe he might protect me, regardless of my fertility status and my lies.

Since the night on the basketball courts, an ideal moment had not yet come. I had been on three tête-à-têtes with him, but each one had been in the training arena, which not only had cameras and recording devices in every corner, but was always occupied by at least one other contestant, also training. Any time I saw him in the evenings, Heath or Lida was there, and while they already knew my secret, I was sure that if my revelation turned bad, they would try to intervene, thus endangering themselves.

As the days slip by and no one confronts me, I begin to hope that perhaps Raquelle still has enough decency not to turn me in. When I see her swinging across the monkey bars with the speed and agility of an acrobat and skipping across the boue trench without a single misstep, I am sure she will be able to win the next challenge without sabotaging me.

Her refusal to help me expose Hugh to Xavier has still created a dilemma that I have been pondering since the night I heard him conspiring with Cronus. I thought I had found a way to kill two birds with one stone. Having Hugh locked away for what he has done to Raquelle would ensure that he'd be unable to participate in Cronus's scheme. With their rocky relationship, Xavier would be much quicker to believe accusations leveled against his father than his best friend, so dealing with Cronus afterward would have been comparatively simple.

But now, in order to stop them, I will need to find proof of a plot so sinister that I almost disbelieve it, despite everything I have heard. I am sure that Cronus Xavier and Hugh Grimsby are going to find a way to inoculate the entire adult population of the East with Hugh's immortality enzyme, thus ensuring a human race that can live and reproduce forever. Then, the moment that Denzel and his new wife embark on their honeymoon to the customary spot on the beaches of Florida, airstrikes will eradicate the five cities of Cinq, leaving the Federation as the sole power on the North American continent.

A little over three months remain in the Espousal. In order to stop the airstrikes against Cinq, I need someone in power to call the operation off. But I still have no proof. If I could find and destroy the stock of the enzyme that Hugh was talking about, the Federation's need for Western brides would continue, and the airstrikes would almost certainly be postponed, buying time. But I am afraid to go snooping around alone at night. I want to believe that Hugh did not recognize my fleeing form the night I heard him plotting with Cronus, but whenever I meet his eyes these days, I get a horrible feeling that he does know. And that he is going to do something about it. Soon.

As I swing across the ropes course above the pool today, my disturbed thoughts are interrupted by a commotion below me. I look down to see Zuri jerk the knotted rope on which Bella is dreamily swinging to a stop.

"Stop playing around! Either use it or get off!"

"But I am using it."

"As a rope swing!"

"Yes." Bella clearly misses the fury behind the statement. "I miss the one Daddy built for me in our yard back home. This one isn't very good—it's too high off the ground."

Before I can do anything, Zuri takes a flying leap off the trampolines and catches onto the rope. Bella cries out as Zuri draws her legs up and kicks the other girl in the side. A yell escapes me as Bella's loose grip on the rope slips and she tumbles to the trampolines below, barely missing one of the padded protrusions.

Without thinking, I release the ropes and plunge into the frigid water of the pool below. In a few strokes, I reach the side and haul myself out. Slipping on the trampoline's surface, I make my way to Bella, who has curled up on her side and begun to cry.

"Bells, are you hurt?"

She only cries harder, and I drop to my knees, shaking her shoulder. "Bella! You have to talk to me! Are you going to be all right?"

"That—that was so mean!" Relief washes over me as I realize that she is unhappy rather than seriously injured. Then the relief morphs into rage.

I spring upright, craning my neck to look at Zuri, who is staring down at us with a faintly bored expression. "What was that?"

Zuri's finely penciled eyebrows rise. "Oh, I've been wanting to kick that ninny ever since we arrived. But the reason I finally did it is because I intend to stay in one of the top two spots at the end of this Gauntlet, and a little princess who thinks that the world is a playground and doesn't care about marrying the Elector isn't going to stop me."

Before I can speak, Bella's voice sounds next to me. I realize, with a start, that I have never seen her angry before. "I don't care about marrying the Elector! I'm going to marry someone else. But even if I did want to marry Denzel Xavier, I wouldn't kick people and call them names!"

Zuri's lips twist in a sneer. "Yes, you're going to marry whichever poor suitor places the lowest bid in the bride auction. I pity the man."

"Come on, Bella. You don't have to listen to any of this. Let's go."

Bella scrambles to her feet and begins to wave her left hand at Zuri. For a moment, I think she is making an obscene gesture before I realize that it is her fourth finger that's extended. "Alden promised me that he won't let anyone else pick me at the bride auction. And since he gave me this when he asked me to marry him, I don't think money is going to be a problem."

The ring is gorgeous. Five sapphires are arranged around a golden topaz to create a forget-me-not. Not only is Alden clearly a romantic, but he definitely is not struggling financially. A specially commissioned ring like that must have cost a fortune.

"It looks like Bella is set." I meet Zuri's furious gaze. "Unfortunately, even if you make one of the top two spots, I don't think that the Elector is likely to pick a conniving bully for a wife." I jerk my head toward the camera in the left corner of the room, and Zuri pales as her eyes follow my gesture. "Come on, Bella," I say again. She takes my hand, and we walk slowly along the central aisle toward the elevators. "I'm happy for you," I say quietly, squeezing her fingers lightly.

Her smile is radiant as she squeezes my hand back. "Sometimes I'm so filled up with happiness, I think I might pop."

"Andromache!" We pause. Zuri has dropped to the trampolines and is stalking toward us.

"Meet me downstairs?" I say to Bella. "I want to hear all about the proposal."

As Bella continues toward the elevator, I turn back to Zuri. "What?"

She is offensively close, and I take a step back, slipping on the smooth metal. Zuri grabs my wrist as though to steady me. "The Ascendant doesn't spend his days watching security footage. He won't know about today unless you tell him. That little ninny is too lost in daydreams about her Prince Charming to say anything. I'm warning you. If this gets out, I'll know who should pay."

"Stop it," I say. "You're giving me goose bumps."

Then I yank my wrist from her grasp and stride toward theelevators.

CHAPTER 26

"Euroyen for your thoughts."

The words startle me so much that I swing toward the speaker with a doubled fist before registering who is talking to me. "Whoa!" He holds up his hands. "I've been waiting for physical contact from you, but this wasn't exactly what I had in mind."

Blood rises to my face. "How are those gallons of ice cream treating you?"

He leans against the balcony beside me. "What are you doing out here? I thought I'd find you in the gymnasium, beating up a punching bag."

"I thought you had a makeup tête-à-tête with Zuri Pendleton."

"Zuri Pendleton has been confined to her room for the next three days as a disciplinary measure."

"What?"

"Footage came to light of her physically attacking and attempting to intimidate other contestants in the training arena."

I stare at him. It's not that I object to Zuri getting her just desserts. And I'm not exactly afraid of her. But this will solidify her animosity toward me, and people who hate me seem to be cropping up at an alarming rate.

"Did you see the footage?"

He smiles slightly. "You have a talent for making enemies, Kanoska."

"Thanks."

"You still haven't told me why you aren't in the gymnasium."

"It's harder to motivate myself without Raquelle there, yelling that only losers stay on their butts."

"Why did she stop teaching you?"

The sky above the bay is blazing. "She views me as the competition now."

"They should all view you as the competition." He isn't looking at me, but warmth rises up my neck again.

"What that really means is that they all view me as the enemy," I say. "Oh, except Bella. Did you hear that Alden asked her to marry him?"

"Mhm. I don't know him well, since he spent most of his teen years at a military base, but he's a good guy. The best one in the group besides Hugh."

There is no good response to that. "Did the Department of Correction get closed down after Lothar Grimsby was arrested?" I say finally.

"From what we can tell it was a one-man operation. He had controls on his device to direct a small squad of 'punishment bots' within the White House complex. The fleet of AI drones that have been attacking certain ships were normal patrol planes whose systems were hacked to allow commands from outside the military, but since Lothar's imprisonment, there have been no more airstrikes. I verified it."

Hugh must have similar controls on his device. If I can find a way to get my hands on it, there Is my proof.

"What were you up to today?" I say, tucking the inspiration into the back of my mind until I have time to create a real plan.

"Kanoska, pick a topic."

"What? I'm just interested in your life."

"And extremely bad at conversation."

"Newborns don't talk. I didn't get a whole lot of practice."

"What about the newborns' mothers?"

"That was mostly screaming and swearing."

"Sasha?"

I pause, considering. "This will sound strange, but we talked less than you would think for living and working together. She's the only person I've ever met where we could communicate without words."

A euroyen clatters onto the railing next to my hand. "You never told me what you were thinking about."

"One thing I was thinking about was what it would mean to be Consort."

"A lot of meetings. Foreign delegates. Committees on public health. Food supply. Infrastructure. The works."

"Wow. Sounds thrilling."

He turns so that his elbows are resting on the railing. "You know, until you came, I thought I would loathe my life as Elector."

"How did I change that?"

"You have the vision I need," he says quietly. "I can get stuff done. I don't mind making people angry. But you? You see the opportunities for good that power provides."

Before I can talk myself out of it, I place one hand on his neck and press my lips to his cheek. His hand rises to cover mine and for a moment, I am sure that he is going to turn his head and kiss me on the mouth. But he just says, "If you really want to know what it's like to be Consort, I think I know someone you could talk to."

"Do you still get to sew at all, Excellency?"

Xavier is right. He *can* get stuff done. The day after our conversation on the balcony, a hologram appeared beside my plate at breakfast, requesting my presence at tea that afternoon with Consort Boadicea Xavier.

Now I am sitting in a semicircular room with floor-to-ceiling windows, sipping tea and nibbling tiny cakes, tarts, and sandwiches while an automaton hovers behind me, speeding forward whenever I stop eating to offer a different selection of delicacies.

"My apologies," Boadicea says. "This one must have been programmed to be a little overzealous. Ginger 111!" The automaton turns its face inquiringly toward her. "Please return to the kitchen and recommence your duties there."

She takes a sip of tea before saying, "I sew every evening. Even if it is just a few stitches. Being Consort is not all sunshine and teacakes, and sewing has always been a place of peace for me."

"Did you want to be Consort?"

For a moment, Boadicea is silent. Then she says, "When I first arrived here, all I wanted was to be loved by a man. The wounds from my father's abandonment ran deeper than even I realized. I was in a dangerously vulnerable position."

I run my fingertip unconsciously around the edge of my teacup. I have no idea what to say to this. Or if any response is expected at all.

Boadicea clears her throat. Her face is still, as though carved from stone. "Immediately after my arrival, one of the bachelors caught my attention. He was funny. He was clever. We struck up a friendship almost at once." Boadicea clears her throat again. "I quickly fell in love with him. But about three months in, Cronus began to pursue me. He has a way of getting what he wants. And at the time, I thought that as long as I was loved, it didn't entirely matter which man I chose." A cloud passes over the sun, and the light from the window dims. "You asked if I wanted to be Consort. I wanted to be loved. And now I am Consort instead." She continues, "But I don't think you'll have to make that choice."

When I meet her gaze, a genuine smile lights up her already lovely face. "My son is quite taken with you. And he is not his father."

"Do you think I can make him happy?" I'm not sure where the question comes from.

Boadicea touches my cheek. "My dear girl, the fact that you ask that means that your chances of success are great." She sits back. "My son and daughter are my world, Miss Kanoska. If I thought that you would ever knowingly bring harm or sorrow to Denzel, I would make it my mission to destroy any chance you might have with him."

Won't it break him when he learns he will never be a father?

I sit up straighter in my chair and force myself to meet the Consort's eyes. "Understood, Excellency."

Whack. My fist connects with the punching bag in the gymnasium.

I can't do this.

Whack.

I need to get out of here.

Whack.

I can't marry Nicholas Pendell.

Whack.

I can't marry Denzel Xavier.

Whack.

Not without telling him.

Whack.

And I can't tell him.

Whack.

He said to Evangeline Langley that they could run away to the Midwest.

Whack.

Maybe I can get him to tell me how to get out of here.

Whack.

Then I'll take Heath and Lida and we'll go.

There must have been creaking. The sound of chains slipping.

One hundred and twenty pounds of red leather crash into me as the bag falls from the ceiling, and I am hurled backward.

My elbow slams into the corner of a treadmill. The last sound I hear is my bones shattering before my head strikes the plastic edge, and everything goes black.

CHAPTER 27

Lights swim above me, gradually coming into focus. My head feels as though it has been stuffed with cotton, and I know from the dull ache at the edge of my consciousness that there must be an enormous amount of drugs in my system, holding agony at bay.

I turn my head slowly, trying to take in my surroundings. I am lying in a bed in a completely white room. There is a smell that I cannot place and a needle in my left arm that is connected to a machine by a long rubber tube. That must be where the meds are coming from. I feel a slight tug at the back of my neck, and my eyes drift down to my right arm, which hangs immobilized in a sling. I turn my head a little further to the right. A man is slumped over in a chair, fast asleep.

"Xavier?"

He raises his head. A smile breaks across his face, and the irrational, probably drug-induced thought flits across my mind that if anyone ever found a way to bottle Denzel Xavier's smile, they could sell it as a pain reliever.

The legs of his chair scrape across the floor as he pulls it up to my bedside. "Kanoska. How do you feel?"

"Like I'm going to be in a lot of pain if anyone takes the morphine away. What happened to me?"

"The punching bag in the gym came loose somehow and fell while you were using it. You have a shattered elbow and a mild concussion. They just finished operating on the elbow."

"Where am I?"

"In St. Juno's. When the White House physician recommended surgery for your arm, you were transferred here." He drops his head into his hands. "Armageddon, Kanoska, what were you thinking?"

I stare at him, noting with mild interest that if I look at the same spot too long, his edges begin to blur. "I'm sorry?"

"How on earth did it escape your notice that the punching bag was slipping?"

His tone is beginning to aggravate me. "Do you look up every time you walk underneath a chandelier, just in case it falls on you? It's not exactly something a person expects to happen."

"I would look up if I heard creaking and grinding!"

"I was punching that bag, Xavier! It was creaking and grinding as it swung back and forth! Instead of blaming me, you might want to look into whether a punching bag falling on your number one contestant is coincidental or not!"

His head snaps up. "Why do you say that?"

"Because it will be a miracle if I'm able to complete the second Gauntlet now." As the words cross my lips, their reality settles over me. Even if I'm cleared to compete in the second Gauntlet, I'll be competing one-armed. I'll come in dead last.

Xavier's fingers close around mine. "I'll talk to my father. Surely the Council will postpone the Gauntlet until you're healed."

I'm less sure than he is that his father will help me. "Even if they do, I won't be able to train."

"Even if you come in last, you could still be in the top two spots if you win the last Gauntlet."

"And if I don't come in the top two? Who will you pick?"

"I don't want to talk about it, Kanoska."

"I suppose I'll marry Nicholas Pendell." Some wicked part of me wants to goad him into speaking, into telling me, like he told Evangeline Langley, that he'll abdicate, that we'll run away together. That we'll find some way around the laws of this cruel, advanced country. "At least then, I'll be guaranteed a marriage without any awkward silences."

"That's not funny."

"Laughter and tears are brothers. In the dimness of sorrow and the blinding radiance of joy, one is oft mistaken for the other." The Western proverb is one I've heard Sasha murmur during countless births as we watch tear-stained mothers laugh with delight while caressing the faces of their newborns.

"Are you about to start crying over the thought of losing me, Kanoska?" There is something familiar about the irony in his voice, a tone I've heard so often before that a lump rises in my throat, unbidden.

So, partly because I'm terrified that I will start crying and partly to wipe the half smirk off his face, I lean forward and kiss him on the mouth. When I sink back against my pillows, his face is blank with shock.

"Bet you didn't see that coming." The words are meant to be teasing, but they come out wobbly and uncertain.

He leans toward me. His lips part and my eyelids drift shut, waiting for the fire of his kiss. Instead, I hear a whisper. "Was that the drugs?"

My eyes fly open, and laughter explodes out of me in hacking, rasping gasps, almost indistinguishable from sobs. By the look on his face, I know he is sure that I am having some sort of medically-induced episode, but at this moment, I don't care. I take his chin in my good hand and kiss him again. His hands rise, cupping my face and tangling in my hair as he kisses me back. And I am glad that I've never been kissed before, because even if I lose him, I will never lose the wonder of this.

When we break apart, his fingers stay in my hair. "I have a strict policy against marrying girls shorter than six feet or with less than ten letters in their names. It's going to have to be you, Kanoska."

Happiness doesn't last. I've always known this. But being in love makes you a fool. And you believe, despite all the evidence to the contrary, that that starry, soaring-through-the-clouds feeling will last forever.

As Patricia 003 and two other droids escort me from the medical vehicle through the front doors of the White House two days later, Zuri appears from a hallway, dressed in athletic gear with strands of her short dark hair plastered to her face with sweat.

"Oh, that looks so painful!" The concerned purse of her lips is exaggerated. "How long before the cast comes off?"

I endeavor to keep my voice neutral. "The surgery went well, so with physical therapy I should be back to normal in seven or eight weeks."

"I can't believe how positive you are. I don't think I could do it."

"I'm all ears, Zuri." I know how cold I sound, but I don't care. Pretending is her game, not mine. "Just say whatever it is you want to say."

"I heard that Denzel really tried. But he has no power over the Council."

I know what is coming, but I'm not going to give her the satisfaction of asking.

"They said that moving the date for the second Gauntlet would push the entire timeline and delay Denzel's ascension to the throne, which could put the Federation in a precarious position in relation to its international allies and rivals. So I'm afraid that you'll be going through that obstacle course with one arm in two and a half weeks."

"I'll bet that breaks your heart," I say. "The fact that the contestant who won the first challenge will in all likelihood flunk the second."

She smiles. "Why, I didn't even think of that. But now that you mention it..."

"I'm glad to hear that you didn't think of it," I say, my voice as insincerely sweet as hers. "Which is why I'm sure that if we check the gymnasium footage from the day of my accident, we won't see you loosening the chains on the punching bag that everyone knows I use every night at seven o'clock."

It might be my imagination, but I think I see her smile slip. "You're paranoid, Andromache."

"Maybe," I say. "But you know what else I am, Zuri? Stubborn. I've got two and a half weeks to become the best one-armed competitor this country has ever seen, and you better believe I'm going to use every second of it."

CHAPTER 28

"Andi, no boy is worth permanent brain damage." Lida leans against the door to our suite.

"I never thought I'd see the day when you would become the voice of reason in my life," I say, trying to tease her, but her expression only grows more sour.

"Neither did I, and believe me, it's not a role I want to keep, girlie."

"She has to go, Lida," Heath pipes up from his chair where he is playing some sort of racing game on the suite's electronic pad. "She only has two weeks to learn how to do one-armed pull-ups and flips and stuff. She'll never manage it if she rests for a week."

"One-armed flips? Are you out of your mind?"

"Lida, he's right. If I want any chance at not coming in last, I have to learn how to get through an obstacle course one-armed."

"You're taking advice from a seven-year-old?"

"Lida—"

"Andi, you've protected me from myself. Always. Do you think I've forgotten all the bottles you pried out of my hands? All the days you fed me when I'd spent every eu-royen I had on drink? All the mornings you got me cleaned up and shoved me out the door to find work? It's my turn to protect you from yourself. You're going to get injured. Maybe permanently. Don't do this."

"Lida, if I don't come in the top two at the end of the three Gauntlets, it won't matter how Xavier feels about me. The law will prohibit him from picking me as Consort."

"Why would that be so bad? You'd still get to marry one of the other rich airheads."

"I don't want to marry any of the others, Lida."

"Andi! Are you listening to me? He's not worth landing on your head and messing up your mind for the rest of your life. He can't be."

"Someone wants to keep me from becoming Consort," I say, pushing my sunglasses onto the top of my head so that I can look Lida in the eye. "Punching bags don't just fall from the ceiling. And if someone is that determined to keep me out of a position of power, then maybe that is exactly where I need to be, Lida. You know what I've told you. Someone is trying to eradicate Cinq. I know who it is, but becoming Consort is the only way I think I could actually have the power to stop them. This isn't just for me, Lida. It's for our entire country."

"What did our country ever do for us?" My surprise must show on my face, because her tone softens slightly. "I mean it, Andi. Our country signed a treaty that guaranteed our deaths. Yours and mine. We were expendable resources. Why should you risk yourself for them?"

"Because there's no 'them', Lida!" My voice rises. "The babies I delivered—do they have anything to do with the injustices we suffered? The mothers and fathers who go hungry every single day to put food in their children's mouths—is that treaty their responsibility? The street urchins and homeless women—are they trying to hurt us? The prostitutes who are desperate enough to give up every scrap of dignity just to survive—do you really think they haven't suffered enough? Our lives are no more valuable than theirs. Every life is precious. And if we say otherwise, we are using the exact same logic as the people who believe that you and I don't deserve the air we breathe."

Lida wilts before my furious gaze. In the throbbing silence that follows my tirade, she steps slowly away from the door. She suddenly looks very tired.

Guilt stabs at me, but this is not the time to try to use speech to repair the damage my words have already done. I have to go. The seconds of my precious two weeks are slipping away. As I pass Lida on my way out the door, I wrap my good arm around her. After a moment, her arms come up, clumsily hugging me back. It's the best we can do for now.

"What do you think you're doing?"

I don't answer, concentrating every particle of my mental and physical energy on dragging myself upward. My left bicep screams in protest, and even with the exercise band supporting my feet, my body doesn't rise.

After a moment, I sag, kicking to extricate my feet from the band so that I can drop to the floor. But the band tangles, and I grunt in helpless frustration, fighting the tears of exhaustion and despair that prick my eyes.

Large hands grasp my waist, and I still before releasing the bar. My weight collapses against Xavier's bracing shoulder. He steps back, allowing the exercise band to slide off my ankles. With gentleness that causes the lump in my throat to thicken, he lowers me to the floor, propping my back against the wall before crouching in front of me.

"You're supposed to avoid physical strain for at least a week."

"Time is one thing I don't have, Xavier. That, and a working right arm."

His shoulders sag. "I tried, Kanoska."

"I know."

"I presented my case to the entire Council. And I talked privately to both my parents. I was so sure they would postpone the second Gauntlet. But the only person who agreed with me that these were special circumstances calling for a delay was my mother."

Boadicea. Gratitude flashes quickly, only to evaporate in the cold mist of my despair. "If I can even manage to complete the obstacle course, I'll come in last, Xavier."

"Who wants to hurt you, Kanoska?"

"What?"

"I looked at the gymnasium footage from the day of your accident."

Hope swells. "And someone tampered with the bag?"

"Of course."

"Then you know who wants to hurt me."

"The footage was tampered with too. Someone looped the lunch hour to repeat itself. Whoever has a grudge against you either has resources or a very unusual skill set, Kanoska."

There are three people who have something to gain by preventing Xavier from picking me as Consort.

Hugh.

Cronus.

Raquelle.

And Zuri promised to make me pay if Xavier found out about the incident in the training arena. Hugh and Cronus, who might be working together, both have the resources and influence to make incriminating footage disappear. I have no idea about Raquelle's skills in the area of erasing camera footage, but she is the person most comfortable with a punching bag, and she knew my kickboxing routine better than anyone else.

In some ways, Zuri is the least likely, but she also made no secret of her glee at my elimination as a serious competitor.

"Kanoska. You must have some idea who it could be."

"I have ideas," I say slowly, "but no proof."

"I'll help you find it."

I want to maintain my bubble of self-preservation. I want to work alone and refuse to expand the boundaries of my trust.

But if, by some crazy stroke of luck or the working of some unknown Divine Power, we are able to be together, is that how I want our relationship to be? Full of lies? Constantly divided by secrets? Giving him my body but never allowing him to touch my soul?

"Zuri believes that I told you about what happened in the training arena," I say. "She promised to make me pay if you found out." I force myself to go on. "Raquelle is desperate. She believes that marrying you is the only way to avoid a marriage to someone she despises." Xavier's lips part, but I have to go on or I will lose the smidgen of courage I have managed to muster. "You remember that night we met on the basketball court? I overheard your father talking to…Hugh Grimsby." I feel Xavier's body stiffen, but there is no going back now. "They were planning an attack against the cities of Cinq during your honeymoon. I sneezed, and I think Hugh might have seen me running away. It was dark, but my height is a bit of a giveaway."

He doesn't speak. I can't look at him. I don't want to see disbelief, or worse, anger in his face.

Finally, Xavier says, "You're accusing Hugh?"

"I'm not accusing anyone," I say. "Because like I told you, I have no proof. But you asked who might want to hurt me."

I'm trying to trust you, I want to say. *Can't you see how hard this is for me?*

But I've used up my courage.

"Will you look at me?" His voice is exasperated, but I don't hear anger in his tone. "Why are you tensed up like a dog that expects to be kicked at any moment?"

"Because I just accused your father and your best friend of trying to hurt me?"

"You forget, I've watched my father intentionally hurt the woman closest to me for almost twenty years."

"And your best friend?" It takes all my nerve to ask the question.

"I'll look into it." His voice makes it clear that he is not going to say any more.

"Unless we can somehow recover the footage from the gymnasium or trick the guilty party into confessing, there is no way to prove who it was," I say when he doesn't go on. "Or the person might try again. But if I come in last on the obstacle course, the chances of my being one of the top two are so slim that they might stop viewing me as a threat."

"You're not going to come in last."

I raise my eyebrows at him. "Well, now that you've decreed it..."

His lips curve into a grin, and he jumps to his feet, reaching a hand down to me. "Come on. Wasn't it you who told me that only losers stay on their butts?"

CHAPTER 29

Whoever thought a party with excessive amounts of heavy food and alcohol the night before a difficult race was a good idea must have an incredibly warped sense of humor.

I stand in the shadows, clutching the untouched flute of champagne that I only took to stop the Gingers from constantly approaching me with offers of refreshment.

Music blares through speakers over the outdoor dance floor. I can see Bella and Alden in the middle. Their dancing is exuberant and unconventional, but somehow it works, because they are utterly at ease. Alden's whole focus is on the girl in front of him, and I know with sudden certainty that she will be safe. She will be happy. There is one person I don't have to worry about anymore.

Near them, Xavier is dancing with Hugh and his younger sister, Enid. As I watch, Xavier bumps Hugh's shoulder, muttering something, and both burst out laughing. The momentary joy I felt evaporates.

"You ready for tomorrow?" The voice makes me stiffen.

"As I'll ever be."

"I saw you doing one-armed pull-ups in the gymnasium yesterday. You're getting really good."

"Oh, drop the act. You couldn't be more thrilled that I've been eliminated as a threat."

"You think I had something to do with it."

"Did you?" I turn and meet Raquelle's eyes. This is the first time I've seen her up close in almost a month, and I realize, with a start, that she looks ill. Gray and so thin that her cheekbones are knife-sharp through her papery skin.

"No, but I'd say that even if I had done it."

"How hard have you been training?" I try to sound unconcerned but don't quite succeed.

"Hard enough to win. But it doesn't matter whether I get a top spot or not. Xavier's too decent to pick the girl he thinks his friend is in love with."

Pity smothers the angry heat in my chest. "Raquelle, if we work together, we can show him what kind of person Hugh is. Then Hugh will be imprisoned, and you'll be able to marry one of the others, or else return home."

"I've already taken care of it." Her voice is toneless. "After how I treated you, I didn't think you'd want to help me, so I dealt with it on my own. Hugh won't legally be able to marry me by the time all this is over."

"What have you done?" My heart picks up speed. "Raquelle?"

She doesn't answer, and I'm about to demand an explanation when a shadow falls on my shoulder. Turning, I see Xavier, the top button of his magenta dress shirt open to expose a flash of dark skin and a golden necklace. His hands are in the pockets of his peach-colored slacks. It is extremely irritating that rather than looking ridiculous, the outfit works for him.

"It's a good thing that dancing isn't on the list of the Elector's duties, because you'd be shirking right now."

His eyebrows rise, and his dimples pop out. "Oh, being a good dancer is essential. All those state and international functions."

"Saturn's flaming rings, that's unfortunate."

"Oh yeah?" His fingers close around mine. "Come show me how it's done, Kanoska."

"I'm an invalid."

"I've seen you do the monkey bars one-armed."

"I'm talking to Raquelle."

"You're boring her stiff. I'm doing Raquelle a favor."

"You really are," Raquelle says, and for an instant, I hear the sparkle of the girl I knew for a few short weeks. The girl unbroken by Hugh Grimsby.

Pretending to glare over my shoulder, I allow myself to be dragged onto the dance floor. Xavier begins to cut loose, and I start to dance too, the music finding its way into my bloodstream.

Live for this moment. It's all you're guaranteed. Western street wisdom spray painted on a crumbling brick wall across from the market flashes through my mind. Watching Lida and Jez had made me certain it was abject stupidity, a sure way to ruin your life by gratifying every whim.

But now, I think that maybe there is a place for it after all. Perhaps soaking up the golden moments is the best way to honor Whoever sends them. Or maybe releasing worry over the future, if only for a moment, is the only way to keep from going stark raving mad.

All I want is to put my arms around Xavier's neck and kiss him on that crowded dance floor as though we are just two normal people in love, not the boy who will be Elector and the girl whose only dream in life was to remain in the shadows.

Unexpectedly, Xavier takes my hand and begins to lead me through the crowd.

"Where are we going?" I call above the pounding music.

He must know this song, because he hesitates just long enough for the last notes to fade before shouting back, "Up to my room."

The last three words echo out over the silent dance floor, and I hear titters as people pointedly stare anywhere but at us. Blood pours into my face. I catch a final glimpse of the ballroom, with people leaning together to whisper how like his father the Ascendant is, while Zuri stares after us, her expression murderous, before the door clicks shut.

"Where are we really going?" I say as we trot along a silent hallway.

"To my room."

"To do what?"

"What do you think?"

"I'll have you know that someone as good as I am at one-armed pull-ups is not to be trifled with, Xavier."

He laughs. "Duly noted."

I've never been in this part of the complex before. We pass a doorway through which I catch a glimpse of a recording studio. A bank of glass windows exhibits a solarium.

"You really have everything here," I say, a Western pauper briefly overcome by the splendor around me. "You'd never have to leave to find anything you'd want."

"Except freedom." His profile is stern. "When all's said and done, an opulent, comfortable, luxury-gilded cage is still a cage, Kanoska."

When we finally stop, Xavier steps close to what looks like a peephole in the center of a door. For a moment, nothing happens, and then a green light flashes, and I hear the click of a lock.

"A retinal scanner? On your bedroom door?"

But the words trail away as I follow Xavier into the room. The room is circular and windowless, every inch of the walls constructed of curving shelves lined with books. I crane my neck, wondering how high the shelves go, and just when I think I'm going to topple over backward, I catch a glimpse of a dome and through it, a glowing, silvery orb.

"That's—that's the moon," I say stupidly.

Xavier doesn't respond as he fiddles with a knob on the wall until perfect golden mood lighting fills the room. In another moment, soft music begins to play. I turn on the spot, trying to find the speakers among the books. I can't see any, but they are clearly there, and I wonder, with a squeezing sensation in the pit of my stomach, if there are cameras just as cleverly disguised.

To hide my discomfort, I walk to one of the bookshelves and gently run my fingers along the contours of the spines. "It looks like you have the whole complex library in here."

When he answers, his voice is so close that I turn, my spine flattening against the spines of the books behind me. "I was thirteen when my father decided to make the library digital. I begged him to let me have the books, and he agreed as long as I could fit them in my room. With the help of a bot crew, I completely remodeled the space in a month."

He's moving closer, and I am suddenly afraid of where this is going. "Xavier…"

His palm flattens against a book right next to my ear. His lips brush my cheek, and the fear inside me recedes at the gentleness of the touch, replaced by a yearning for something I don't dare to quantify.

"Xavier—"

Something cool slides into my good hand.

"Look." His voice is a breath against my ear. "Hugh's device."

With a shock, I remember him dancing with Hugh and Enid, bumping his friend's shoulder as he whispered in his ear. I look down at the small screen in my hand as Xavier continues to kiss the side of my face, and I realize that he knows exactly where the cameras in this room are. My thumb swipes along the screen and an image pops up.

"Thumbprint," I murmur, trying to ignore the warmth that tingles through my body as Xavier's fingers brush a strand of hair off my neck. This is just a ruse. Something for the cameras.

His other hand closes over mine, and the screen flashes luminescent green. "We promised each other we'd never use it." His voice is carefully detached, and I know, with a sudden, deep clarity, that I am the reason for this betrayal.

I glance down at the device in my hand, looking for a clue to lead me to the proof I need. But then Xavier says, "We've been out here long enough," and I feel the books behind me give way and I am falling, staggering, thrown even more off balance by my lopsided arms.

Xavier's hands close on my shoulders just as I am giving up hope of righting myself. There is a click as the secret bookshelf door closes, and my thigh bumps against something soft in the darkness. Lights flicker on, illuminating the closet-like space we are in, which is entirely taken up by a queen bed.

"I—" I start, with no idea how to finish the sentence. My eyes bounce between him and the bed. "Xavier, I don't think—"

Then I register the smirk tugging on the corners of his lips. "Not without a ring, Kanoska." He sits down on the edge of the bed and begins tugging at his shoes. "I managed to convince my father that having cameras in here was perverted. But the cameras in the rest of the suite will have picked up our little show, which will remove any suspicion about why we're in the bedroom." He pulls himself backward on the bed, propping his lanky frame against the backboard and patting the covers beside him. "There's not really anywhere else to sit, sorry."

I scramble up beside him and begin to scroll through the files and applications on the device in my hand. "What are the chances that he has a second device?" I ask as I search.

"Very slim. Every citizen of the Federation is issued a device on their tenth birthday, and the Bureau of Electronics keeps strict tabs on them. There are obligatory appointments every year to get your devices serviced or upgraded, and penalties, including losing service to your device, if anyone fails to keep their appointment. And while it is possible to get devices on the black market if you can pay enough, it is next to impossible to connect them to the country's network without detection."

"When your device is getting serviced, does the Bureau record anything about the content?"

He nods. "It's a way to suppress seditious activity. But when I asked a contact of mine about unusual activity on Hugh's device, he said that there was none. Hugh has normal apps—calculators, calendars, games, messaging—"

"Wait."

"What? Did you find something?" Under the usual deep calm of his voice, I hear a thread of disbelief. Despite making inquiries and stealing his friend's device, there was still a part of him that believed we wouldn't find anything on it.

"A game." My finger hovers and then clicks on the application for a game involving fighter planes. "Because that's all this is to him. A game he intends to win."

Xavier snatches the electronic pad from my hand, and I don't protest but watch his face. For moments that feel like hours, he stares at the screen, swiping back and forth. Then his face twists, and he drops the device onto the bed as though it has burned him.

"It's not just a game, is it?"

His head moves slowly left and right before sinking to rest in his hands. "It's controls. I don't know how he got them. Hugh's never been any good with computers. Or at least that's what I've always thought. His device is connected via satellite to all of our AI-piloted surveillance planes on the West Coast. Using this, he can override the AI and send movement and attack commands."

All I've wanted for months is for Xavier to know the truth about Hugh. But instead of elation, the look on his face makes me feel as though a punch from Raquelle has just landed in my gut. "I'm sorry," I say quietly.

He doesn't answer, and for what feels like a long time, we sit without speaking. Finally, I say, "What are we going to do?"

"I don't want to talk." The harshness of his tone stings. I stare at his hunched form before sliding off the bed. As I'm reaching for the lever next to the hidden door, his voice stops me—softer, almost vulnerable. "I need time to realize it."

"I know."

"Go to bed, Kanoska."

"You promised you wouldn't give me orders."

"It's not an order. Just advice from someone interested in you doing your best tomorrow."

I force myself to smile. "An extra hour of sleep will make all the difference in keeping me out of the bottom spot."

He smiles back, but it is strained. Last is not an option. But we both know it is the most likely outcome.

CHAPTER 30

The limo ride is silent. Even Bella is sitting quietly, twirling the ring on her left hand, after a glare from Zuri silenced her humming. Butterflies whir in my stomach, making me terrified that I am about to lose the single piece of toast that was all I was able to choke down for breakfast.

Two and a half weeks is not enough time to adapt to the loss of one of your arms.

Numbers swirl in my head. If I get last place, my score will be ninety-eight. My bet would be on Raquelle to win, which would bring her up to 226. Zuri will probably be second, with a score of 216. Then Clotilde, 151. Bella, 119.

The last Gauntlet will advance in increments of ninety-seven. If I lose this challenge, the only way to guarantee getting into one of the top two spots would be by coming first in the third. Unless Raquelle and Zuri completely flunk the final Gauntlet—which I do not anticipate—even coming second will not be enough to reverse the damage done to my score.

At least Xavier knows about Hugh. My failure will only lead to a broken heart, not the demolition of my country.

"Destination reached," intones the vehicle's automated voice. The other contestants hurry to exit, but no one says anything. For a moment, as the car door slams behind Clotilde, I wonder what will happen if I just stay in the vehicle. "Please disembark," says the voice, and I obey.

We are on an island. In the distance, I can see a bridge, which we must have driven over in order to get here, but I was too preoccupied to notice at the time. The mainland shore is clearly visible from the beach on which we stand, but the shortest swim, which I would guess to be about a mile, leads directly to a sheer cliff face.

"Ladies." The sound of Cronus's voice makes me start. A hologram of the Elector emanates from the chest of one of the automatons. "Welcome to your second Gauntlet. Your objective is to return to the front gate of the White House complex, which is roughly ten miles from where you stand as the crow flies. This is a race, pure and simple. The highest marks will be awarded to the contestant who arrives first. Since observation and attention to surroundings are vital qualities in a ruler, no route is marked, and we trust that you were paying enough attention on the ride over to be able to make your way back. However, in case you were daydreaming, I will give you two hints.

"Firstly, the path of most resistance is also the most direct route to the complex. Secondly, should you stray too far, one of the drones patrolling the area will alert and redirect you. As you may have noticed, there are a plethora of our robotic friends in the sky, on the ground, and in the water. All of these are equipped with cameras, which will allow myself, the rest of the Council, the Ascendant, and the other suitors to watch your contest. Be warned, we will also see any attempts to hamper your fellow contestants, which will be regarded as grounds for disqualification. The second Gauntlet begins...NOW!"

A sound like a horn blast echoes over the beach. I race toward the water as, ahead of me, Raquelle throws herself into the waves and begins to stroke toward shore.

I must have swum hundreds of laps in the frigid pool in the training center, but this is different. It is not a particularly windy day, but there are still waves buffeting against me as I swim with all my might. Several times when I rise to draw air, water sloshes into my open mouth, causing me to gag so badly that I have to stop swimming. Before my injury, swimming a mile would have been moderately challenging, but now I can feel my strength draining away with each feeble, one-armed stroke as my legs begin to cramp, unused to compensating for my upper body.

As the shore remains stubbornly distant, I am tempted to just give up. To lie back in the waves and wait for one of the water bots to pick me up and tow me to shore. But the drive to keep going, the stubborn refusal to quit—these are instincts now, something primal in my core, and so my one arm keeps stroking, and my feet keep kicking until finally I am bobbing beneath the cliff, craning my neck to catch a glimpse of dry, solid ground.

The rock face is not as sheer as it looked from the beach. It is pockmarked with gouges and outcroppings. But it will still be a treacherous climb. Far above me are two small figures, recognizable as Raquelle and Zuri. A glance to my right shows me an easier, more gradual ascent, about a quarter-mile swim along the shore. Clotilde is just clambering up onto the first few boulders. To the left, the shoreline continues steep and uninviting all the way to the metal bridge pilings.

I reach up and grab on to a rocky ledge above me, dragging myself out of the water. Cronus said that the path of most resistance was the quickest way back to the White House complex. If I can manage to get up this cliff, I'll have a chance to catch up to Clotilde, whereas, if I attempt to swim over to the place she is climbing, I will certainly not. I don't see Bella, so she is probably still in the water. If I can beat both her and Clotilde, I will get third place in this challenge, which will make the top two spots an attainable possibility.

This thought is like a shot of liquid adrenaline that carries me through my entire terrifying, grueling climb. My wet fingers and feet slip more than once. Each time, I barely manage to hang on, my broken arm clenching uselessly within its waterproof sling as though trying to catch my fall.

When I finally pull myself, trembling and sweating, onto the grass at the top of the rock face, I turn for a final glance down. Bella is about halfway up the cliff.

"Hi, Andi!" she calls happily, removing one hand to wave. I strangle a cry of warning. If I startle her, she will almost certainly fall.

"Focus on climbing, Bells," I call, striving to keep my voice level. I glance over my shoulder, and my stomach plummets as I see Clotilde crest the cliff and begin to run toward the buildings of the city. I should run after her and leave Bella to fend for herself, but something keeps me at the cliff's edge.

Bella is just out of my reach when she slips. My insides seem to be in a vice as I watch her fumble for a hold, a scarlet gash appearing on her cheek as her face bangs against the rocks. "Andi, help me!" Her voice is high and thin. "I can't find anywhere to put my feet. Andi!"

I need something to throw down to her.

My eyes roam the surrounding area and land on a droid shaped like Patricia, standing motionless at the cliff's edge.

"Patricia!" I race toward the robot.

"You are mistaken." The robot's voice is deep. "My identification nomer is Eugene 324."

"Eugene, then! There's a girl trying to climb up the cliff. She needs help!"

"We are not permitted to offer assistance except in cases of fatal peril."

"Her peril looks pretty fatal to me!" The automaton deliberately turns away from me, and I see its back panel, which screws open to allow mechanics access to the thick cable that runs like a spinal cord up and down the frame.

"Andi!" Bella's scream makes my blood run cold.

"Hang on, Bella!" I yell, and then I drop to the ground. My fingers close around a rock roughly the size and shape of an egg. "Oi! Eugene!"

The droid turns, and I hurl the rock with all my might, straight into his left eye socket. In my hours hiding from Nicholas, I had checked out a random book about robot design, which stated that in the earliest models, the place of greatest weakness was in the left eye socket. The skull was made in one solid piece, but the eye socket had a seam which allowed mechanics to work on the cranial areas should the need arise. My entire plan relies on this flaw still being present in Eugene's generation of automatons. The rock needs to have damaged his control system.

Time freezes before Eugene topples to the ground. I spring at him, yanking the small, multipurpose tool that was all we were allowed to carry out of the pocket on my leg.

I never would have believed it, but I owe you one, Nicholas.

Part of me expects the drones soaring above to converge on me, shock guns blazing. But nothing happens as I pry open Eugene's back panel and reach into the internal cavity to sever the ends of the cable and pull a section free.

"Andi!" Bella's cry sends me flying back to my original position. There are bloody scrapes all along her forearms now, and she is barely clinging to the rock with the fingertips of one hand.

"Bella!" Throwing myself onto my stomach and bracing the shoulder of my injured arm against a rock conveniently embedded in the ground, I inch the cable down toward her free hand. "Grab this." The sudden force of her weight nearly yanks my arm out of its socket, and I bite my lip to keep from yelling at her. "I can't pull you up with one arm, Bells. You need to use this as an extra handhold and try to climb up to me."

"Okay." The weight on the end of the cable shifts as she inches slowly from side to side. "I found a foothold!"

The minutes drag as she carefully picks her way up the cliff face before finally collapsing next to me on the grass at the top of the cliff. I wish we could just lie there in the sun and fall asleep—pretend all of this is a horrific dream—but I struggle to my feet.

"I have to keep going."

Bella scrambles up. "Let me come with you! Maybe I can save you next."

"Come on," I say, ignoring the weight in my gut that tells me I have lost any shot at third place.

I follow the road, praying that I am going in the right direction since even if time weren't an issue, I'm not sure I have the strength for twenty miles instead of ten. Behind me, Bella's run has an almost skipping cadence, and the sound grates against my already raw nerves.

The first sign that I am on the right track appears after roughly two miles of running. A huge chasm cuts across the center of the road, filled with yellow liquid and speckled with rocks, most of which are slick with moisture. I pause, breathing deeply.

"Is that urine?" I ask myself aloud.

"If it is, that would be disgusting to fall into!" Bella says cheerfully. "But I don't think it is pee. It doesn't smell like it. Should we try to go around?"

I glance left and right. There is no visible end to the canal, and besides, following the route delineated by the obstacles is our only chance of not getting hopelessly lost. "Hopscotch time," I say, and step onto the first rock.

I'm most of the way across the channel when I discover what the yellow liquid is. Landing badly after a jump, the tip of my rubber-soled shoe dips briefly into the fluid. There is a hissing sound, and the tip of my shoe dissolves. I make my last few jumps, only letting out my breath as my feet land on solid ground on the other side of the canal. Turning to look back, I see Bella skipping from rock to rock, oblivious to the acid pooled beneath her.

I have to allow her to do this on her own. I can't protect her from everything.

With one last backward glance, I take off running, cool air tickling my toes through the hole in my shoe. By the time I see the next obstacle, a cramp is beginning to prickle along my right shoulder. Clearly, my body objects to me trying to swing my arm in a running motion while it is mostly immobilized by a sling.

My heart sinks at what I see in front of me. The way forward is through an alleyway between two buildings, which narrows until the only possibility is to go up, shimmying with a hand on each wall. Except I only have one hand.

I stride down the alley, relishing the last few seconds of being able to move freely. The concrete walls draw closer and closer together, until I can feel them brushing my shoulders, rough through the fabric of my almost dry suit.

I slow to a stop and turn sideways, planting my back against one wall and the toes of my rubber shoes against the other. Slowly, I walk my feet up until they are almost level with my waist. Then I push, sliding my back upward.

The rough material grates against the skin of my back, and I know that I will be bleeding by the time I reach the top. But for now, I focus on the rhythm that is taking me toward my goal.

Step, step, step.

Push.

Step, step, step.

Push.

About a third of the way up, I hear scuffling sounds begin below me. Bella. I don't look down, but the pattern takes on a bit more urgency.

Step, step, step.

Push.

Step, step, step.

Pain is blossoming in winding tendrils across my back, but I am halfway there.

I think I can smell the sharp scent of my own blood, but the sky is drawing near.

As, at long last, my shoulders rise over the top of the building's roof, I freeze. I have no idea how to drag myself up onto one of the rooftops when the only thing that is keeping me from plummeting to the ground below is being wedged between two walls. I glance down, and the reality of how great the drop is crashes over me. Cramps shoot up my thighs, but I can't move.

I don't know how long I stay there before I hear Bella's voice below me. "Andi? Need a hand?"

Something brushes my legs, and her head rises between my knees. "I'm in a stable position," she says. "Here, I'll use my shoulder and arm to support your rear. Keep sliding up. You won't fall. I've got you."

I move up, and she moves with me, her shoulder supporting me as my back loses contact with the wall and finally, I slide backward onto the rooftop, scooting away from the edge so that she can clamber up after me.

It feels as though I left my breath on the ground thirty stories below. With an effort, I pull air into my lungs and say shakily, "You were right. This time, you saved me."

She smiles—her signature, effortless grin—then climbs to her feet with a moan. "Everything hurts. And I'm so tired. I hope we're close. What do we have to do now?"

I stand too, and look around the rooftop. Five round, evenly-spaced trampolines have been embedded into the roof of the building. Above each one is a metal frame shaped like a doorway. The frames vary in height, with the tallest set over the middle trampoline. Right in the center of what would be the lintel in an actual doorway dangles a harness, swinging from a zip line.

"We have to jump up and get ourselves zipped into one of those?" Bella asks.

"Looks like that's the way to get a quick ride down," I say as flippantly as I can. "And the one in the middle must be the quickest way."

"Okay, you take that one. I'll take the one next to it."

"Are you sure?"

"I don't care if I lose," Bella says brightly. "I just want Alden to be proud of me. That's the only reason I did any of this. He helped me train." She shrugs. "But it's probably better if you don't lose. If you want Xavier to be able to pick you. Don't worry, I'll make sure you cross the finish line before I do."

A lump swells in my throat, and I have to swallow a few times before I can say, "You're really something else—you know that, Bells?"

Her eyes widen in confusion. "Something else than what?"

I give her a one-armed squeeze before stepping onto the buoyant surface of the middle trampoline. Looking up, I can see that the harness is hooked to the doorframe by some sort of catch. Apparently, the idea is to jump up into the harness without braining yourself on the doorframe and then release the catch system once you are securely buckled in.

Taking a deep breath, I begin to bounce in place, each bounce a little higher than the last. When I get high enough, I reach up with my good hand and latch onto the armhole of the harness. I pull up, my body swinging wildly as I attempt to wriggle my arm through the vest. My elbow knocks into something.

I've been afraid almost all my life. Ever since I've been old enough to know what a crazy, messed-up place this world we call home is. But I've never felt fear like this.

I scream as the harness pulls away from the doorframe, gathering momentum. As it plummets, I cling with the grip of death to the armhole of the vest, winds buffeting me as I plunge downward.

My smashed remains are going to be scraped up off the asphalt of Washington DC's streets.

The shrillness of my voice slices the air as I scream again and again, twirling like a toy on the end of a string.

I don't know if it is a miracle or dumb luck, but my body faces forward just in time to see the sheet of plywood with a cutout of a spread-eagled human racing toward me. There is no way that I can get through the cutout while holding on to the harness with one hand. Glancing down, I see the ground about ten feet below me, drawing nearer. Waiting until the last possible second, I throw a prayer skyward that if there is Anyone out there, they will allow anything to happen rather than me re-breaking my almost healed elbow.

I force my numb fingers to release the harness.

My body curls into a ball as I fall, wrapping protectively around my immobilized arm. Pain explodes up my left leg as it absorbs the ground's impact and, lopsided as I am, I stumble, my ankle twisting as I crumple to the ground.

You do have a warped sense of humor, don't you? It feels like I just snapped my ankle, but, hey, you kept my elbow safe.

Gingerly, I push into a sitting position, biting my lip to keep from moaning as the movement jiggles my ankle. Staring around, I see that I am in the center of what appears to be a park. Perfectly manicured grass spreads out around me. In the distance, I can see the silhouettes of skyscrapers, but here, trees and squirrels and geese are strutting languidly along. For a moment, it feels like I have managed to break out of the perfect, gilded cage I've been living in for the last four months. Until I notice that there is not one twig on the ground. Not a speck of goose poop. Not a dandelion or a fallen leaf.

I don't see the maintenance bots, but I know they are there, working in the shadows, keeping this place perfect. Too perfect. I don't know why the Federation bothers to keep up this charade of flawlessness, since every human being in this city is royalty—constrained to live within the White House complex, only allowed out on specific occasions. Kept safe, they say. Controlled, I know.

The unnatural cleanness of the ground poses a problem greater than pure aesthetics. I'm not going to be able to walk if I can't find something to splint my ankle, which is sprained if not broken. Eventually, I push up onto my hands and knees and begin to crawl, dragging my ankle behind me and following the path of the zip line. I have to keep moving. Bella's zip line will have taken her on a less direct route, and if I can just keep going, I'll still have a slim chance of getting fourth place rather than fifth.

After a few minutes, a pond comes into view, with two rowboats perched on the shore. I crawl faster, ignoring the jolts of pain as my ankle bounces over the ground behind me. Not only will rowing a boat allow me to sit down, but after getting across the pond, I can use one of the oars as a makeshift crutch.

The distance, which could be covered easily running or even walking, seems infinite on hands and knees. Finally, I am dragging myself across the sand, until my hands latch on to the edge of one of the rowboats. I grab one of the oars and use it to push myself into a standing position, then hop to the back of the boat and drag the craft into the water before scrambling aboard.

This is the easiest obstacle so far. My sling leaves my hand free, so I am able to grasp both oars. My range of motion is limited, but by using my torso, I am able to propel the boat across the water with relative ease. When I reach the other side, I pull myself onto the concrete ledge and wriggle under the wire fence separating the pond from a walkway, dragging one oar with me.

Looking up, I see something that makes my throat close up. A pearly wall is shining in the distance, speckled with windows reflecting the light of the midday sun. It's the back of the White House. Less than a mile away.

My mother was almost as petite as Sasha, barely managing to clear five feet. But at 6'10", my father never met a human taller than he was. Now, as I turn the oar and stick the blade into my armpit, I am happy to be my father's daughter.

It is not comfortable, but it is effective. After a few strides, I manage to find a rhythm, reaching forward with the handle of the oar, planting it on the ground and then swinging myself forward, keeping any weight off my damaged ankle. The oar blade digs into my armpit, but I ignore the discomfort, focusing on one thought.

I can still get fourth.

I'm almost there.

Bella said she wouldn't try to beat me

I can still get fourth.

Seconds slip by, punctuated by the rhythm of the oar striking the ground. I am out of the park. I am on a road. There don't appear to be any more obstacles. Probably the Council considered exhaustion and perhaps injury to be each contestant's obstacle in this final mile. I am at the edge of the White House complex, following the shimmer of the force field in the air as I head toward the front gates. The complex feels endless, but I know that each click of the oar handle and each painful dig into my armpit is bringing me closer to my goal, and if I don't stop, I might still get fourth.

Rounding a corner, my heart leaps. I can see people in the distance, surrounding the open gate of the complex. They are shouting, and for a moment, I think they have seen me and are cheering me to the finish. Then I see a blonde figure ahead of me, her walk breaking into a slow jog in response to the crowd's cheers. I know that she is sure I have already crossed the finish line, because unless I was crawling, there is no way she could have beaten me there.

"Bella!" But my voice is thin as a string, my throat raw from my screaming on the zip line. "Bella!" The cheers of the crowd are too loud, and even as I increase my speed, I know that I will never catch up to her.

The crowd's cheering swells to a roar, and I see a sensor in the archway flash green as she crosses the finish line. She turns, scanning the crowd, and her eyes find me, staggering toward her on my makeshift crutch. The look on her face is too much. When, minutes later, I totter through the gates, tears are streaming down my face. I don't care that the entire nobility of the Federation sees, because there is no way that I will be their Consort now.

The oar clatters to the ground.

The pain, which my adrenaline has held at bay, comes crashing over me.

Spots of dark and light pop before my eyes, the dark spots growing bigger and more numerous. Through them, I can see people rushing toward me, but I don't recognize any of them.

As I feel myself tipping, sliding forward into the darkness, the worst agony is the reality of my own failure.

I tried so hard.

But it didn't matter.

I lost him anyway.

CHAPTER 31

I am a little girl again.

It is a rare holiday for Sasha—no clients, no births, no prenatal care, no doctoring ailing infants. We are on the beach, with her lying on a blanket basking in the warmth and me dancing in and out of the waves. Seagulls and Federation planes soar above us, but neither concern me because I don't know yet that I am a societal outcast, haunted by a secret that will wreck my life if it is ever discovered.

An Enforcer approaches Sasha, almost certainly to see why she is loitering on a beach rather than working, but after a quick glance at her midwife papers, he drifts away, only pausing to watch me working on my sand replication of the White House complex.

"Maybe you'll be picked to go there someday, girlie."

"Why would I want to?" My voice is scornful in the way that only a nine-year-old's can be.

"You're about young Xavier's age. You could be Consort. Most powerful woman on the continent."

"And leave all this?" My airy gesture encompasses the garbage-strewn sand, Sasha on her blanket, the smog-dimmed sun, and the distant, crumbling buildings.

"Most people would give their right arms to be able to leave all this, sweetheart."

"And I'd give my right arm to stay," I say, crossing both arms across my chest defiantly.

"Kanoska?"

Consciousness is fighting to come, and I fight back, struggling to hold on to my dream.

"Kanoska?"

It's all fading away—Sasha and the Enforcer, my sandy White House and the blue Pacific waves—and tears come, slipping from beneath my closed eyelids.

"Sweetheart, don't cry."

Someone is calling me sweetheart, but it is not the Enforcer, it is the boy the Enforcer was talking to me about. But the Enforcer was wrong. I will never be the most powerful woman on the continent. My chances of becoming Consort have been broken, crushed like a sand structure beneath an ocean wave.

I feel someone brush my cheeks, wiping my tears away. I open my eyes. I am lying on a bed in an unfamiliar room. The sheets of the bed are crisp, like at St. Juno's, but the walls of this room are pale blue. The lights are dim with soft music playing in the background and a pleasant smell lingering in the air.

"Where am I?" My voice is raspy, and I see Xavier's eyes flicker with concern.

"In the White House hospital suite. Apparently, your ankle isn't broken, just badly sprained."

"Did Raquelle win?"

"Is this really what you want to talk about right now?"

"How will talking about it later change anything?"

"This entire day was brutal for you. You should just rest."

"Then why did you wake me up?" Misery is morphing into anger, and I grasp at the feeling because the warmth of anger is better than the cold of despair.

He hesitates. "I was concerned. You just collapsed after the Gauntlet. I wanted to make sure...I don't know...that you were—"

"That I'm what, Xavier? Completely devastated? Don't worry, I am. Physically and mentally at the breaking point? Check. Ready to inject poison into my veins if it will allow me to leave this messed-up place? Pretty much."

"Don't say that."

"Oh, is the truth painful? Here, I'll ease the agony. I never would have been able to give you an heir. So it's not so bad that you'll have to marry Raquelle or Zurl in a few months. You're lucky really. Life just dealt you an ace."

Despair and recklessness are brothers. I've known this all my life. That's why caring is so dangerous—because if you value anything too much, its loss will make you feel as though losing other things doesn't matter at all.

When Xavier speaks, his voice sounds conversational. "So that's why you cared so much about ships of infertile women being destroyed. You're one of them."

"No, I care so much because a person doesn't cease to be human simply because they can't reproduce. But yes, I am 'one of them'."

"How do you know you can't have children?"

"What does it matter? It's no longer your concern."

"I beg to differ."

"Oh, of course. Even if I'm not supposed to produce an heir, it's still important to repopulate this desolate, machine-dominated excuse for a nation."

"And you accuse us of having warped minds." The laugh he gives is harsh and humorless. Seemingly unable to remain seated, he pushes to his feet and strides around the room. After a moment, he turns back to me, eyes glittering. "It doesn't matter what I do, Andromache." His use of my first name is like a slap. "I've trusted you. I've listened to you. I've turned against not only my family, but my best friend, to stand beside you and your people. Again and again, I have shown you that I care for you, not because of anything you can do for me, but because of who you are." He pauses, chest rising and falling. "And still, you refuse to trust me in return, and your first assumption is always that I am using you in some way."

He turns away from me and, as the truth of his words hits me, I open my mouth, only to close it again as tears prick the corners of my eyes. His back is still to me, but when he speaks, every word is clear. "I'm a fool. Because even though you've thrown it in my face again and again, I keep coming back, trying to make you see..." The sentence trails off, and the tears that I can no longer restrain begin to slide down my cheeks, though I hold my breath to keep from making any sound.

The room is silent. Then, Xavier walks slowly to the door and pulls it open. "I should let you get some rest," he says, and the dullness in his voice mirrors the ache in my soul. As the door is closing, I finally let out my breath in a choking sob and bury my face in my hands. But instead of hearing the click of the latch, I hear his voice. "I woke you up because I wanted so badly to hear your voice. And all my life, I've dreamed of being a father. It's just hard to have a dream die."

The door closes softly, and I cry until sleep's gentle arms envelop me.

CHAPTER 32

"I'm so, so sorry, Andi."

I glance back as Bella's hand grips my elbow and see that she is close to tears. "Don't, Bells." I take her hand and draw her to the side of the hall. I lower my voice as Zuri sweeps by, her expression smug. "None of this is your fault. I'm not sure I would have gotten onto the roof of that building without you. I was just too slow."

"It's not fair!"

My eyes catch on a camera in the ceiling, not ten feet away.

"Bella." The sharpness in my voice makes her look up in surprise. I give a tiny jerk of my head toward the black circle above us. "Don't worry," I say with as much heartiness as I can muster. "I think my invention is going to be a big hit with the judges. But we really should both go or we'll be late for our tête-à-têtes."

I give her hand a final squeeze before limping away down the hall. The rankings came out exactly as I had predicted they would. Raquelle, Zuri, Clotilde, Bella, me. Which means that my only chance of securing one of the top two spots is by coming first in the last Gauntlet.

My invention is good. The serum formula is finished, with only a few minor tweaks needing to be implemented. Its effects have yet to be tested on humans, but mice who received a dose before being exposed to a pathogen had milder symptoms than mice that did not receive the serum. Given the Federation's history, I am sure that it will rank highly with the Council.

But highly enough? Everyone has been very secretive about their inventions for fear of being copied, so I have no idea what any of the other contestants have been working on. With no knowledge of what I am up against, it seems foolhardy to base my future plans on coming first.

Even if, by some miracle, I do manage to come in the top two, would Xavier pick me? My stomach squirms with guilt as I remember our last interaction three days ago in the hospital suite. Everything he said was true. He has shown me again and again that he cares, that he is trustworthy, and I've taken every gift he's given me while continuing to hurl accusations and assumptions at him from behind my own shield of distrust.

A sound jolts me from my reverie. Retching sounds are proceeding from a door to my left. I hobble to the door and tap hesitantly. "Hello? Everything all right in there?"

There is no response apart from more retching. I reach down to try the handle and, finding that it is not locked, inch the door open. "Hello?"

I am looking into a small powder room. Raquelle is kneeling in front of the toilet, her red hair hanging in curtains on either side of the porcelain bowl as her body shudders with the violence of her vomiting. Limping quickly into the room, I close the door and prop my crutches against the wall before dropping to my knees beside Raquelle. I sweep her hair back from her face and sit beside her until her body finally stills.

After a moment, she pushes back from the toilet, rubbing one hand across her mouth before sinking back against the wall. Staring into her face, my heart skips a beat in dismay. Raquelle looks worse than she did on the beach. Her skin is waxier than ever. Her hair is no longer glossy, but lank and stringy. Her cheekbones look so sharp against the papery skin of her face that I am scared they will slice right through. Her eyes, as the lids flutter open, are glassy.

"Raquelle, you need to see a doctor." I scoot closer to her. "Something is clearly wrong. How long have you been like this?"

"Leave me alone."

"No. I'm calling a Custodia."

"Andi! Don't! Please!" Her fingers scrabble at my ankle as I start to rise, but the exertion of shouting is too much, and she doubles over the toilet again.

I sink down beside her, sweeping her hair away from her face again, but there is really no need. Her body retches vainly, expelling nothing but a thin dribble of pinkish fluid.

When she falls back against the wall, eyes closed, I ask, "Why don't you want to see a doctor?"

It is obvious that she doesn't want to answer, but equally clear that she knows I will go for help if she doesn't give me a good reason not to. She licks her lips, trying to moisten them, but it appears that her body is too depleted of fluids to continue saliva production. "I don't want any tests to be run on me," she says finally.

"It's a little hard to make a diagnosis without running tests."

"I don't need a diagnosis. I already know what's going on."

"Then just tell them and ask for treatment."

"The reason I don't want tests run is because no one can know, Andi." Before I can interrupt, she hurries on. "They'll all know soon enough. I just need to make it through the third Gauntlet. Then I can go home."

"There's no way they're going to send you home, Raquelle."

A spark of her old defiance appears in her eyes. "They will when they find out."

"Find out what?"

She refuses to break eye contact. "That I'm pregnant."

"What?"

"You heard me."

"Hugh...did he...?"

She gives a rasping laugh. "Hugh wouldn't risk losing the opportunity to terrorize me for the rest of his life. He's done everything to me *except* that. No, there's an old scientist in the complex who has frozen sperm samples from before the Genetica-Tores virus. He runs a roaring trade with noblewomen who are worried that their husbands are the reason they aren't getting pregnant. I found out about him when I was trying to figure out what would happen to you if you never got pregnant." She draws in a long breath. "The law stipulates that Western brides must be virgins. After the third Gauntlet, when I reveal that I'm not a virgin, I'll be sent home in disgrace. No one can find out before because Hugh might—I don't know—slip me something to make me miscarry or something."

My mind is whirling. "So you have pregnancy-induced hyperemesis gravidarum."

"No idea what you just said."

"Midwife's assistant," I say. "It's a condition in pregnancy that leads to a dangerous level of vomiting. I only saw a handful of cases in all my years working with Sasha, but the women who survived were those rich enough to go to hospitals and get IV fluids." I pause. "Has no one else noticed how sick you are?"

"No one else has seen me like this." Raquelle gestures limply around the powder room. "And makeup and shape-less clothing will do wonders. Hugh thinks I've developed an eating disorder. But he doesn't care. He says I needed to lose some fat."

I ball my fingers into tight fists. With all the suffering in this world, how is it that Whoever rules this blue planet hasn't yet struck Hugh Grimsby with some painful plague that will cause him to end his life in agony?

The thought of Hugh's crimes makes me remember something. "You don't want to go back West. Not right now."

"You think I've become too much of a fine lady? Think I won't be able to deal with a little less food and giving up fancy foot massages?"

"Of course not," I say, pausing as I debate whether to tell her the full truth.

"You think I'm going to miss the man who has forced himself on me and torn my dignity to shreds? You think there's nothing for me there? There's nothing but misery for me here!"

It is clear her distress is about to make her start dry heaving again. "The West will be a smoking pile of rubble the day after Denzel Xavier leaves for his honeymoon!"

The words are a shout, an attempt to quell her hysteria. It works. Raquelle stares into my eyes, her face, if possible, grayer than before. "What?"

Before I can say a word, someone begins to pound on the bathroom door. My heart leaps into my throat as a voice I recognize commands, "Open this door immediately."

CHAPTER 33

As I inch the door open, I expect to see a crowd. But the hall outside is empty apart from the knocker.

Boadicea is dressed simply today. Her black jumpsuit is clearly made of expensive material and fits her body perfectly, but her only ornament is a silver chain with two bars dangling from it. Squinting slightly, I make out "Denzel" on one and "Enid" on the other.

"Miss Kanoska." Boadicea's expression is, as always, unreadable. "I would like a word with you."

I do not look back at Raquelle, huddled on the floor behind me. Is it possible that Boadicea doesn't know who is in here with me? That she only heard the tail end of our conversation?

"Of course, Excellency." I slip out the door and close it carefully behind me. Without another word, Boadicea strides away, and I follow, my heartbeat pumping in my ears.

We go up flight after flight of stairs. Even though I use the railing to support my weight since my crutches were left behind in the bathroom, tingles of pain are beginning to snake up my ankle by the time Boadicea turns down a hallway that I recognize. We walk toward the door of Xavier's bedroom. For a mad moment, I wonder if she is taking me to him, but then Boadicea stops and taps at a screen beside a plain black door. After a pause, she taps again and there is a clicking sound before the door slides seamlessly into the wall.

"After you," says the Consort of the Federation, and I walk past her into warmth and verdure. The door slides shut behind us, and I turn on the spot, fascinated by the flawless illusion of being in a real garden. The floor is a mixture of rock paths and springy turf. The walls must be embossed with high-definition photos instead of paint, and strategically placed climbing plants and trees complete the fantasy. Butterflies flit through the moist air, and I can see flashes of gold in the fountain that indicate the presence of fish. Glancing up, I catch a glimpse of blue and wonder if the ceiling is glass or only cleverly painted.

"The glass is opaque." I turn to look at Boadicea, who has followed my gaze. "Cronus wanted the sunlight but no chance of anyone looking in." There is a pause as she moves to a bench beneath the trailing fronds of a palm tree. "He used to bring me here."

I follow her to the bench and sit down on the corner farthest from her. "That was when we were first married," Boadicea continues. "Then, gradually, he stopped bringing me anywhere. But he continued to go out. One night I followed him and watched as he brought another woman up here." A butterfly alights in the space between us before taking off again.

"He was obsessed with the idea of love in a garden. He would always say it was what humans were created for. That the oldest myths and stories show humans cavorting in a world unspoiled by technology or politics." I stare at the dancing droplets of the fountain across from me, trying not to focus on the meaning of what she is saying, but a pit of nausea is forming in my stomach. "Some nights, as I lay alone in our bed, I almost went to find the man I had loved before him. But I knew that if I was caught, my children would be taken away from me. So I've been a good wife. A faithful wife all these years."

I don't want to hear any more. But if she keeps talking, perhaps she will forget the real reason she brought me up here. "The man you loved before—is he still alive?"

She gives a soft, bitter laugh. "The man I once loved was destroyed long ago, poisoned by a longing for power and a desire for revenge. But his shell is doomed to end its days as a lab rat, testing technologies that might make the Federation stronger."

"You were in love with Lothar Grimsby?"

Her eyes meet mine, full of pain. "He was my first friend when I came here. He was kind then, brilliant, funny. I didn't know a thing about computers or technology, and he taught me. He was a genius at coding—and hacking, though not many people knew that. We would spend every spare minute together. I loved learning from him, and he said once that it was love at first sight for him when he saw me. For three months, we were happy. I was doing well in the Gauntlets, but I didn't care, because Lothar was going to pick me.

"Then Cronus noticed us. He's a jealous man. And he loves a chase. So he began to single me out. He was charming, in a way that only he could be—charismatic, hypnotic, magnetic. I was flattered by the attention from the man who was going to be Elector. He made me believe that I was his soulmate, that without me he was lost. So I submitted my suit design in the third Gauntlet, even though Lothar begged me not to, telling me that if I forfeited my chance at the top spots, we could still be together. When I won and Cronus picked me, I believed that I was about to step into a fairy tale. Not the nightmare my life has been for the past twenty years."

Silence falls, broken only by the splashing of the fountain. I know that the smart thing to do would be to ask more questions, try to keep Boadicea talking, but I can't think of anything to say. After a long moment, she says, "Why will the West be a smoking pile of rubble the day after Denzel leaves on his honeymoon?"

I consider making up a story. Then I glance at the woman beside me, and I don't see the Consort of the Federation—instead, I see the daughter of a seamstress from Los Angeles. "Hugh Grimsby and the Elector have a plan to make the Federation the most powerful nation on this continent," I say. "Hugh has discovered an enzyme that stops human aging. The plan is to inoculate every adult in the Federation before Denzel's instatement as Elector. The need for Western brides will be eliminated, since the people of the East will be able to live and reproduce forever.

Hugh has hacked into the AI on the fighter planes patrolling the West, and the day after Xavier leaves for his honeymoon, he plans to bomb the cities of Cinq out of existence, blaming the attack on China when the newlyweds return."

I expect Boadicea to ask me how I know this. Instead, she says quietly, "What an opportunity for Cronus. The chance to bed a different woman every week for eternity."

"Excellency, if we went to the Council, if we could show proof—"

"That won't save Cinq." Boadicea's even voice cuts across me. "While those fools are dithering around trying to determine the facts, Hugh Grimsby has the capability at his fingertips to press a button and obliterate the West. No, I need you to bring me the device that you found Hugh's controls on. He almost certainly only has one. The cost of getting an unregistered device is astronomical. And we don't need to worry about Cronus. He doesn't understand the first thing about computers, so he was certainly relying on Hugh's hacking abilities for this part of the plan."

I meet her gaze. "I'll get the device. How should I contact you when I have it?"

Boadicea gives me a small smile. "You're close with someone who has 24/7 access to me. I'd ask him."

CHAPTER 34

"**I** thought I'd see you more now that you messed up your ankle."

I turn from pulling on my one shoe to see Heath staring at me resentfully from the couch.

"You really thought a twisted ankle would stop me?" I try to tease, but he just glowers. "There are some things I need to deal with, buddy. We'll do something tomorrow during my free time."

"When are you going on your next tête-à-tête with Xavier? Can I come along for that?"

"You want to come along on one of my tête-à-têtes?"

"Not with just anyone," Heath hastens to say. "Only Xavier. If you took me on one of your tête-à-têtes with Nicholas, I'd probably kill myself. Or him."

"I see. You just want to see Xavier. I'm going to be a third wheel on my own tête-à-tête."

"He's so busy," Heath says. "Sometimes we shoot hoops early in the morning before anyone else wakes up, but most of the time, he can't even do that. Coming along on one of your tête-à-têtes just seems like a good way to make sure we all see each other."

"I'm sorry, did you just say that you've been sneaking out in the mornings to shoot hoops with Denzel Xavier?"

Heath raises his eyebrows at me. "Andi, I survived alone on the streets of San Francisco for years."

"This isn't San Francisco, Heath! There are cameras everywhere! Lida and I are the only people who care about you!"

"That's no different from San Francisco. Except here, Xavier cares about me too."

"Heath, you can't just go sneaking around here. It's dangerous." I limp across to the sofa and drop down beside him with a sigh. "I know it's hard, buddy. I know you're used to freedom, to being able to roam around calling your own shots. But that's not possible here." My shoulders slump. "If you want me to, I can arrange for you to go home. You could live with Sasha. Or at least go to her if you ever need anything."

His head burrows against my arm. "Going back home would mean leaving you, Andi."

I lift my arm and wrap it around him, drawing him against me. "And I'd hate that. But I don't want to force you to live in captivity just because I have to."

He's quiet. "You know what I'd like?" he says after a moment. "I'd like it if we could just head into the Wastelands and see what's out there. No people except you and me and Xavier and Lida, but probably there'd be animals, and we could hunt and build a cabin in the woods and live there together. It'd be like discovering a new world. Like those guys two thousand years ago, Lark and Clervis."

"You mean Clark and Lewis."

"Whatever. It'd be awesome."

For an instant, I close my eyes and allow myself to see his new world—rocks and ground just starting to produce vegetation again, rivers finally beginning to run clean. He's right—it would be a new beginning, freedom like none of us have ever experienced. But it's also a pipe dream.

"I have to go, buddy."

"Next tête-à-tête with Xavier? Otherwise I'm hopping on the next plane out of here."

"Ask him. And no more sneaking out. At least tell me or Lida so we know where you are."

As I close the suite door, I glance down at my device. 7:02. Just over two hours before curfew to get help for Raquelle and somehow make amends to Xavier. When I reach the door to the hospital suite and press the buzzer, an automated voice responds, "Name and ailment."

I take a deep breath. "Andromache Kanoska. I fell down today and think I might have re-twisted my ankle. The pain is making me really nauseous. Could I get some anti-nausea medication?"

There is a pause. Then the voice says, "Please hold while I relay your complaint to the on-duty physician."

A few moments pass, and I fidget. The story is as lame as I currently am, but before coming here, I thought it would make sense to link my request to a verifiable medical issue I already have. Now, as I stand waiting, it seems obvious that claiming food poisoning would have been a much better lie.

With a click, a small drawer next to the buzzer pops open. A bottle rests on the silver tray. I snatch it up as the automated voice says, "Please report to the infirmary if the pain does not subside within twenty-four hours."

"I will. Thank you!"

I hobble away as quickly as possible, irrationally frightened that the door will open behind me and the physician will appear to call my bluff and force me to return the medication. When I reach Raquelle's door and knock, it flies open so quickly that I stumble back. Raquelle is standing there, a finger pressed to her lips. She looks slightly less ill as a result of the makeup coating her face. She slips into the hall with me, closing the door quietly behind her.

"Hugh is in there, passed out on my bed," she says wearily. "He came back from Achilles Pendell's high as a kite on nirvana and ranting about Achilles cheating in whatever VR game they were playing. I slipped some sleeping pills into the drink I gave him, and he just dropped off. The sleeping pills usually guarantee three or four hours of sleep, and with how wound up he was before then, I'd guess it'll be longer." She slumps back against the wall. "The last thing I want is to go back in there and sleep next to him." Her eyelids flutter. "But I'm so exhausted. I really need a bed."

As her words sink in, my mind begins to race. "Raquelle, I brought you some anti-nausea medication," I say. "I told the infirmary that pain from my ankle was making me nauseous. You should go to my room and take some, then try to get some fluids into you and take a nap on my bed. I won't want to sleep for a few hours."

She meets my eyes, a sparkle of something almost like hope appearing in hers. "You're all right, Andi," she says gruffly. One side of my mouth tips up as I hand her the bottle and watch her hurry down the hall to my suite. Lida pokes her head out, and I give her the thumbs up before she leads Raquelle into the suite and the door closes.

I silently count to twenty before opening Raquelle's door and slipping inside. The suite is dark, and I stand still for a moment, allowing my eyes to acclimate before I can see that the layout is identical to my suite. The bedroom door across the main living area is ajar, and I push it open, pausing as the door gives the tiniest creak.

Hugh Grimsby is sprawled face down on the bed, his torso moving rhythmically in slumber. I prop my crutches against the doorframe and limp toward the bed. My hands are shaking as I reach slowly to touch him, terrified that he will start up and grab me. But as my fingers graze his shoulder, he only stirs slightly and then snores on. Emboldened, I slip my hand into each of his pants pockets in turn. Nothing.

With the feeling of placing my hand inside a metal trap that could spring closed at any moment, I worm my fingers between his chest and the bed. Just as I feel a lump in his breast pocket, he stirs again. "Raquelle?"

"It's all right," I whisper, running my other hand soothingly along his back. "It was just a dream. Go back to sleep."

I wait until his breathing deepens again before pulling gently on the device, attempting to slide it out of his pocket. It doesn't budge. I pull again and it slides into my hand.

Forcing myself to move calmly, I withdraw the hand holding the device inch by inch before slipping to the door, gathering up my crutches, and exiting the suite.

As soon as the door closes behind me, I blow out a long breath and set off to look for Xavier. It only takes fifteen minutes of riding the elevators and hopping down hallways for me to realize two things—one, that it would be quicker to message him and ask where he is, and two, that I left my own device in my room.

When I finally push open the door to my suite, I see Xavier sitting on the couch next to Heath, playing a game with him on the suite's electronic pad. I limp over and plop down on the other side of Heath.

"This looks like fun." I make no effort to keep the irritation out of my voice.

"Oh, it is." Xavier doesn't look at me.

"Come on, come on," Heath moans, scrabbling at the datapad, then groaning and flopping back. *"Armageddon!"*

"Heath Insley!"

"Sorry, sorry," Heath glances at me sheepishly. "Want to play again, Xavier?"

"Xavier and I need to talk, Heath."

"Ooh." Heath scoops up the pad and heads for his room. "Have fun."

I turn to Xavier, who is staring down at his hands. "Could we go somewhere?"

"If you like."

"Xavier, I'm sorry."

He looks at me then, eyes hard. "For what?"

You're not going to make this easy, are you?

"For treating you like the enemy. When you've been noth-ing but a friend to me. Except at the very beginning, I guess."

"A friend? That's what I've been to you?"

And suddenly, I am furious. Because I didn't ask for any of this. Because in the last few months, my armor of indif-ference has been stripped away. And now I have all the pain that caused me to don that armor in the first place.

"What do you want me to say, Xavier? That I'm in love with you? That the thought of watching you pick a different girl makes me sick? That my own infertility hurts worse than ever because I want to be able to have your children? Is that what you want to hear? Does it make the fact that we'll never be together better?"

The couch cushions shift, and his arms come around me. "That's exactly what I wanted to hear," he whispers into my hair. Something between a laugh and a sob erupts from me as I bury my face in his shoulder.

I wish we could just stay here. Like this.

"We have to go."

"I haven't accepted your apology yet."

"Well, I can't afford to sit around waiting forever, Xavier."

"Oh yeah?" he whispers and takes my face in his hands. When he kisses me, I put my arms around his neck and kiss him back. I kiss him like it is the last time I ever will, because for all I know, it might be.

"We really have to go." The words are a little breathless, spoken after I don't know how long. "I have Hugh's device."

Immediately, he helps me to my feet, handing me my crutches. We make our way out the suite door, and only when we are in the hall does he say, "How?"

"I'll tell you on the way. We have to find your mother."

"My mother?"

"She can disable Hugh's AI connection."

"My mother?"

"You're starting to sound a little like a scratched CD, sweetheart."

He begins to walk slowly up the hallway, matching his pace to mine. "Start talking, Kanoska."

By the time we knock on a door near the top of the complex, he has received both an abbreviated version of my talk with his mother and a synopsis of how I got Hugh's device, with the major detail of Raquelle's pregnancy omitted. The door opens to reveal Boadicea in a robe and slippers, her silver-threaded hair hanging in long braids down her back.

"Denzel, Andromache. Come in."

Despite her casual attire, she is still every inch the Federation's Consort. As I limp after Xavier into the room, I wonder what it would be like to grow up with a mother whose first and primary role was as the leader of a nation.

Boadicea sits down behind the sewing machine that occupies most of the tiny room and rests her hands lovingly on the purple gossamer material draped across the table under the needle. "Enid's dress for your wedding," she says, smiling at her son. "I thought an A-line might suit her better, but she has eyes and ears only for the fashion broadcasts."

Xavier's arm brushes mine, and I follow his gaze up to the camera in the corner of the ceiling. Clearly, the phrase "eyes and ears" is a code between mother and son to let the other know when their conversations are being monitored.

"I just love the fabric though," I say, slipping Hugh's device out of my pocket and into Xavier's hand before limping over to the sewing machine. "Is it locally made or imported?"

"Imported from Greece," Boadicea says, lifting a swathe of fabric as Xavier steps up beside me and slips the glowing device onto the table. His mother allows the fabric to fall in a pool around the small screen. "Do you mind if I keep working while we talk? Enid will be devastated if the dress isn't finished in time."

She restarts the sewing machine. We continue to chat, loudly, to hear each other over the clatter. Out of the corner of my eye, I watch Boadicea, amazed at her ability to sew with one hand while the fingers of her other hand fly over the screen of the device.

After a relatively short time, Boadicea stops the sewing machine. "That's one seam done," she says. "But I think it's a little crooked. Denzel, my love, what do you think?"

"Straight as a rocket's trajectory, Mother." He leans over the dress, and there is a brief flash as the device slides into his pocket.

"Good." Boadicea leans back in her chair, rubbing one hand across her face. "Did I ever tell you, Denz, that though my mother was a seamstress, she didn't own her own sewing machine? She rented it from a local pawn shop, and we had to return it every night. Every single night. In perfect condition, or the owner would charge us extra. I always felt relieved when he inspected the machine and didn't notice anything amiss."

"You look tired, Mother." Xavier moves around the table and bends over, wrapping one arm protectively around her. She leans her head against him for a moment, closing her eyes. Her lips move slightly, and I know that she is breathing some final message to Xavier. Then she says, "I really do have to finish this, son."

"We should go," I say. "It'll be easier to get work done without us distracting you."

"My children will always be my favorite distractions." Boadicea smiles at us. "But I wouldn't want Enid to kill Denzel over a dress, and it's almost curfew, so perhaps you'd better head back."

The sewing machine has started again as we slip out into the hall. Only when we are several floors away and between cameras do I dare to whisper, "So?"

"She said the West is safe. And Hugh won't notice what she's done as long as we make sure to get the pad back before he wakes up."

I pause to allow my leg to rest. "But he will find out. When he learns that the West hasn't blown up."

"It won't matter. I intend my first act as Elector to be exposing his and my father's crimes and bringing them to justice." I wonder if there is a part of him that feels he will be avenging his mother.

"What about your honeymoon?"

"Would you mind terribly if we postponed it?"

"Right at this moment, the chances of my opinion mattering seem very slim."

"Your opinion will matter. I intend to spend the next month finding a loophole in the law that says that I can only pick one of the top two contestants. And if you spend the time making your invention completely flawless, that wouldn't hurt either."

CHAPTER 35

"**W**hat a treat—to finally be able to dress you without worrying about a bunch of casts and slings," Lida says sarcastically, as she buttons the back of my creamy, long-sleeved dress. "And it would probably be bad luck for a bride to hop up the aisle on crutches. But it doesn't exactly seem like a real wedding when there are going to be five couples, and you don't know which man you'll be marrying."

I smooth my fingers along the front of my dress. It is lovely—simple with a high neckline and lace sleeves, and a scooped back exposing a hint of skin. My hair is pulled back into a low bun at the base of my neck with a frosty lace veil fluttering down from a silver circlet. Before the Invitation, I could never have imagined looking like this on my wedding day. But as Lida says, the fact that it is my wedding day feels surreal since I don't know if I am about to wed Denzel Xavier or Nicholas Pendell.

I have spent the past month exactly as Xavier advised, running tests on the lab rats and perfecting my immunity serum. Any spare minute I had, I combed through the digital library, sometimes with Xavier and sometimes on my own, but neither of us was able to discover any precedent allowing the Elector to select a contestant who didn't make one of the top two spots.

"We can always start a new precedent," Xavier told me grimly last night, and I gave him my best fake smile and agreed. But I knew that if Xavier chose to defy the law and marry me, the most likely outcome would be that he would be forced to abdicate as Elector. And in that case, he would be unable to stop Hugh and his father.

Even if I do not win the last Gauntlet, the West is safe. The attacks on infertile and elderly women have stopped, and Xavier has promised to do everything in his power to put an end to the shipments to Paradise. Cronus Xavier and Hugh Grimsby will be imprisoned for life, and their hopes of an immortal race will die with them. Heath and Lida will be safe under Nicholas's protection, and I will be under much less scrutiny for not producing a child if I am not the Federation's Consort.

The only thing lost will be a chance at life with the man I love. But that is almost fitting, really. Andromache of long ago lost her love too.

"I can't believe I don't get to come to your wedding," Heath says gloomily from the couch. "The announcement this morning said that the entire human population of the

Federation was supposed to attend. Apparently I count as a robot now."

I drop down beside him in a rustle of silk. "Honestly, I wish I could skip my own wedding and stay here with you, buddy."

"Because you think you'll be marrying Nicholas Pendell?"

"It seems pretty likely, Heath."

"Xavier won't let that happen," Heath says confidently. "He's too in love with you."

"If Xavier marries me when he's not supposed to, he'll be made to step down as Elector."

"That would be great!" Heath bounces up and down. "We could all go live in the Wastelands then!"

I laugh and hug him. "I have to go. But if you want to see my wedding, just turn on the suite's electronic pad. The third Gauntlet will be live streamed to all devices." Standing, I reach for Lida, but she pulls away. "No hug? On my wedding day?"

"I don't want to mess up your dress," she says stiffly.

"You're a marvel of a stylist, you know?" I pause to look down at her on my way through the doorway.

"I've got eyes," she says sourly, and I laugh again as I sweep out, holding my skirt up in both hands.

The third Gauntlet is to take place in the banqueting hall where my dress ripped on my first night in the Federation. Everything is decorated in white and gold, and as I make my way slowly to the head table, I see that my four fellow contestants are all arrayed in bridal finery.

Zuri is dressed in a strapless, bedazzled gown with a tiara resting atop her short dark hair. Beside her, Clotilde wears a sweetheart neckline and pats nervously at her golden pompadour. Raquelle's dress is an empire waist with a silver belt and a long chiffon skirt, and her red curls hang loose, topped by a veil that hides her face. As I slide into my chair, I glance at Bella, who is sitting beside me, half her hair braided into a crown while the rest hangs in curls down the back of a timeless gown with cap sleeves and a flowing skirt.

"Oh, Andi, you're gorgeous!"

"So are you," I say. "Excited?"

She gives a little shiver of delight and glances toward Alden, who is dressed in his red and white military uniform and looking at her as though he has never seen anything so beautiful in his life.

The sight of their unadulterated happiness is too much. I look away, my eyes meeting Nicholas's. This is a mistake, as he immediately begins talking. "You look absolutely ravishing, Andi. The simplicity of your gown denotes great taste. It is for the same reason that I chose this suit cut in a charcoal gray. Simplicity and elegance..."

His prattling is cut short by the roll of distant drums. The small circular stage of the first night rises before us, but instead of Lothar Grimsby, Cronus Xavier stands atop it, clad in a reserved black suit.

"Ladies and gentlemen." Stillness descends over the hall, and Cronus smiles. "This is the night we have all been waiting for. Boadicea and I have been waiting for the opportunity to gracefully step aside and allow our son to ascend into a role of leadership. Denzel has been waiting for a woman who will not only be his companion and soulmate, but a fellow ruler over our glorious nation. These four young men"—he gestures toward the suitors—"have been waiting for wives to carry on this strong, proud breed of humans who have survived disease and near-extinction. And all of you"—his arm encompasses the entire banquet hall—"have been waiting to see which of these gorgeous young women will take her place by my son's side as Consort of the Federation."

He pauses, allowing the silence to swell. "The wait is over! Allow me first to present the inventions created by these beautiful ladies. The judges will then reveal the scores, at which time my son will emerge and choose his bride from the top two contestants."

A second platform rises slowly beside the one on which Cronus stands. Spotlights join together to illuminate the item resting on a small table. "Ladies and gentlemen, Raquelle Mortimer, who currently holds the highest score, presents a headset consisting of glasses and an earpiece, which will allow the wearer to hear the conversation of anyone within sight, since the glasses are equipped with a new technology capable of reading lips. Miss Mortimer?"

Raquelle makes her way to the edge of the stage and steps onto the platform, holding her invention. She takes the headset and positions it on her head.

"We will now allow her to demonstrate the device's capabilities," Cronus says. A spotlight appears, drifting over the crowd. "Stop," Cronus says, and the beam pauses over a table. "Now all of us will converse among ourselves. In a moment, Raquelle will relay the conversation from that table."

Chatter breaks out through the hall. After a moment, Cronus proclaims, "Quiet, please." He gestures to Raquelle.

"The man in the lavender suit told the lady in the silver blouse that they had better not say anything they don't want the entire hall to hear in case my device really does work. The lady responded that she thought that sounded like he would usually say incriminating things. The woman in pink was talking about a new skincare product rumored to be undergoing testing in Europe, which can make you look thirty years younger, and the man in green responded, 'Oh yeah? How would it make you look if you were fifteen years old?'"

"Is Miss Mortimer correct?" Cronus calls.

Everyone at the nearby tables swivels to look at the group. The man in lavender looks appalled, the woman in silver smug, the woman in pink mildly impressed, and the man in green amused. "Yes!" he calls out.

Applause breaks out, and I join in, which causes Zuri to shoot a condescending look down the table. "Very impressive, Miss Mortimer," Cronus says. "You may return to the stage. Let us move on to our next contestant. Currently in second place, Zuri Pendleton presents a multipurpose ball gown with strategically placed zippers, allowing the skirt to be converted into pants, giving women the capability of swift motion in any social setting."

Surprised, I glance toward Zuri as half-hearted applause sounds through the room. Clearly, Zuri had thought to follow in Boadicea's footsteps by presenting a garment, but lacking Boadicea's skill at sewing and her innovation, her 'invention' could barely be classed as such and would be of little use to the Federation. I had expected something much cleverer from her.

Zuri steps onto the pedestal where a mannequin stands, garbed in a gown the same shade of red as the pantsuit she was wearing when we first met. With many unnecessary flourishes, she uses the zippers to change the dress. Despite her posturing, the demonstration is so anticlimactic that the audience does not start applauding until she is already back on the stage.

"Thank you, Miss Pendleton," Cronus says. "On to our third contestant. May I present Clotilde Katzmiller's offering, a self-refilling water bottle that uses a miniature refrigeration system to pull moisture from the air."

Clotilde steps onto the platform beside her invention. "The only downside to this water bottle," she says nervously, "is that it takes about eight hours to fully refill. So, it is difficult to demonstrate. However, I did make a graphic of the mechanism."

A screen lowers from the ceiling above the stage, and an image appears. Clotilde explains briefly how the mini-refrigeration system in the walls of the bottle causes condensation to form due to the difference between the temperature of the air and the walls.

Applause rings out, and I begin to feel hopeful. I am almost certain my invention will beat Clotilde's and Zuri's. I might have a chance after all.

"Bella Santos has developed an emotional regulation device." Cronus's tone is patronizing. "It can be worn like a necklace, and when the pendant senses an increase in heart rate, it will produce slow, rhythmic pulses designed to slow the heartbeat down to a normal rate."

Bella climbs onto her platform and picks up the necklace. "Hello!" she says brightly. "I will need a volunteer for this." A spotlight swings out across the crowd. At first, I think that no one will help Bella, but then a middle-aged woman with styled curls slowly raises her hand.

"Good!" Bella says as her platform descends to allow the woman to climb up beside her. "Now, I am going to need you to do some jumping jacks." The woman looks at her, aghast. "Just to raise your heart rate," Bella says. "I didn't want to emotionally distress you."

The woman slowly begins to jump in place, her arms limp and unengaged. "Good!" Bella says again after several minutes. "Does your heart rate feel elevated?"

"Yes," whispers the red-faced woman, who looks as though she wants to sink into the floor.

"This will help," Bella says, fastening the necklace around the woman's neck. "Just allow the pendant to rest inside your dress."

The effect is striking to watch. After a moment, the look of embarrassment and annoyance fades from the woman's face, replaced by a look of relaxation and enjoyment.

"Do you feel better?" Bella asks.

"I need one of these for my quarters," the woman says, smiling at her. "It would help when my children are being particularly provoking."

Laughter rings out from the audience as the platform lowers to allow the woman to return to her table. I clap for Bella's invention until my hands smart, stopping only when I hear the grind of a fifth platform rising from the ground. "Andromache Kanoska," says Cronus, "has developed an immunity serum designed to significantly raise the ability of the human body to fight disease. As of yet, it has only been tested on rats, but the results have been statistically significant."

I stand and walk to the edge of the stage, wiping my sweaty palms surreptitiously on my skirt. I could really use one of Bella's necklaces right now. "It would be difficult to demonstrate the effects of the serum right now," I say to the crowd. "However, I would like to show you two of my study participants. Both were exposed to rabies. One had received my immunity serum the month before, the other had not."

I gesture to the screen, and a video appears. "This is footage from yesterday," I say. A rat appears on the screen, walking in wobbly circles. Strings of drool are hanging from its snout, and it suddenly turns and lunges at the camera, teeth bared. The next video shows a plump rat calmly eating from its food dish. Another rat scampers by, and the rat turns and gives chase, pouncing playfully, wrestling and nuzzling the other rodent.

"The only difference in these test subjects was whether or not they received the immunity serum," I say. "As you can see, the results were very different."

Listening to the applause, my stomach clenches. They don't seem particularly exuberant. But I only have to convince the Council. Not the audience. "Thank you, Miss Kanoska," says Cronus's voice. "Please allow the Council a moment to deliberate. We will then release the scores."

A buzz of talk breaks out as Cronus steps off the platform onto the main stage and joins the table adjacent to the one at which all the contestants and suitors sit. I stare at my fingers, straining to hear a sound from the table behind me, but there is nothing, and I realize that they must be taking a simple vote without any discussion.

Please. God? First Cause? Creator? Let me come first. It's not to save the world anymore, and I know no one needs this but me. But sometimes I think that you wouldn't have made such a beautiful planet if you didn't care a little bit about the people who live here.

After what feels like an eternity, Cronus steps back onto his platform. As the gears whir upward, quiet settles once more over the banquet hall. "In fifth place comes the convertible ball gown created by Zuri Pendleton. This adds ninety-seven points to your score." There is a smattering of applause. "In fourth place, the self-refilling water bottle created by Clotilde Katzmiller. This adds 194 points to your current score. In third place, the emotion regulation device created by Bella Santos. This adds 291 points to your score. In second place"—my hands are balled into fists so tight, I can feel the nails pricking into my palms—"is the lip-reading device created by Raquelle Mortimer."

Cronus continues talking, but I can't hear him. The world has gone still and silent around me, illuminated only by the blinding truth that I am not Andromache of Troy. I am Kanoska. Xavier's Kanoska.

The crowd is on its feet, and my temporary deafness melts away in time to hear, "In first place, with a combined score of 614, we have Raquelle Mortimer." The crowd screams as Raquelle rises, an unreadable expression on her face, and sweeps toward the front of the stage. "And in second place, with a combined score of 583, Andromache Kanoska."

I move to stand beside Raquelle. "Denzel Xavier," Cronus calls. "Come choose your bride."

He is walking toward me, and I can't tell what color suit he is wearing because his smile is so wide it's blinding. He stops in front of me. "My choice is Andromache Kanoska, daughter of San Francisco." The words are ceremonial, but then he looks into my eyes and says, "If she will have me?" And I know it is a real question.

"Do you really have to ask?" The answer is quiet, meant only for him, but as Xavier scoops me into his arms with a yell of triumph, the banquet hall explodes around us. Everyone is yelling and cheering, and a band has appeared out of the crowd and is playing the Federation's national anthem. I hear explosions, and a glance out the window shows fireworks exploding over the river.

Thank you.

But as I wrap my arms around Xavier's neck, I catch a glimpse of Raquelle's face, and her expression chills my blood. It is full of hatred and despair. A part of her must have hoped that Xavier would pick her against all odds.

"And now for these other beautiful ladies!" Cronus's voice booms above us as Xavier sets me on my feet. "I have here sealed bids from the bachelors, each of whom placed two bids in case his first choice was also the Elector's."

Laughter rings through the hall, and bile rises in my throat. Heath was right. It is a bride auction. As if Raquelle and Bella and Zuri and Clotilde are cattle rather than women.

"For our first place contender, the lovely Raquelle Mortimer, the highest bid was placed by Hugh Grimsby!"

Hugh rises, his smile predatory. I have to stop this. But before I can say a word, Raquelle's voice rings out over the crowd, shrill and desperate. "I'm pregnant!"

Silence, thick and absolute, falls over the room. "What is this?" says Cronus quietly.

"I'm pregnant." The shrillness is gone from her voice now. "Your laws state that all Western brides must be virgins. Clearly, I do not fit that qualification. Your law further states that all Western brides found not to be virgins before their wedding nights shall be returned in disgrace to their homes and a new bride selected for the jilted suitor."

Muttering, like thousands of angry bees, begins to swell across the hall, but Cronus waves a hand, and it subsides. "Your knowledge of our laws is correct. Eugenes 208 and 213, please escort—"

"I am the child's father." Hugh cuts across Cronus. He makes his way forward and takes Raquelle's hand. I see her try to pull free, and his hand contracts brutally. "What can I say? I have been in love with Raquelle since the first moment I laid eyes on her, and we fell prey to our passions. Will you really send away the woman I love, who is carrying my child, when we can marry tonight and make this right?"

"I am not carrying your child!"

"Then whose child are you carrying?"

Raquelle says nothing. There is no way to respond without incriminating the old scientist.

"We will put the matter to a vote," Cronus says, gesturing toward the table where Boadicea and the rest of the suitors' parents are seated. "All in favor of allowing Raquelle Mortimer to remain and marry Hugh Grimsby?"

Every hand rises but one. Boadicea is staring stonily at her husband, her hands clasped in her lap. "Then it is settled," says Cronus. "In third place, Bella Solantis…"

His words fade into the background as my brain scrambles for a way to save Raquelle. Then I realize that as soon as we are pronounced man and wife, Xavier will be the Elector. He can accuse his father and Hugh, and both will be sent to prison to await trial before eventually receiving life sentences in the labs. Raquelle won't have to marry Hugh.

The other three couples—Bella and Alden, Clotilde and Barek, and Zuri and Nicholas—join us at the front of the stage. "Before I perform the ceremony of unification," says Cronus loudly, "after which, I will no longer be your Elector, I wish to express how much the chance to serve you has meant to me. We are a people small yet mighty, and I believe that we are destined to one day control this great continent, and perhaps later, the world. As my last act of service to all of you, I have conducted research to develop a vaccine against a new virus that is currently devastating Europe. Since our entire nation is gathered here tonight, we will be administering the vaccine to every adult as they leave the room. In order to fulfill our destiny, we must remain strong, healthy. This is my last gift to you." He pauses to accept the applause that fills the room. "And now, on to the ceremony—"

"Andromache Kanoska will never produce an heir for the Federation!"

CHAPTER 36

R aquelle's finger trembles as she points at me. "She's infertile. She's never had a menstrual cycle. She's been sending in blood samples from one of her midwifery clients since she was fourteen."

The words are soft, but even above the buzz of chatter that broke out immediately following Raquelle's announcement, they seem to echo through the hall. I look into Xavier's eyes, and the fear I see there seems to jumpstart my own dormant emotions. No lie will be able to save me, because as soon as my blood is tested, everyone will know the truth. That brief, perfect moment mere seconds ago? It was too good to be true. I knew that all along.

"Miss Kanoska?" I meet Cronus Xavier's gaze. "What is your response to this accusation?"

"She doesn't have to respond." Xavier's voice is a rumble of fury. "This wild accusation of Miss Mortimer's is clearly an attempt to delay the unification ceremony after her pregnancy announcement failed to garner the desired response. Excellency, there will be no order if every groundless allegation is heeded."

"But my son, this is a serious charge. If it is true that Miss Kanoska cannot produce children, then her only purpose as your wife is voided. If it is untrue, then she has nothing to fear from a fertility test, and the unification ceremony will only be mildly delayed."

There is nowhere left to hide. And suddenly I am not afraid anymore.

Gently, I pull my fingers from Xavier's and step off the stage and onto the platform next to my serum. "I am infertile. As far as I know, I will never be able to bear children." The words are like the first notes of a familiar melody, leading to freedom from my secrets and lies. "But when you say that fact voids my purpose as Xavier's wife, you are wrong. The purpose of marriage is not to provide seed and an incubator. Marriage is for companionship. For intimacy. For love and trust that only death can break. I may not be able to bear Xavier's children, but I am able to hold him on the days when the world is hard and cruel. I am able to laugh with him at jokes that only the two of us understand. I am able to encourage his strengths and help him triumph over his weaknesses. I am able to be a mother to the children who come into our home, even if they do not have our DNA. I am able to lead alongside him as I have shown through the Gauntlets which *you* designed to find a worthy Consort."

I pause, gazing out over the stony faces of the men and women below me. "You say that I and those like me are worthless. And you put a euroyen amount—literally—on the worth of others." My hand sweeps toward the four other contestants standing frozen beside their suitors. "Don't you see that when you start to devalue some human lives, there will eventually be someone who sees you as worthless? If we are the handiwork of some Cosmic Artist, are we not all worthwhile because we bear His fingerprints?"

My eyes meet Cronus's again, and now I am Andromache, fighting as I watch my world crumble. I am Andi, brave in the face of my own demise. "You can't have it both ways," I say. "Either we all have worth. Or none of us do. And if we are not intrinsically valuable, then strength is all that matters, and someday that strength will pass to another, who might easily decide that your life is a guttering candle flame that he might as well snuff between his fingers."

Someone begins to clap. I turn and see that Xavier is standing below me, applauding alone as the rest of the hall sits frozen. When he speaks, his voice rings across the silent hall. "If you cannot see that Andromache Kanoska is exactly what our country needs, then you are fools. The lot of you."

My platform begins to lower, but as his hand reaches to help me back onto the stage, the speed increases, and as I fly past Xavier, a downward glance reveals a crowd of armored bots waiting for me on the ground.

"Very touching, Miss Kanoska." Cronus's voice drips with sarcasm. "But let me paint an alternate picture. When cancerous cells develop in the human body, your argument would say that we ought to leave the mutant cells because they are, in some way, human. But left unchecked, they grow and spread, attacking and destroying healthy cells until eventually the entire organism succumbs to the disease. You and those like you are a weakness to society, Miss Kanoska. A cancerous growth, which, if left unchecked, will swell until society crumbles beneath it. The only reasonable response to a cancerous growth is to cut it out. Eradicate it completely."

The droids close in on me, pincer-like hands grasping my biceps. I let out an involuntary gasp as a burning sensation sears across my forearm. When I look down, I see a sequence of numbers imprinted into my flesh.

"Since the Ascendant's choice has been found unworthy and the other top contestant is pregnant by another man, it is impossible for us to complete the unification ceremony tonight." I see Xavier make an angry movement toward his father, but his mother materializes by his side, holding him back. "All Federation citizens should return to their quarters, where complimentary champagne and wedding cake will be delivered later. I, as the current Elector, Boadicea as Consort, and the rest of the Council will decide as soon as possible how to resolve this situation so that my son is able to marry and assume his rightful role as Elector."

"Given these unforeseen events, we will not administer the vaccine tonight." Boadicea's voice rings out. "As a final token of the current administration's care for the Federation, it no longer seems appropriate."

After a moment, Cronus says, "The Consort has spoken," and the syringe-wielding automatons stationed near the doors exit the hall.

"Come," says the clipped voice of the armored droid next to me. "Be warned, resistance will be met with force."

As I am marched from the hall, I glance back, hoping for a final look at Xavier. But he is already gone.

CHAPTER 37

*I*s this a trick to break me?

Seclusion?
Darkness?
Silence?
My imaginations of the horrors in store for me?

To get here, the armored droids led me to an elevator that carried us down, down, down, until I was certain that we must be underground. When the box finally stopped, the head droid tapped a sequence into a pad outside a metal door. As we marched through, the sight of what was beyond brought me to a horrified stop.

To me, labs have always been places of learning. Places of quiet. Happy places where I feel at ease.

This lab? It is a place of nightmares.

Through the glass window to my left, I see an emaciated man dressed in a flimsy gown. Electrodes are attached to his shaved head, and he is shaking and convulsing while a man in a lab coat types into a computer, his expression bored. To my right, I see a woman, as emaciated as the man, clawing at the door to the room she is in, clearly begging frantically. An untouched meal sits on a table next to her hospital bed. What did they give her? Some sort of addictive test drug?

Pain explodes through my back, and I cry out. My abrupt stop caused me to stumble against the droid behind me, which clearly viewed this as an act of aggression and responded with some sort of taser. I stagger forward, trying to keep my eyes trained on the ground. But every glance upward shows me some fresh horror. A glass tank, swimming with what are clearly human hearts, some still beating. A baby with a deformed arm sitting on the floor in an empty, sterile room, screaming with no response, no loving adult to comfort and soothe him. A woman running in terror around her cell, trying to avoid being bitten by the three snakes slithering after her. Are they testing venom antidotes?

I clamp my lips tightly shut, sure that vomiting all over the droids closest to me would be a punishable offense.

Which one of these terrors is in store for me? And then the truly horrific thought comes. *What if Heath and Lida are sent down here?*

They were under my protection. Now that I am a criminal, that protection is gone. We make our way through another metal door into complete darkness. I stumble between my guards, eyes straining against the pitch blackness, trying to discern anything. I don't know how long we walk before the droid in front of me stops. The halt of the whispering sound his metal feet make against the floor gives me a split second's warning so that I barely manage to avoid running into him.

I hear another door open. "Forward," says the disembodied voice of the droid, and I totter forward. The door clangs shut behind me, and I sink to my knees.

That might have been an hour ago. Or five hours. Or three days. I'm pretty sure it hasn't been three days, but it is impossible to calculate time in total darkness. I am huddled in a corner of the room, softly singing a lullaby that Sasha used to croon to newborns, just to keep myself from dwelling on the future and going crazy, when I hear the sound of the door opening.

A white beam of light slashes across my face, and I gasp, clamping my eyes shut and pressing my fists against my closed eyelids, surprised at the pain. "Well, well," a voice says above me. Hugh Grimsby. "You're not as smart as I thought the first day I met you. You should have been satisfied with attracting Denzel's interest, love. Instead, you just had to try to be a heroine."

The back of his hand connects with my cheek so hard that I'm sure if I wasn't already backed against a wall, my head would have whipped from side to side. As it is, my teeth close on my tongue, and my mouth fills with blood.

"That's for getting my father imprisoned," Hugh says quietly. "Luckily, he didn't actually know the extent of Cronus's and my plans. He, like you, thought we were just weeding out undesirables by our airstrikes against the 'Paradise' ships, and establishing authority and respect with the Department of Correction. He and I both had devices connected to the AI on our Western patrol planes. Since Father was arrested, I haven't attacked any more ships so that Xavier would be sure he had dealt with the problem. But I've just been biding my time. See this?"

The device in his hand is open to a screen I recognize. "I've had it all programmed and ready for months," Hugh says. "The moment I press this button, airstrikes will begin on all five cities of Cinq. But you know something about that already, don't you, smart girl?"

There is no point in lying now. "You saw me that night I heard you and Cronus talking, didn't you?" I say.

"Your height gave you away. The only other woman that tall is Boadicea, and there was camera footage from the time that showed her sewing in her recreation room. I thought you probably wouldn't risk going to Denzel right away since it would be your word against the word of his best friend and his father, but that might change if you became Consort. So I loosened the punching bag in the gym a few weeks before the second Gauntlet and kept my sweet little Raquelle away, since you and she are the only ones who use it. My plan seemed to be working beautifully when your injuries caused you to come in last in the second Gauntlet. But just in case you somehow managed to win the third Gauntlet, I had a special syringe with your name on it. Rather than immortality, you were going to get a little dose of the virus that is terrorizing Europe." He laughs, and I sit still, allowing the strands of information to knot together in my brain, a picture beginning to emerge.

"But Raquelle saved me the trouble with her little announcement." The laughter is gone and his voice is icy.

"She thought getting herself pregnant would keep me from marrying her." His tone is cruel. "She's never going to get away from me, but I'm not going to be raising some demon spawn that isn't mine, either. Abortion might be illegal, but there are still ways to end a pregnancy, as she is going to find out tomorrow."

He bends toward me, and I feel his breath tickling my face. "Tomorrow, you'll begin your life as a lab specimen. Tomorrow, Raquelle will learn never to defy me again. And tomorrow," he pauses theatrically, "that dung heap you come from will be a smoking hole in the ground."

His finger hovers for a moment and then touches the button in the center of his screen. I sit numbly as he begins to laugh again, backing out of my cell. "Sweet dreams, love."

CHAPTER 38

When, a short time later, I hear the door again, I clench my eyes shut to avoid being blinded. But instead of the white blaze from before, there is only darkness. And a voice.

"Kanoska."

"Xavier?"

"Come here. This is going to hurt."

"What? What are you—" His fingers close around my wrist, and I sink my teeth into my lip to keep from howling as pain explodes up my forearm. It feels like he is using a filet knife to carve off the top layer of my skin.

"I'm sorry. It's almost done." Through my closed eyelids, I can see violet light, but the pain is so excruciating, I have no brain space left to wonder what it is. After a moment, a little of the agony subsides, and I feel a bandage being wrapped tightly around my arm.

"You're tough as nails, Kanoska." He grabs my hand. "We have to go."

"How—"

"No time."

The purple light is gone, and everything still appears pitch black to me. But Xavier must have some way of seeing because he is striding confidently, dragging me behind him. After a few moments, he pauses, and I bang into his back. "Come on."

"You're the one who stopped, Xav—"

"Not you, Kanoska."

That's when I feel the people pressing around us. "Xavier, what the—"

"No time." There is finality in his voice, and we are moving again. As time begins to fade away into darkness and the shuffling of feet, I wonder if I am dreaming. If not for the pain in my forearm, I'd be sure I am.

The ground begins to slope upward, and we climb on. Just as I am starting to wonder if this will go on forever, Xavier stops again. I hear typing. There is the sound of a door opening, and fresh air tinged with salt washes over my face.

Xavier's hand pulls me forward, and I step out behind him onto a pebbly beach. A full moon is painting the ocean silver. I glance around me at the other people crowding onto the beach, and relief surges through me. Heath and Lida are there, next to Raquelle, who looks ghostly in her wedding dress. Behind them stand Bella, and Alden, who is holding a bundle, and next to them, shifting nervously from foot to foot, is Enid Xavier. All of them have strange goggles hanging around their necks, which I assume must have allowed them to see in the dark.

"Time to climb." Xavier lets go of my hand and gestures to the wall of rocks surrounding the little cove. "Heath, Lida, Enid, you go first."

Questioning again whether I am in some sort of strange dream, I follow the others. In comparison with my one-armed effort during the second Gauntlet, it is as easy as climbing a flight of stairs, and before I know it, I am clambering over a guardrail and onto asphalt. Putting an arm around a panting Heath, I look around and see the silhouette of a black van parked beside the road a few meters away.

"Mother said she'd send a car." There's relief in Xavier's voice. "Come on, everyone."

We pile into the van. Xavier hops into the driver's seat, and I climb over the center console to the front passenger seat. As we pull away from the railing and onto the highway, I say, "Xavier?"

A long breath whooshes out of him and to my surprise, he leans across the console and kisses me full on the mouth. There are groans from the backseat, and he is laughing as he pulls away from me.

"Lucky I don't have to keep my eyes on the road since this is a self-driving car." He pauses. "Just in case you want to get out, I should probably tell you now that we're headed for the Wastelands."

Heath gives a quiet whoop from the back, and I say, "Xavier, how?"

"After the whole debacle in the banquet hall, the first thing I did was go find Heath and Lida. They weren't in your room—"

"We saw the whole thing on livestream and thought someone might come looking for us," Lida chips in from the backseat.

"I wouldn't have known where to look, but Alden met me coming from your room and told me that Heath and Lida were hiding in Bella's suite. We had just gotten inside when we heard a knock on the door. It was Raquelle, who told us that she'd turn Heath and Lida in if we didn't take her with us when we broke you out."

"I'm sorry." Raquelle's voice is strangled. "I...I don't know what made me tell them about you, Andi. It just looked like I'd end up with Hugh and he'd hurt me and the baby for the rest of our lives, and seeing you so happy, it just...made me crazy, I think. But after Hugh came to my room and told me that the baby would be dead tomorrow, I realized that Xavier would almost certainly try to free you somehow and that maybe I could escape with you."

After a pause, Xavier says, "I had most of a plan. My father had told me about the tunnel to that secret cove right before the third Gauntlet, since it is a secret that only Electors, their Consorts, and the head scientist of the human testing lab are supposed to know. Ships smuggling in supplies from Europe for the human testing come into that cove, and droids unload the supplies and load up any of the research results that we are trading. Since it's a secret, that tunnel has minimal security, only a simple passcode and an alarm that is triggered by one of the ingredients in the ink that research subjects are tattooed with." His fingers caress my bandaged arm. "That's why I had to use a laser to remove the tattoo on your arm. Don't worry, all the others had to do it too."

I glance over my shoulder and see several bandaged arms lifted as if in salute. I open my mouth to ask how everyone else was captured as well, but Xavier goes on before I can speak. His words are heavy. "I was planning to stop the human testing once I became Elector. And when I saw what they were doing to those people..." He trails off before saying, "I thought about trying to break as many as possible out and taking them with us. But I didn't want to risk the rest of you being recaptured. I don't know if I made the right choice."

"You did save one of them though!" Bella chirps.

"What?" I say, turning to look into the backseat. Alden holds up the bundle, pulling back the folds of what I now see is a pink suit jacket, to reveal the baby I saw crying alone.

"You got the baby." My voice breaks as I turn to Xavier, who still looks defeated.

"His cell and yours were the only ones that didn't have passcodes. Yours, because they hadn't assigned you to testing yet, and his, because he's too little to get out, I guess."

The sadness in his voice breaks my heart. "Give him to me," I say to Alden. The baby is passed forward until he is close enough for me to take in my arms. He looks to be about seven months old, with fuzzy red hair and wide blue eyes. I wrap the folds of the jacket more closely around him, and he blinks up at me curiously. "Look at him, Xavier."

The man I love turns to look down at the child. His face twists. "I wanted to save them all." The whisper is for me alone.

"But you saved him."

Xavier doesn't say anything. Instead, he reaches out, stroking the baby's head. When he speaks again, his voice still holds a hint of huskiness. "The only thing I didn't know how to access without attracting attention was one of the White House's self-driving vans. So I left the others and went to find my mother. She told me that she couldn't get one of the complex's vans for me, but that by using my father's thumbprint, she could authorize a van from a nearby military base to come for us. Then she told me that I had to take Enid with us. She didn't explain, and I didn't have time to argue with her."

"Wow, that makes me feel really special," Enid says sourly.

"I just thought you'd want to stay."

"Stay and get married off to some younger son of the founding families? No thank you. I can't stand any of them. Besides, Dad hasn't said more than ten words to me in the past five years and Mum is...different since she learned about Dad."

"I went and got Enid. Then I found a pair of military droids and told them that Enid and I had discovered several of the contestants were plotting to escape, and that I could lead them to the room where the culprits were. We went back to Bella's room, and I pretended to arrest the others. The military droids I had with me tattooed everyone, and we brought them down to the lab. As soon as we were in, Enid and I each powered down one of the droids, then everyone hid in an empty cell while I went to find you."

Lida speaks from the backseat. "Who will become Elector now?"

"I'm not sure," Xavier says. "From what Kanoska heard my father and Hugh saying, they are planning to give the entire adult population of the Federation an enzyme that will keep them from aging. Perhaps with Enid and me both gone, and his aging process halted, my father will decide to keep the title indefinitely."

After a beat, "Where exactly are we going?" comes from the backseat in Heath's voice.

"Right now? Out of the Federation. All security at the borders is programmed to keep intruders out since the security of the White House complex is deemed sufficient to keep citizens in. It's a little over a seven-hour drive from DC to the border between the Federation and what used to be the state of Ohio. Once we're over the border, there won't be a way to recharge the car, so we'll be on foot in the Wastelands. My plan was to head south and see what we find. Some rumors say that there are still human settlements in the Wastelands. If not, this van has a decent amount of survival supplies in the floor since it's military grade and, necessity being the mother of invention, I imagine we'll learn to find food and shelter pretty quickly."

"They'll discover we're gone." Raquelle's voice is small, and I feel a fresh wave of hatred for Hugh Grimsby, the one who turned her into this. "What if they follow us? Or send aircraft?"

"If they send aircraft after us, we don't stand a chance." Xavier doesn't look back, his eyes fixed on the dark road ahead. "But it'll be a quick death if that's any consolation."

Quiet descends over the van. After a moment, I reach forward and begin to fiddle with the dials of the radio. Music fills the car, the same song Xavier and I listened to once, about love acting as a bridge through the tumults of life. Xavier's hand reaches over the center console to find mine, and I lean my forehead against the cool glass of the window, suddenly too exhausted to keep my eyes open any longer.

The last thing I hear is the beautiful, soothing melody of the song. The last thing I feel is my beloved's fingers around mine.

"Kanoska!" Xavier's whisper has the effect of a shout, jerking me from slumber. Disoriented, I shake my head, turning to glance into the backseat, where the others are all slumped over in sleep. "Kanoska, look!"

I turn to gaze blearily through the front windshield. The sky is pink and gold, reflecting the sun that is still just below the horizon on the other side of the world. But something is rising from the West. At first it looks like a flock of birds, rising over the skyline and heading straight toward us. Then, as they grow bigger and bigger, I realize that they are aircraft, hundreds and hundreds of them.

"They can't be coming for us, can they? They'd be coming from the other direction..." My voice fades away, drowned by the pulsing roar of the planes passing directly above us.

The insignia of the Federation is etched onto their bodies, tails, and wings. They look exactly like the Fed planes I

watched soaring over San Francisco every day of my child-
hood, patrolling Cinq.

It is only when the rumble of the last plane is dying away
that Xavier starts the van again. I glance into the backseat
and see that Lida and Raquelle are both awake, staring out
of the back windshield after the retreating planes.

"What was that?" Lida says as we begin to drive again.

I shake my head, unnerved. Angels of Death, Cinq citizens used to call those planes. The sight of hundreds of
them filling the sky gives me a strong feeling of foreboding,
like something terrible is about to happen.

A few miles later, we hear the first explosion. Xavier
brakes so hard that we are all thrown forward before whipping around to stare behind us. At first, there is nothing to
see. But as explosion after explosion rings out, a pillar of
smoke begins to rise into the sky behind us, turning the
golden edge of sun creeping over the horizon a violent,
bloody red.

"They're bombing DC." The whisper is Xavier's. "They're
bombing DC. Mother! No!" The last two words are strangled, and I grab his hands as he lunges to restart the car.

"Xavier, we're too far. We can't do anything."

For a moment, he fights me before stilling. "She did this."

The others are exclaiming in the backseat, and only I hear
the words, words that give substance to my own suspi-
cions. I see Boadicea in my mind's eye, handing back Hugh's
device, her expression calmly inscrutable as an ancient
Sphinx. I hear her voice saying, "What a chance for Cronus.
The opportunity to bed a different woman every week for
eternity." She had told me that she remained faithful to
Cronus for her children's sake. But now that her children

are grown, perhaps she felt that the season for faithfulness had passed.

Xavier makes a choking sound, and I reach out to him, pulling his head onto my chest and holding him as his world, the nation he thought he would rule, crumbles into ashes behind us. When Enid begins to sob in the backseat, I reach forward and start the car, setting our destination as the Federation border.

As we move away, I look back one last time.

In the black cloud of devastation billowing up toward the sky, I see the murderous rage that one woman kept pent inside for decades. I glimpse the vindictive fury in her eyes as she watches her husband, seeking desperately for escape, knowing that with one blow, she is destroying not only his nation, but his plans for an eternal race. He planned to wipe out her people, so she wiped out his.

Hundreds of innocents are dying. But to her, their lives were worthless in the balance of her thirst for revenge.

Is this how it has to be?

Humanity burned and crushed into the ground before a remnant realizes the value every human life holds?

Maybe this is why we are here. Maybe we nine are survivors for a purpose. To create a haven, a place of safety for the Creator's beautiful, broken masterpieces.

My parents named me Andromache.

And I have learned to fight for those I love.

My friends call me Andi.

And I have learned to leave my fear in the shadows, to step bravely into the light.

I will need to be brave in the months ahead. To fight to forge a new future.

But I am ready for tomorrow.

Because, as far as I know, there are only nine other people left on this side of the continent.

And each of them I love enough to die for.

Epilogue

I t's been fifteen years since I've seen Pacific waves.

But this eastern ocean is all right too.

The sun is sinking behind our house, painting a soft orange glow across the waves. When I told Xavier that building a house on the very edge of the beach was a recipe for flooding, he said, "I'll risk getting a little damp if I can watch the sunrise over the ocean for the rest of my life." My rocking chair creaks a little against the porch deck, causing the baby in my arms to stir, and I cuddle her closer, straining my eyes to see if I can discern Heath and Xavier coming up from the docks yet.

"I can take her if you get tired of holding her," my daughter-in-law, Moira, says, as she sinks into the rocking chair next to me.

"You're the one who looks tired, honey."

"Getting a toddler into bed ought to have been one of the Gauntlets for the prospective Western brides. That's a true test of mettle."

I laugh, leaning down to brush my lips against my granddaughter's downy head. "You know I never get tired of holding babies, since the Creator never allowed me to have one of my own."

"You got to raise Yancy and Ella from the time they were babies."

"And I count that as one of the greatest privileges of my life. I got to have part of Yancy's babyhood, though he was already sitting and crawling by the time he came to us. But I think losing her mother during the birth gave me so many feelings of guilt that I wasn't able to enjoy Ella's infancy as I otherwise would have done. There was a part of me that always felt responsible for Raquelle's death, as though my longing for a baby had killed her."

"You did everything you could to save her, Mama Andi. My mother told me that she thought Raquelle didn't have the will to live anymore."

"I will never forget how surprised I was the first time I saw your mother. For a second, I had the mad idea that she was the most life-like droid I'd ever seen. Then the rest of you came popping out through the trees of the orange orchard, and I knew that after almost a month of trekking through the robot-inhabited remains of the Federation, we had finally found other humans."

"Mother and Father were as happy to see you as you were to see them. You were the first adults they had seen since the Federation sent them down to try to deal with the outbreak of brown rot that was attacking the North

Carolina orange orchards ten years ago and then forgot about them."

"I think the person happiest to see you all was Heath," I say slyly.

"Are you kidding? He detested me for the first eight years you were here. I was the one who was hopelessly smitten. I couldn't believe it when he finally started being nice to me."

"Kanoska!"

Moira and I both start out of our rocking chairs, straining to see through the gloom. "Xavier?" I call and see a dim figure waving.

"He's hurt, Mom." Heath's voice sounds from the same direction as Xavier's.

"Your father?" Moira plucks the baby from my arms, and I start down the porch steps.

"Not Dad. We found someone."

I quickly turn and hurry back up into my brightly lit kitchen. Ella is standing at the sink, humming as she dreamily swirls suds over a dish. "Someone's hurt, El." I say.

"Who?" She drops the plate into the dishwater, and I hear a cracking sound that causes me to groan inwardly. "Oops."

"Throw that away and drain the sink, honey."

I hurry into the living room, turning on lamps and shooing an exceedingly indignant cat off the sofa. Yancy looks up from the piano where he is improvising. The birth defect that only gave him one finger on his left hand made him more determined to excel in life. Hearing the songs he composes makes me wish that there were some way to get him onto a concert stage, to show his talent to the world. "What is it, Mum?"

"Dad and Heath found someone, son." Yancy starts to close the piano, but I shake my head at him. "Keep playing, Yance. Something soothing."

Behind me, I hear footsteps entering the kitchen and turn back to see Heath and Xavier carrying an ashen-faced young man with a nasty-looking cut across his temple. His eyelids are fluttering, but he doesn't appear to be fully conscious.

"In here."

They carefully deposit the young man on the sofa. Ella comes behind, full of questions and interest. "Where did you find him? How'd he get that cut? Is he going to make it?"

"El, he needs help. Get Mom the bandages instead of talking," Heath says.

My fingers are already probing gently along the edges of the wound. "This'll need stitches." My mind goes to Sasha, like it always does when I am doing anything medical. As far as I know, she is still in San Francisco. There is no way to be sure. But her absence is a constant ache in the back of my heart.

"On it!" Ella sings from the kitchen, and I hear her scrabbling in my medicine cabinet.

"We found him on the beach when we were walking back from putting out the crab pots," Xavier says in my ear, and I feel the pleasant flutter in my stomach from his nearness that fifteen years of marriage haven't managed to quell. "There was some sort of a crude boat wrecked nearby. He must have run aground on those rocks near the point."

Ella piles bandages, a bowl of hot water, antiseptic, needle, and synthetic thread on the table next to me. "Anything else I can help with, Mum?"

"You could put a kettle on, sweetheart. And if you want, you can toast some bread as well just in case he wakes up and is hungry."

The stitches are completed easily, and as I'm scanning the boy's body for other signs of injury, he begins to mutter and stir. Xavier, who is sitting quietly in an armchair nearby, leans forward, and Ella barely avoids dropping the plate of toast she is just carrying in from the kitchen.

The boy's eyes open, hands rising to his forehead to feel the bandages I have wrapped like a crown. "Where am I?" he mutters. Then, before anyone can respond, he begins to move restlessly, hands groping, head rolling from side to side. "My boat... Took me almost six months to build... Need to be able to fish... Have to take care of myself..."

"Shhh." I put a soothing hand on his shoulder, and he stills, sea-blue eyes meeting mine. "You're safe," I say.

"But my boat..."

"We'll help you build another boat, laddie." Xavier's rumble is low and soothing.

The boy's eyes rove the room, finding Ella with the plate of food in her hands, Heath and Moira with the baby in her arms, hovering in the doorway, Yancy coaxing a beautiful melody from the battered piano, Xavier smiling at him from the armchair. His eyes come back to me, and one of his searching hands finds mine and grasps it.

"Where am I?"

I follow his gaze around the room before gently squeezing his hand. "We call it Haven," I say. "You're home."

Acknowledgements

There's someone who needs to be thanked first and foremost because she believed in this book before I had written a word of it. Her name is Madame Publisher. AJ, thank you for giving this book of mine a home and for being the epitome of understanding and grace through the publication process. I am blessed to not only call you my publisher, but also my friend.

To Kyle - thank you for building a home with me where life and dreams can thrive. Being your wife is my favorite. Micah, Caleb, and Jules - getting to see the three of you as flickers on a black and white screen cemented even more deeply the knowledge that life is precious from its inception. I love you with all my heart, dear ones.

To Mom - you help me to tighten and refine my stories, but more than that, you inspire me to continue writing them. Your support means everything.

Helena, I never truly appreciated how much time and effort went into producing an audiobook before I saw you do it. And, Matthew, your expertise made it all come together. Thanks a million, guys.

To Amanda, Denica, Brigitte, and Stephany, thank you for your insights in the editing process.

To the incredible authors who took the time to read and endorse this book - I cannot say enough how grateful I am. Having your words on this book is an honor.

And to the Creator of this spinning blue planet, thank you for numbering the hairs on our heads. Your image gives us value, and we are incomplete apart from you.

About the Author

L.E. Richmond is a lover of lore and fairy tales. Her YA fantasy duology Chronicles of the Undersea Realm is a spin-off of *The Little Mermaid*, and most of the other stories bouncing around her head connect to a classic tale of some kind.

When she is not writing, she spends her time having adventures with her three delightful little Muggles, running races with her Prince Charming, and brewing a magical elixir that mortals know as kombucha.

The One whose image gives each human life value is the reason for every story she pens.